IN PLAIN
SIGHT

OTHER BOOKS AND AUDIO BOOKS

BY CLAIR M. POULSON

Checking Out

Framed

I'll Find You

Relentless

Lost and Found

Conflict of Interest

Runaway

Cover Up

Mirror Image

Blind Side

Evidence

Don't Cry Wolf

Dead Wrong

Deadline

Vengeance

Hunted

Switchback

Accidental Private Eye

IN PLAIN
SIGHT

A NOVEL BY
CLAIR M.
POULSON

Covenant Communications, Inc.

PROLOGUE

To passersby, he appeared to be just another homeless man traveling along the side of the highway with his nondescript gray mutt. The dog contentedly rode in a small cart being towed by the man on the bicycle. The sun beat down unmercifully on the pair; the man was sweating profusely, his shirt sticking to his back, his sloppy felt hat wet and dark around the sweatband. The small backpack on his back wasn't exactly bulging nor were the two saddlebags that straddled the back wheel of the bike, but he had enough high-energy bars and food to sustain him and his dog for several days. He also carried a change of clothes, a knit cap, a soiled jacket, and a small US atlas. Because of the limited space, he refilled the water containers every time he could, knowing that ahead of him were often long stretches of open country.

Occasionally, someone with a pickup truck would stop and offer the pair a ride. When that happened, the bike, the small cart, and the packs went into the back. If the drivers who stopped had known about the small twenty-two caliber pistol and close to a hundred hollow-point long rifle bullets in the backpack, they would probably have been less likely to offer help. Others, had they known that the fellow wore a money belt beneath his tattered, dirty brown shirt, might have tried to overpower him to get to the roughly three thousand dollars hidden there. The man didn't carry a wallet. He kept his driver's license, debit card, and passport hidden beneath the inserts of his worn hiking boots.

Other than those things, he carried a secret that was far too dangerous to divulge. In fact, it was *that* secret that had compelled him to adopt the lifestyle he was living. It had caused him to grow out his dark blond hair and wear a shaggy beard. It even forced him to allow himself to smell bad—probably one of the reasons he didn't ride with anyone for very long before they found an excuse to let him out. He'd gotten used to the unpleasant stench and his dog didn't seem to mind in the least, but it must have been terrible for those few good souls unfortunate enough to offer him a ride.

It was likely that those who passed him by on the road assumed him to be a lazy man with a low IQ. But they couldn't have been further from the truth. He was ambitious, had an IQ of over 160, and was only doing what he was doing because of circumstances beyond his control, circumstances which had produced the burdensome secret he hoped one day to have removed from his shoulders.

CHAPTER ONE

Donte Noble sat at the side of the road, resting against a signpost, eating a power bar, and sipping water from his dwindling supply. His dog wagged its tail and poked its nose against the hand holding the water. "You must be thirsty too, Dude," Donte said, reaching into his backpack for a small tin dish he had picked up at a Goodwill store. It served as both a food and water dish for the dog. He poured Dude a drink, which the dog quickly lapped up.

The traffic on the highway was fairly light, and no one even slowed as they passed. He wasn't trying nor did he expect to get a ride, although that would have been welcome on this hot afternoon. His water supply was running short, and his atlas told him it was probably around thirty miles to Tonopah, the next town to the north. He knew he had to ration the water carefully. He put the tin dish, water bottle, and atlas back in the soiled backpack. He'd already ridden his bicycle close to thirty miles that day, towing the small cart and the dog. He didn't relish another thirty in this intense heat, but he could do it if he had to. He'd done far more than that in the past three months although not in such intense heat.

Dude watched Donte for a moment before dropping his shaggy gray head between his paws. Donte chuckled. "I know, it's a long ways, but at least you get to ride—I have to peddle," he told the pup. "We don't want to be stuck in the middle of nowhere for the night if we don't have to." Donte kept his head down, and for a moment, he vacillated between getting up and staying put. He chose staying put. "Okay, five more minutes, Dude, and then we'll get going."

His watch read 1:15. The worst heat of this mid-June Nevada day was yet to come. He closed his eyes, thinking that if he was in the shade, he'd allow himself a short nap. But there was no shade on US Highway

85 between Las Vegas and Tonopah. He'd already spent one night a few hundred feet from the highway somewhere north of Lathrop Wells and didn't want another one, especially if he ran out of water.

The five minutes he'd promised his dog had not yet passed when he heard a vehicle slow. He opened his eyes, shoved his old felt hat back, and glanced up. "You look hot, mister." The man in the late-model brown Ford pickup looked to be about thirty. "I'm going to Tonopah. Could you and your dog use a lift?"

Could he ever! The heat this near Death Valley was almost overpowering. "Thank you, sir," he said. Gratefully, he got to his feet, grabbed his backpack, and hefted it in the back of the pickup bed as the driver got out of the cab. The man lowered the tailgate and helped Donte load the bike and small trailer. Donte tapped the tailgate, and Dude jumped in. Then Donte joined the man in the front.

They pulled onto the highway as the driver asked, "Where you headed to?"

"Tonopah is fine," Donte said, not supplying a final destination—he didn't know that. He was chasing a ghost, or so it seemed after three months. He was going wherever the ghost led him, hiding in plain sight from those who would take his freedom away.

"By the way, my name's Clive Granger. What would yours be?"

His name was Donte Noble, but that wasn't for everyone's knowledge. Frankly, he'd never thought he looked like a Donte, but his sister told him that their mother had once dated a dark and dashing man by that name. She claimed Donte was named after the man, and apparently their dad never knew anything about where the name came from; he'd just gone along with their mother's suggestion. At any rate, Donte wasn't about to use his real name now, so he said, "Dave."

"Nice to meet you, Dave," Clive said with a smile. He didn't ask for a last name, so Donte didn't bother to invent one. Had he done so, it would have been a common one like Smith or Brown. He usually used common names so he would be less likely to forget while he was in the company of someone he had just deceived.

"How old's the mutt?" Clive asked next.

Donte tugged at his dark blond beard. The color matched his hair, hair that was now beyond his collar, not something that he was used to. He'd never grown a beard before and had always worn his hair quite short, about the same as Clive's. Not anymore. Donte couldn't afford to be recognized. He thought about Clive's question as he tugged. Finally, he answered, "I honestly don't know. First time I ever saw him was about eight weeks ago. I was sleeping beneath a tree alongside a road in Wyoming. When I woke up, he was there. When I started out on my bike, he followed me. I finally stopped and said, 'Where you headed, Dude?' He wagged his tail and hurried up to me. There was no collar on him. I tried to shoo him away, but he wouldn't go. I still call him Dude, and we've been together ever since."

The fellow smiled. "Maybe he's your guardian angel," he said. "It can be dangerous out here by yourself."

"You're right about that," Donte agreed. "Angel or not, Dude's good company for a wandering man like myself. And even though he's not too big, he has a tendency to make most people keep their distance."

"Not too old," Clive muttered after five minutes of silent travel.

"What's not too old?" Donte asked. His mind had been elsewhere, analyzing the trouble he was facing, wondering what his future held.

"Your dog," Clive said. "He doesn't look too old to me. Does he follow you when you're on your bike?"

"Oh, no. He tried that at first, but he couldn't keep up," Donte explained. "So I bought that little cart we threw in the back of your truck. Most of the time he rides in that, but he does like to get out and run from time to time. It slows me down—not that it matters since I'm not in a hurry—and he seems to enjoy the exercise."

"An old dog couldn't do that," Clive said. "Yeah, I'd say he's fairly young."

"I'd guess he's maybe three or four," Donte agreed.

"Probably," the fellow said. Then they lapsed into silence for a time.

"I appreciate the ride, Clive," Donte finally said, enjoying the feeling of the air-conditioning blowing the intense heat from his body. It also caused the smell of his unwashed body to circulate, probably bothering his benefactor.

"I don't know what you're running from or what you're chasing, but I'm glad to give you a lift," Clive said with a smile.

Donte couldn't tell anyone that he was biking around the Western states, constantly looking over his shoulder for the shadowy killer of his fiancée's brother or that he was running from those who wrongly believed him to be that killer. She didn't know he knew, but his fiancée was one of those. He knew that because, shortly before he fled, he overheard Kasiah talking to his sister. He'd been shocked to hear her say, "I know you don't like to hear this, Sara, but it *was* Donte that killed my brother." Sara, bless her heart, argued with Kasiah, but she hadn't prevailed.

Kasiah Aklen and Donte had been engaged for three months before her worthless brother, Walker, had been murdered. Donte had thought he loved her, but in retrospect, he realized that it was her beauty that he loved. He vowed to never make that mistake again—if he ever escaped the accusation hanging over him, if he could ever live a normal life again.

As if reading Donte's mind, Clive said, "You must be thinking about a girl."

Donte started at that. He was glad his head was turned, or Clive might have seen something that told him he was right on the mark. Before Donte came up with a way to deny the guess, Clive said, "She must be pretty."

Donte decided not to say anything and nodded. After he got out of the truck in Tonopah, he'd never see the man again. It really didn't matter what he thought. But Donte couldn't help but continue to think about Kasiah. With long blonde hair, sparkling green eyes, high cheekbones, a pert nose, a lovely smile, smooth flawless skin, and a figure that turned men's heads, she was a beautiful girl. But that she could so easily think of him as a killer after the plans they'd made to spend their lives together angered him. He had decided, these three months he'd been biking around the West, that she was a shallow girl. Her beauty was only skin deep.

He was just hoping and praying that by some miracle the real killer would be found and arrested and that Donte would be free to go home and resume his life—a life that did not include Kasiah.

"You sure are deep in thought, my friend," Clive said.

Donte, who had been gazing out the window at the passing desert, turned his attention to Clive. Donte smiled, although it was an effort. "Yeah, I have a lot to think about," he said.

Clive chuckled. "I'm into mysteries," he said. "I write novels, mystery novels. You and your dog have given me some ideas. I hope you don't mind."

Donte felt uncomfortable. He hadn't expected anything like that. "Of course not," he said, although he sort of did. Surely Clive, who was kind enough to offer him a ride, wasn't somehow tied in with Kasiah or the police who were looking for him. That thought made him shiver.

"Seriously, Dave. I'm a writer, and I'm driving around the country to visit different places and to meet new people. That's how I come up with some of the ideas and locations for my stories. I lost my wife a few years back, so now I just drift around and look for ideas. My books, by the way, are doing quite well."

"That's great," Donte said, wondering how much to believe.

Clive chuckled again and looked over at Donte. "A guy who hauls his dog around in a cart behind a bike—now that is something to write about."

Donte couldn't argue with that. If this guy was for real, he'd be shocked to know the truth about why Donte, a man who had been accepted into medical school, was now a sloppy, longhaired, bearded, homeless wanderer. "Yeah, I guess you don't see that every day."

"I'd say not."

It was silent again for a few minutes. Donte was nervous, yet he couldn't help but like Clive. Throwing out a few more questions, Donte decided to wait and see what kind of answers the guy threw back.

"You lost your wife?" he finally ventured.

Clive took his eyes off the road long enough to glance at him. "I'm afraid so. She was a good girl. I loved her more than I can express."

"Do you mind if I asked what happened to her? Was it cancer or something?"

"That would be easier for me to deal with than what actually happened," Clive said. He touched his eye with the back of his hand, and it came away wet. Donte found himself more at ease at that display of emotion. The guy just might be what he claimed to be. Donte didn't say anything, wondering if Clive would continue. He did after a moment. "She was murdered," he said with a catch in his voice. That word made Donte jump, but he said nothing, just waited for what else Clive might say.

Without turning his head, eyes glued to the long, black pavement that stretched straight ahead, heat waves rising from the surface, Clive asked, "Do you ever see or hear the news?"

"Occasionally," Donte responded. "I pick up a paper on occasion, and I do spend a night in a cheap motel once in a while so I can get rid of this smell that is probably driving you nuts. When I do, I watch the news."

"Don't worry about the smell," Clive said. Then he went on. "There was a massacre at a shopping mall in Omaha several years ago—six to be exact. We were living there at the time, and I was writing for a local paper. My wife had gone to the mall to get her hair done at a salon she liked. Anyway, some madman who had lost his job at one of the stores there went in with a gun. He killed a dozen people. One was his former boss. The others were just people in the wrong place at the wrong time." Clive choked up again.

Donte said, "And your wife was one of them. I'm so sorry. That's horrible."

"You can say that again." Clive took a deep breath. "It took a long time, but I've moved on. The killer is dead, and I have a new career. It was that horrible incident that got me thinking about doing something more than just writing stories for a newspaper. It's worked out, and so now, since we didn't have any kids, I'm alone, and I spend my time writing or traveling and getting ideas for books."

"It must be hard, something like that. How can someone do something so awful?" Donte asked, though he was also thinking about how some people—Kasiah in particular—thought he was that kind of person.

Clive again pulled his eyes from the pavement ahead. "I've forgiven the man. I had to. It was what my wife would have wanted me to do, and it's what the Savior has commanded me to do."

"It still must take a lot of courage," Donte ventured.

"I guess, but my religious beliefs have kept me anchored to what I know I should do. And I try to do it." Clive pointed to the glove box of his truck. "There's a book in there," he said. "I'd like you to have it, Dave."

Donte hesitated, glancing at the glove box in front of him. "Oh, I can't do that."

"No, really. I carry several of them to give to people I meet. It explains a lot about who I am and how I think. Go ahead," Clive said, pointing. "Take it. And when you get a chance, read it."

Puzzled, Donte opened the compartment. A blue, soft-cover edition of the Book of Mormon was lying on top of whatever else Clive kept in there. Donte pulled it out, held it up, and said, "Thanks, Clive, but I carry all of the Standard Works with me. They're in the saddlebags on my bike."

"You're Mormon too?" Clive asked, his face a picture of astonishment.

"I am. I served a mission. My small set of scriptures gets used every day. They're my anchor to who I am, or at least, who I used to be."

"Where did you serve your mission?" Clive asked.

"You probably won't believe this. I was in Omaha. In fact, I was there when that massacre occurred. It was on a Monday. My companion and I were in that very mall that morning. They locked the mall down, and we were stuck there for hours."

Clive stammered for a moment, and then he said, shaking his head, "This is incredible. There is a reason that you and I met today. I just wish I knew what that reason is."

"Maybe I do," Donte said softly.

CHAPTER TWO

"Tell me about it," Clive suggested earnestly. "It's clear that you wouldn't be biking around the country looking like you do if something terrible hadn't happened to you."

"Actually," Donte began, "something terrible happened to someone else." He paused, not sure even yet how much he dared tell this man who already seemed so much like a friend.

"Please continue, Dave. You can trust me, and if there happens to be anything I can do to help, I will."

Donte hung his head for a moment, and then he said, "It's been three months since I've told anyone. My name is not Dave. My name is Donte Noble."

"It's nice to meet you, Donte," Clive said with a smile. "So tell me, what terrible thing happened that has altered your life so dramatically?"

"I . . . I don't know where to start," he stammered. "I feel like I can trust you. It would lift a great burden from me to have someone to trust. I can't go on like this much longer. It's driving me insane. If it wasn't for Dude, I'd have probably lost my mind by now. Actually, my sister has helped too. She's a great girl. We communicate from time to time, even though we have to keep it secret. She believes in me."

"It's always good to have someone you can confide in," Clive said. "If it wasn't for my parents, I don't know if I could have made it after my wife was killed. But I'm interrupting you. Go ahead, Donte. I'll listen."

"Thanks, Clive. My parents are both dead. There's just my sister and me, but we're very close. Anyway, I guess I can start with who I really am and what I was doing before the . . . the terrible thing happened." Donte paused. Clive nodded but kept his eyes on the road. He said nothing, so Donte continued. "My sister and I lived in the house our parents left us.

Sara's never married, something I'm not quite sure I understand. She's a very attractive girl. Of course, she's not exactly an old maid—I didn't mean to imply that. She's only twenty-three, one year younger than me. Anyway, she works as a legal secretary in a law firm in town, and I was taking some time off from school, working in a local bank as a teller."

Donte looked over at Clive, who was smiling. "I know, not exactly a pre-med job, but I needed something, and I found I quite enjoyed the work."

"Where did you go to school?" Clive asked.

"The University of Utah," Donte replied. "I was pre-med and had been accepted into medical school there. I was supposed to begin in August. I'm afraid that won't happen now. Anyway, Sara and I were both living in the home we grew up in. It's in Provo, not too far from the temple there. One day, Sara introduced me to one of the other legal secretaries in the law firm she works for. I fell head over heels the moment I saw her. I asked her out, and she, to my surprise, agreed."

"Why were you surprised?" Clive asked. "I suspect that if you cut your hair and shaved, you'd be a reasonably handsome guy."

"That's just it, Clive. I'm not such a handsome guy. But Kasiah," Donte said as he pictured her in his mind, "is gorgeous. I mean, she could be a model or a movie star. She's got this perfect figure and a face that is simply unbelievable. She's not anyone who I ever thought would date me. But she did. After we'd dated for a while, I asked her to marry me."

Donte paused, thinking what a mistake that had been. Clive again took his eyes off the highway and asked, "Did she turn you down?"

"No," Donte said. "And I was stunned. I couldn't believe I was so lucky. But now, as I look back, I realize that all she wanted was to be a doctor's wife. I had been fool enough to think I loved her, but I don't think I ever really did. It was her physical beauty that caused me to sort of . . . well . . . lose my head."

"I take it you're no longer engaged," Clive said, cocking an eyebrow.

"She still has my ring, but I wouldn't marry her if she were the last girl on earth. I thought she was a good girl, but she must be pure poison," Donte said bitterly.

"Is that the terrible thing?" Clive asked. "I mean, was it something terrible that made your fiancée into someone who is not a good person?"

"That is terrible, but whatever it was must have happened long ago. She was only putting on a show for me. Like I said, she just wanted to be a doctor's wife, and I was handy—a future doctor," Donte said. "No, the something terrible was murder. Someone killed her older brother. And she told my sister that I did it."

"Oh my!" Clive said. "That is terrible."

"Yes, and that's why I am where I am and doing what I'm doing. Kasiah's convinced the police of my guilt, or at least that's what Sara thinks, although she doesn't see Kasiah anymore. Apparently she quit the law firm shortly after the murder. Anyway, Sara told me that it doesn't look like the cops are even looking for anyone else. They're after me." He began to feel the old familiar despondency creeping in. "Sara keeps saying that she wants to try to figure it all out, but she'd be in way over her head. So I've asked her not to. She's all I have left, and I don't want her to put herself in danger."

"Donte, maybe I can help," Clive said. "Maybe that's why the two of us met today."

"Clive, I can't ask that of you. If you would just be someone who believes in me, that would be great. I don't want you to put yourself in danger for me. It wouldn't be right," Donte said. "No offense, but just because you write mysteries doesn't necessarily mean you could solve real-life ones, does it?"

"I don't know, Donte, but I sure would like to try. Please, let me help. I really want to," he said, pounding his fist lightly on the steering wheel.

"I don't see what you could do," Donte countered.

"Well, for starters, you could send me to meet Sara. She could point me in the right direction without having to be involved herself," he said, his enthusiasm mounting.

Donte thought about it. As much as he wanted the killer caught, he wished the police would take care of it so that others would not be put in danger.

"Hey, if nothing else, maybe I can get the cops to look for someone besides you," Clive urged.

That was too good to pass up. "Sure, Clive, that would be great. Just get them working and you won't have to be involved and neither will Sara. But how are you going to do that? You're not from Provo. You're—"

"A man with a very big imagination," Clive said with a grin as he cut Donte off midsentence. "I'll figure it out. I'm excited just thinking about it. But I'll have to know more about Kasiah, her brother, and so on. We'll be in Tonopah in a few minutes. I'm hungry, and I'll bet you are too. We'll find someplace to eat, and then you can talk and I'll take notes."

***

The girl kneeling next to the brand new headstone in the Grand Junction, Colorado, cemetery was sobbing and wiping at her eyes. She was a beautiful creature with long blonde hair, dazzling green eyes, and a perfect figure. "I'm so sorry, Walker. This never should have happened. Sawyer and I will make Donte pay. I promise, Walker. He will pay. If I'd known that he would do something so terrible, I would never have brought him into our lives. I'm so sorry."

Kasiah hunched over and sobbed for several more minutes. Finally, she straightened up and continued, her voice choked up. "I've got to get back to Provo, big brother. I'll make sure the cops find Donte." Her face grew hard, and she added fiercely, "And I'll make sure he gets the worst punishment there is for what he did." With that she rose to her feet and walked quickly to her dark blue Chevy Malibu. Climbing in, she looked back toward the grave and then drove away.

***

"Sara, can you step in here for a moment?"

It was the voice of her boss, Attorney Winn Bertram, summoning her via the intercom. She quickly saved the document she was typing and then headed for Winn's closed door. She opened it and went in. "What can I help you with?" she asked politely, brushing her long brown hair across her shoulders.

"Please sit down, Sara," he said as a scowl appeared on his face.

Her stomach gave an uncomfortable twist. He was apparently displeased with her over something. That was unusual. He was usually trying to flirt with her. She wondered nervously what she had done.

He didn't keep her in suspense for long. "I just got a call from Detective Fields. He tells me you're stonewalling him."

Sara wrinkled her brow. "Stonewalling?"

"Yes, Sara. He says you know where your brother is and won't tell him."

"That's not true. I don't know where he is," she countered hotly, even as she hoped he didn't ask if she had talked to Donte recently because she didn't know how she would answer that. Actually, she could say that she hadn't actually *talked* to him because all of their communications had been via e-mail. She couldn't, however, honestly say that she had not been in touch with him. She hoped no one would ask because she would have to lie for Donte's sake.

Winn didn't ask. "I'll let Fields know."

"Thanks, but I already told him that."

"Apparently he doesn't believe you, Sara, but I do." The scowl was gone. Winn smiled and said, "Why don't we talk about it over dinner this evening?"

"I don't want to talk about it at all," she said. "I'd rather—"

Winn didn't give her the chance to say what she'd rather do. He simply said, "Then we won't talk about it," he said, "but we will eat a nice dinner. I'll pick you up at six."

She'd had a feeling this was coming. It didn't feel right. She felt trapped, wondered how to turn him down without creating a problem, and finally heard herself say, "Okay. Is that all?"

"Yes, Sara. And thanks," he said, rising to his feet as she stood up. "It'll be an enjoyable evening."

When she sat down at her desk, she wondered why she had said yes. He was a nice man, a good boss, and quite good looking. They shared the same religion, but she was still uneasy. It wasn't that he was divorced but rather that he was her boss. She wasn't at all sure how that would look to other attorneys in the firm.

She finally shrugged and began typing vigorously. Maybe it wouldn't be so bad, she thought as she worked. After all, she hadn't been asked out since way before Kasiah's brother had been murdered. She should just go and try to enjoy herself, not worry about what others might say or think. After all, Winn was a great guy.

It wasn't more than a few minutes before her iPhone buzzed, indicating an incoming text. She glanced around, making sure no one else was watching, and then pulled it from her purse, wondering who was texting her. She knew it wasn't Donte—he didn't carry a cell phone and only contacted her by e-mail using different addresses. It would be too easy for the police to locate him if he had a cell phone. She wondered if it might be Kasiah. She didn't want to hear from Kasiah. Sara had been so relieved when Kasiah had left the law firm so that they didn't have to see each other every day. Kasiah was totally convinced that Donte had killed her brother. She wouldn't listen to reason. And she had the case's lead investigator hooked on her theory.

She looked at the screen on her phone. She couldn't tell who it was from. The message was short and succinct. *Look for an e-mail tonight around six.* That was it. If this did have something to do with Donte, it would be almost impossible for her to do that. Winn was picking her up at six. She couldn't be checking her e-mail, not even on her phone, in front of him. What could she do? After once again surveying the room, she deleted the message and stared at the phone in her trembling hands. It must be very important if Donte had used someone's phone to send her a message.

Her stomach began to hurt. She looked at the blank phone in her hand and then slipped it back inside her purse. She'd no sooner put her purse back beneath her desk than Winn stepped out of his office. Her stomach was already upset with worry, but now her pulse began to pound when she considered how closely Winn had come to seeing her with her phone in her hand. What if he'd been a few moments earlier and seen the message? He might have read between the lines and figured out it was from Donte.

"Sara," Winn said with a smile, "can we make that five thirty instead of six? I called for reservations, but the restaurant's booked from six thirty until eight. We could both go home a little early to be ready in time."

What could she do? She had to check the e-mail as soon as she could, but she couldn't risk letting Winn see it, no matter how nice a guy he was. Her palms began to sweat, and she had to fight the urge to wipe them on her pants. She could feel tiny beads of perspiration breaking out on her forehead. Instead of ducking back into his office, Winn stepped beside her desk. "You look uncomfortably hot," he said. "I could turn the air conditioning a little lower if you need. I don't want you to be uncomfortable."

"I'm fine," she said, not about to tell him how *un*comfortable she really was, but it wasn't from the temperature.

"Are you sick?" he asked, extending his hand and placing it on her forehead like her mother used to do when she was a child. "You don't feel like you have a fever."

"I'm fine," she repeated. She forced a grin. "Maybe I've been typing too fast."

Winn grinned at her. "Maybe. But I'm glad you're okay." He patted her on the shoulder, his hand lingering. When he withdrew it, he said,

"If you need to go home earlier so you can be rested for our dinner, feel free."

"Thanks, Mr. Bertram," she said. "But I really am okay."

"Sara, I am Winn to you. I've told you that before. We are good friends, and good friends don't call each other Mister or Miss."

They were also boss and employee, she thought, but she kept that thought to herself. She really didn't mind Winn and Sara. "Okay, Winn, but honestly, I'm fine. I'll just need to get home in time to change."

"I'm glad you're okay because I would sure feel bad if you weren't feeling well for our first date," he said, and with that he returned to his office, flashing her a grin just before he closed the door behind him.

She began to hyperventilate. She took several deep breaths to calm herself, even as she reflected on his words. He'd said *first* date—implying that there were more to come. The idea was frightening, and yet, she had to admit, just a little bit exciting. But the timing was really bad. Donte needed her, and even though she would open the e-mail whenever she found some privacy, Donte would probably be sitting in a library or an internet café waiting for a response.

This was almost too much. Of course, ever since Donte had been forced to flee, it didn't take a lot to upset her. She wiped her brow and then clenched her hands, trying to stop them from shaking. And finally, she left her desk and went to the restroom, where she wiped a paper towel soaked in cold water across her face. She gradually began to feel normal and finally returned to her desk. She settled back into her work, still worrying about Donte and about her upcoming date with her boss, but once again in control of her emotions.

***

"You can e-mail her from my phone or my laptop," Clive said as the two of them drove up to a hotel entrance. "In the meantime, let's get a room."

"If you're sure," Donte said as he looked for a sign that might indicate if pets were allowed.

"Of course I'm sure. I want to help in any way I can, Donte. What time does Sara get home from work?"

"Usually she's home between five and six," Donte said, glancing at his watch. "That's why I told her six. So we still have a few hours."

"What do you do with your dog when you check into a motel or a hotel?" Clive asked.

"I don't check into ones that don't allow him in the room. I don't see any signs here, so I suppose I'll just have to go ask at the desk."

"I'm sure you don't have much money," Clive said. "I'll pay for a room, and we can both stay in it."

"That's fine, but I do have money," Donte said. "I just wish I could go home and get on with my life."

"As do I, and maybe with the Lord's help it will soon happen," Clive said, sounding quite upbeat.

CHAPTER THREE

"So," Clive said as they sat in a café eating. "Why aren't you driving a car instead of riding a bike? Strike that. You couldn't have used your own car because Kasiah would have told the cops about it and they'd be looking for it."

"Not only that," Donte responded. "They have it. It was impounded right after Kasiah told them I did it. Fortunately, Sara knew what was up and alerted me on my cell phone. I was able to catch a cab and get away. I ditched my cell and caught a ride with a trucker who took me all the way to Los Angeles. I hid out there while my hair grew longer and my beard got a good start, but I couldn't stand just laying around doing nothing. I thought about buying another car, but I decided that I'd be less likely to attract the attention of the cops if I was riding a bike and looking like a scrounge."

"So you bought a bike and just started traveling around?" Clive asked.

"Yep. I found it from a newspaper ad in LA. And about a week later Dude found me. By then I had biked all the way to Wyoming. I bought the little trailer and started towing Dude around. But I've tried to stay fairly close to Utah in case the cops decide to do their job and look for the real killer. So far, that hasn't happened."

"With my help, maybe we can get that to happen."

That evening, as the two men and the dog lounged in their hotel room—one that allowed pets—they shared more of their pasts. Finally, as five o'clock approached, Clive said, "It will be six o'clock in Provo soon. Let's get the e-mail ready."

Clive opened his laptop and within a few minutes, Donte had a short message typed and ready to send to Sara. Using one of his dozen alias e-mail addresses, he fired the note off to her. "I hope she can open it soon," he said hopefully.

"I hope she'll agree to meet me," Clive added. "If she does—since it's not too late—I might want to head that way tonight."

"We've got the room. You can wait till morning," Donte said. It was so nice to have a human to talk to and confide in. He was reluctant to have his new friend leave.

Dude got up from his resting place near the door and padded across the slightly worn carpet to Donte. The dog nuzzled Donte's hand. "Yeah, I know, Dude," Donte said. "I've got you. And you are good company. You're a great listener, but I wish you could talk. It's been good having someone who can talk back. "

***

Her cell phone was on vibrate, and since it was in her purse, Sara knew that she wouldn't know when the e-mail came. She glanced at her watch. It was only one minute before six, and she and Winn had just finished ordering their meals. He was being very sweet, and if it wasn't for worrying about the message from Donte, she would be having a nice time. But she was tense, worried, and not sure she would be able to eat when her meal came.

"Winn," she said, smiling at him as sweetly as she could muster, "would you excuse me for a minute?"

"Of course," he said, and as she pushed her chair back, he also stood. "Don't be too long; our appetizers will be here shortly."

"I'll be right back," she promised, hurrying toward the restroom.

She locked herself in a stall and pulled her cell phone from her purse. She had three new e-mails. One was from Kasiah. The second from Kasiah's oldest brother, Sawyer, a man who was as vulgar and mean as their dead brother, Walker. She couldn't imagine what he wanted. She disliked the man, just as she had disliked Walker.

She left both of those e-mails unopened and went to the third, the one she was quite certain was from Donte. This message was short. She read: *Hi Scrunch. There is a man who wants to meet you. His name is Clive. I think you will like him. He is a helpful person and a mystery man. If you need help with anything, he can do it. Will you meet with him? Slurpee.*

He never used their given names, just nicknames no one else knew. Even though he used a variety of e-mail addresses, he always used those childhood nicknames. Their father had called her Scrunch from a habit she had of scrunching her eyebrows when she was thinking deeply.

She, in turn, used his nickname. Slurpee was also their father's invention. Donte, even to this day, always made sure he got every ounce of whatever he was drinking from the cup. He often made a slurping noise, which had irritated their mother something awful, but which their father had always laughed about.

She scrunched her eyebrows now as she thought about the message. She guessed that he was waiting for a reply and that, whoever the mystery man was, he was also waiting. That was why Donte had told her he'd make contact after he was sure she'd be home from work.

She typed on her iPhone: *Yes, Slurpee.* Then she sent it off. She knew Winn would wonder what she was doing if she was too long. She didn't want to give him a reason to ask, but she really wanted to see what Kasiah and her repulsive brother wanted. So she opened Kasiah's message. It had been sent while Sara was at work. It simply said that Kasiah was on her way back from Grand Junction and would like to talk. Sara wished that Kasiah would simply vanish from her life like she'd vanished from the firm. Sara decided she could wait until she was home to reply.

She also opened the other message, the one from Sawyer Aklen. She read it quickly and then deleted it, shuddering. But as she washed her hands and then hurried back to join Winn, Sawyer's words kept running through her mind. He had told her that he'd be in Utah in a couple of days and needed to talk to her about his brother's murder. He said he believed that it wasn't Donte who had killed Walker. He wrote that their conversation would be best done over dinner. He told her that it was very important that she listen to what he had to say if she really wanted to help Donte. Why it was best done over dinner, Sara had no idea—unless it was the only way the creep could get her to go out with him. That was what had made her shudder. And yet, even as Winn stood to welcome her back to their table, she knew she would do as Sawyer had requested. If there was any chance at all that she could learn something that would prove Donte's innocence, she had to do it.

***

"You don't have to leave tonight," Donte said, but Clive's mind was made up.

"I can drive a good three or four hours and then stop for the night," Clive said. "I want to contact your sister tomorrow. The sooner we get the cops on the right path, the better."

Donte couldn't argue with that, but after a few hours of human companionship, the thought of being alone again was depressing. "I appreciate what you're doing," he finally said. "But, please, don't put yourself in danger to help me."

"Quit worrying, Donte. I'll be fine, and so will your sister. Now, you and I need to keep in touch."

"Let's just do that through Sara," Donte suggested. "I think that's the best way."

Five minutes later, Clive was in his Ford truck and on his way. Donte took the dog outside and checked the hotel's small laundry room. It had two washers and two dryers. Both washers were in use. He had to use them that night if possible so all his clothes would be clean before he began biking the next morning. While he waited for the machines to finish, he walked around town with Dude. The air was still simmering. Donte was soon sweating profusely. He'd already taken a shower, but he was looking forward to another one soon.

Back at the hotel an hour later, he again stopped by the laundry room. As he stepped in the door, a young woman with long, curly black hair was backing toward him with a basketful of wet clothes. She didn't see or hear him but effectively backed into him in the cramped confines of the room even as Dude pushed his way in. She began to fall backward and would have gone clear to the floor if Donte hadn't caught her. But her basket of wet clothes did fall.

"I'm sorry," the young woman said as she stood upright and turned to face Donte.

"No, I'm sorry. It was my dog's fault. He doesn't always have the best of manners."

"But I backed right into you," she said. "And look at what I've done to my clean clothes. Now I'll have to wash them again, and I'm sure you're waiting for the machines."

"I'm in no hurry. I can wait," Donte said as he looked at the attractive girl. "I don't have much to wash."

"No, you go first," she said as she bent down to retrieve her things.

Donte knelt down and helped her. When she had everything in her basket again, he gently took the basket from her arms and turned to the washer. "Okay, now in they go."

She let him, but when he asked if she had soap, she said, "I think they'll just need to get rinsed again. They didn't get that dirty on the floor. In the meantime, you can get your things and bring them here. That way, no one else can beat you to the washer when my stuff is done."

"What about that other washer?" he asked. He could tell that it was on the spin cycle.

"That's my white things," she said. "They're almost done. You can have both machines if you hurry."

Donte did as she suggested and hurried to get his small bunch of clothes, thinking about how nice she was. She hadn't seemed repulsed by him like most girls he'd come into contact with since becoming a bearded wanderer.

He left Dude, his dark glasses, and his sloppy felt hat in his room and hurried back down to the laundry room, running his fingers through his hair.

"I saved it for you," the young woman said as Donte stepped back inside. "Is that all you have?"

"I'm afraid so," he said, feeling his face flush. "But I do need to put them into two separate batches." As he dropped his load into the machine, he remembered he didn't have any soap.

The girl must have been watching because, when he dug in his pocket for some change to buy detergent from the dispenser on the wall, she said, "Here, I have some soap. You can use mine." She picked up a box that was sitting on the counter next to the dryers and put some soap into his washer.

"Thanks," he said. "You didn't need to do that."

After he got the colored clothes loaded and the washer started, he turned away from the washing machine. The young woman had one of the dryers going. She smiled at him and held out a hand. "My name is Chey Beckett. It's nice to meet you—embarrassing but nice."

"I'm Donte Noble," he said then realized he hadn't used a false name. He couldn't believe he'd made such a mistake. But then, he told himself, he'd be gone in the morning and never see her again. It probably didn't matter.

"That's an unusual name," she said. "But I like it."

"So is yours, but it fits you." He wasn't sure what he meant by that, but somehow, as he studied her attractive face, short, slight figure, curly black hair that hung below her shoulders, and deep blue eyes, he couldn't think of any other name that would do any better.

"Thank you," she said. "Are you just passing through town?" she asked.

"Yes, I'll be leaving first thing in the morning. And you?" he asked in return.

"I'm here with one of my roommates from school. We're just taking a little vacation. She doesn't feel well and is in our room sleeping. I think the heat's getting to her. We need to head back home, I guess."

"Where's home?" he asked by way of keeping the conversation going. He was glad for someone to talk to again, even if it was nothing but meaningless dribble. And talking to such a sweet and attractive girl was especially nice. Of course, she wasn't beautiful in the sense that Kasiah was, but there was just something about her. And he was still amazed that she hadn't looked repulsed.

"I'm from Vernal, do you know where that is?"

Donte nodded and said, "I've been through there before."

"Nice place, huh?" she said with a grin.

"I'm sure it is."

"Where you from?" she asked.

That wasn't a question he wanted to answer. He'd already told her more than he should have. Even though she seemed like such a nice girl, he dodged the question. "I'm from wherever I was the night before," he said.

That brought a puzzled look from her, but she didn't comment on what he'd said. Instead, she said, "I think my clothes are almost done again here. The spin cycle is almost over."

He couldn't help but watch her as she unloaded the washer again, put the clothes in the basket, then moved them to the dryer. She was small. She couldn't weigh more than a hundred pounds, he thought. He judged her to be maybe five-three to five-five in height. And he didn't think she could be but nineteen or twenty years old.

She almost had all her clothes in the second dryer before he realized he wasn't getting his own laundry into the washer. He only had a small handful of white things, and he quickly threw them into the washer.

Donte reached once again for her box of detergent. "Thanks again for the soap."

"It's not a problem," she said. "You seem like a nice guy. Why do you travel around like you do?"

"It's just my lifestyle," he answered awkwardly, looking down at his badly worn hiking shoes.

She stood there in the tiny room studying him, just the hint of a smile on her face and her hands on her hips. "You aren't who you look like," she suddenly said.

"I am who I am," he countered. He was ready to go back to his room. This girl—sweet and pretty as she was—had succeeded in making him nervous and uncomfortable.

"Aren't we all?" she replied cryptically as her tiny smile blossomed into an enchanting grin. "Hey, you like ice cream, don't you? My roommate would probably prefer not to be disturbed for a little while, so how about if you and I go find someplace to sit down and have a shake or a banana split or something?"

He knew he should say no, but out of his mouth came something altogether different. "That would be nice, if you don't mind being seen with a hobo."

"Donte," she said as she took his arm and guided him out of the laundry room, "I can see from your eyes that you are not the person you look like. Come on, let's find some ice cream. It's on me."

"Do you mind if I bring my dog?" he asked. "I don't think I should leave him alone in the room too long."

"That's fine," she said.

Ten minutes later, Dude was tied up outside a small fast-food restaurant while Donte and Chey ordered shakes.

CHAPTER FOUR

KASIAH WAS ON THE FREEWAY, just a few miles out of Grand Junction, when her cell phone rang. It was her oldest brother, her only brother now. "Hi, Sawyer," she said into the phone. "Any luck?"

"It worked, Kasiah." He sounded excited. "I sent the e-mail like we talked about. I told Sara that I had information that would help prove Donte didn't kill Walker but that I needed to meet privately with her in order to tell her what I knew. She agreed to go to dinner. That's luck, wouldn't you say?"

"Yes, and shrewd manipulating. We've just got to make sure she doesn't find out that you're married. I know she wouldn't go through with it if she knew, and it's important she go through with it. I'm positive that she's somehow communicating with Donte. If you can get her to believe you, maybe you can find out where he is," she said with a sinister smile on her gorgeous face.

"But you really think she knows?" he asked.

"I'd bet on it," she said. "I know her, Sawyer. And I could probably get her to tell me if I hadn't been so outspoken about my belief that he killed Walker. It's too late to change that now, but I think she'll let her guard down for you. I think she'd do just about anything to prove his innocence."

"Okay, I'm counting on that, sis," he said.

"What will you tell her?" Kasiah asked. "You know it was him. You told me that yourself."

"Yes, it was him all right. What will I tell her? I don't know yet, but I'll think of something," he said.

"Good. I want the cops to catch him. He sure had the wool pulled over my eyes. He seemed like a decent guy," Kasiah said. "When will you be back in Provo?"

"A couple of days, three at the most. I'll get ahold of Sara as soon as I get into town."

"She works, you know," Kasiah reminded him.

"If I have to, I'll contact her at work. You gave me the number. I'll get back with you."

He ended the call before she could say anything more. She put the phone down on the seat beside her. As she drove, she thought about how lucky she was to have a brother like Sawyer. Together, they would make Donte pay.

***

After finishing their shakes, Donte and Chey walked back to the hotel, with Dude trailing along behind. Donte was feeling more depressed than usual. Leaving in the morning was going to be difficult. This girl had touched something in him that was going to be hard to walk away from. But walk away he must, so walk away he would. Anyway, he kept reminding himself, she was just being nice to him, an unfortunate man. That was clearly the kind of girl she was. But it was nothing more than that.

At the hotel, she got her clothes out of the dryers, and he put his in. She lingered for a moment, her large basket of clothes in her hands. "I hope my roommate is feeling better now," she said. "I guess I could avoid having to disturb her for a few more minutes if I folded my clothes here."

That was certainly okay with Donte. Maybe they could talk some more like they had while consuming their shakes. Nothing personal was discussed. Chey asked him nothing more about where he was from or why he was traveling. And he didn't volunteer it.

Dude was behaving himself, and Chey kept reaching down and patting his head. When her clothes were folded, she put them all in the basket and said, "Well, I guess now I have to go back to my room."

"Let me carry that for you," Donte said and reached for the basket of clothes.

When Chey entered her room a minute later, Donte was out of excuses to spend time with her, but at least it gave him something good to think about as he continued his aimless roving. He went back to his room, changed into the newly washed and dried clothes, and hurried back to the laundry room to wash and dry the ones he'd been wearing.

The next morning, Donte decided to eat breakfast before he got on his bike and headed for—wherever. Maybe he'd continue north until he got to Battle Mountain. It was as good as anyplace. He had planned to get up early and beat the heat, but the bed had felt so good that he had not succeeded in his designs. He'd slept in. Now it was nearly eight o'clock, and the heat was already getting intense. He tied Dude to the bike, which he had left locked against a fence railing behind the hotel. He patted the dog on the head and said, "I'll bring you a treat too."

As Donte turned away and started across the parking area to the street, he glanced at the windows along the lower floor of the hotel. He knew Chey's room was somewhere in the middle. He saw the curtain fall back into place in one of the rooms as if someone had been looking out.

He walked around the back of the hotel. There was a café a short distance away, the one where he and Clive had eaten. He entered and sat down, putting his felt hat on the seat beside him. A plump middle-aged waitress with a bright smile brought him a glass of water and a breakfast menu. "Do you need a moment?" she asked pleasantly. Like Chey, she didn't show any disgust at the way he looked. That was unusual.

"Yes, thank you," he said.

As he looked at the menu, he sipped the water, thinking about his water bottles. They were still in the hotel. The last thing he planned to do before checking out and getting on his bike was to fill the bottles with ice, top them off with water, and put them in his saddlebags.

The bell above the door rang as he was studying his menu. He looked over, and his heart jumped. A pretty, petite young woman with long, dark, curly hair had just stepped in. Chey looked around the room, spotted Donte, and headed his way. "Mind if I join you, Donte?" she asked as he got to his feet.

"That would be nice." It was more than nice, he thought. It was great.

They both sat down, and the waitress came over, handed Chey a glass of water and a menu, and said, "I'll be back in a minute."

"Where's your roommate?" Donte asked as Chey scanned the menu.

"She's still sick. I'm starting to get worried. I'm thinking maybe I should take her to the emergency room. She says she just needs to stay in bed and that by tomorrow she'll be okay. But I'm not so sure. It seems like she has a really high fever."

"Maybe I could take a look at her after we eat and give you another opinion," he suggested. He was far from a doctor, but he had spent a lot of time working in a hospital while pursuing his pre-med studies. He thought he might be able to help the young ladies decide what to do.

"That would be good," Chey said, but as she spoke she gave him a bit of a strange look. It was a *who-are-you-really?* look.

"I'll do it then," he said and once again concentrated on the menu. He made a decision just as the waitress reappeared. "You go first, Chey," he said.

She ordered, and then he did the same. After giving the waitress his order—a huge breakfast of sausage, bacon, eggs, grits, and hotcakes—he added, "And would you also give me two sausage patties to go."

"Won't they spoil in all this heat before you eat them?" Chey asked with concern.

Donte chuckled. "I don't plan to eat them. They're for—"

"Dude, right?" Chey broke in with a grin. "I guess he does need to eat."

Donte nodded. "Yep, he gets hungry, just like we do."

"You're a good man, Donte Noble. Why don't you tell me a little bit about yourself?" she asked.

"Not everyone thinks I'm a good man," he said, wishing he could share his sad story, like he had with Clive, but he decided that there was no need to do that. He didn't need to involve her in what was now his miserable and dangerous life.

"Then they don't know you very well," she said.

"Neither do you," he countered, but he did it with a smile and a wink.

She didn't pry again nor did she seem to be offended, and they simply talked quietly while they waited for their breakfasts to arrive.

After they finished eating, Donte again offered to go with Chey to her room. "Sure, after you give the sausage to your dog. Is he in your room?"

"Oh, no, he's tied out back. I never leave him in a room alone for more than a few minutes. Not that we have a room very often," he said.

She gave him a sideways look, one eyebrow lifted. But all she said was, "Oh."

They walked together around the hotel and to the parking lot in the back. Donte led the way to where he'd left the bike secured and his dog tied. He glanced at her as he held one of the sausages out to Dude. Her mouth was hanging open. For a moment, she just stared at the bike and the little trailer, then she said, "May I give Dude the other piece?"

"Be my guest," he said and handed the sausage to her.

She held it out to Dude, who took it gently from her hand and gulped it down. She chuckled and said, "All dogs do that, don't they?"

"Do what?"

"Gulp their food down without even taking time to taste it," she said. "I like to enjoy my food."

"I guess they enjoy theirs differently than we human folks do," he said as she went back to studying the bike.

"Like my transportation?" he asked.

"Yeah, it must keep you in great shape."

"It does at that."

"What's the little trailer for?"

"That's for Dude to ride in. He can't keep up if I make him run all the time," Donte explained.

"That's good of you, but it must be hard pulling the cart along with everything else you have," she commented.

"It's not too bad. I've gotten used to it," he said. "Should we go check on your roommate? What's her name, by the way?"

"Jessica Birkel. We're the same age. We graduated from high school together in Vernal. She's a really sweet girl, but she is really sick. I do think I need to take her to the emergency room."

When Donte followed Chey into the room, he knew at first glance that Jessica was indeed very ill. She way lying in bed, her eyes closed, her face pale and damp with a light sheen of perspiration. Donte quickly strode to the bed and placed a hand on her forehead, alarmed at the heat that he felt there. Without a thermometer he couldn't be sure of her temperature, but he knew from experience that it had to be well over 100 degrees, most likely near 105.

He removed his hand, and her eyes fluttered open. She gave a gasp, and her eyes registered fright. "It's okay, Jessica," Chey said as she stepped beside Jessica and touched her face with her hand. "This is Donte, a friend I met. He's staying here at the hotel."

The alarm faded from her face, but Donte could still see pain in her eyes. "Where do you hurt?" he asked.

"My stomach," she groaned.

Donte looked at Chey and then said, "Do you guys mind if I poke around a little?"

Chey shook her head and pulled the sheet down. Without disturbing her pajamas, he prodded gently on her stomach. It was only a moment before he was pretty sure he knew what was wrong. "She has appendicitis," he told Chey. "We need to get her to a hospital right away."

He then looked down at the sick girl and said, "You're going to be fine, but you need medical attention." He pulled the sheet back up and said to Chey, "Let's find out where the nearest hospital is." Then he signaled for her to follow him to the far end of the room, where he whispered, "The appendix may have already ruptured. I don't want to alarm her, but she needs help fast."

Chey matched his volume. "Let me grab my iPhone and find out where the nearest hospital is." She was already heading to the small table, where she had put her purse down. As she worked with her phone, Donte went over to the bed and again put a hand on Jessica's forehead. He couldn't be positive, but he was pretty sure he was right. And he knew that speed was urgent.

"There's a hospital right here in Tonopah," Chey said as she stepped beside them. "My phone will direct us to it. Will you help me get her in my car?"

"Of course," he said. "Are you two LDS?"

"Yes," Chey said. "Why?"

He was already digging in his pocket. Out came a small container of oil. "I'm an elder. I'd like to give her a blessing."

Chey was apparently too shocked to speak, for all she did was nod. He went ahead. When he had finished, he said, "There, she'll be okay. But we still need to hurry. Where's your car?"

"It's not far from where your bike is parked. Let me give you the keys, and you can bring it around front while I get her dressed," Chey said.

"There's not time for that," Donte countered. "She can go in her pajamas. Let's get her up and help her out right now."

As soon as they had Jessica seated in the car, Chey asked, "Will you come too? I need moral support. I'm sorry that there isn't room in the car."

"You go. Dude and I will be right there," he said.

When Donte and his dog peddled up to the hospital a few minutes later, Chey's silver Malibu was parked behind the emergency room entrance. He parked beside it, securing both the dog and the bike to her bumper, and then ran into the hospital.

He told the staff at the desk that he was there with the two young ladies who had just come into the emergency room. "They're friends of mine," he said to the older lady at the desk. She looked him over suspiciously, and before she could say anything, he said, "Call back there, please. Ask for Chey. Tell her Donte's here."

The woman, after glaring at him for a moment, did as he requested. It wasn't but a moment until Chey came running in. "Come back with me, Donte," she said urgently. "You were right. The doctor thinks her appendix may have burst." She threw herself toward him, sobbing. "You saved her life. They took her into surgery just a minute ago. The doctor said it was lucky we got here when we did. Thanks for checking on her. I knew she was sick, but I didn't realize she was this sick."

"Should we find a waiting room?" he asked.

"I don't mean to make you hang around here. You probably need to be on your way," she said.

Donte chuckled. "Not really. I'm a nomad. I go wherever I feel like on any given day. Sometimes I flip a coin to decide which way to go."

Chey was giving him a mysterious look. For a moment, he thought she was going to start asking more about him, but she didn't. She just brushed her long, curly hair from her eyes and said, "I need to move my car. Where are your bike and your dog?"

"Tied to your car. I hope you don't mind," he answered. "I'll go out with you, and we can move them. Maybe I'll ride back over to the hotel and let them know that I plan to stay for another day or so."

"You don't have to do that," Chey said, but the look she gave him said otherwise. He was pretty sure she would prefer that he stay.

While she moved her car, he peddled back to the hotel and gave Dude a drink before going inside and extending his stay for a couple of days. He found the best shade he could for his dog, put a little water pan next to him, and returned to the hospital. He found a place to secure his bike and headed for the entrance. Out of the corner of his eye, Donte thought he saw someone watching him. He turned, and a man with a blue ball cap, gray shirt, and gray pants turned away.

Resisting the temptation to look back again, Donte walked into the hospital. But once inside, he did look back through a large glass window. The man was just standing between a black Dodge Ram pickup and a small blue Honda. Something about him gnawed at Donte. He was almost sure he'd seen the man somewhere before, but for the life of him, he couldn't remember when. Suddenly, the guy looked toward the hospital and walked quickly to where Donte had left the bike. Once the man reached it, he again looked about furtively, opened one of the saddlebags, and thrust his hand inside. Donte suppressed the urge to run out and confront the guy. Unless the stranger actually started to strip the saddlebags off the bike or tried to cut the chain, there wasn't anything to steal. Everything was in the hotel room or on his person.

The fellow withdrew his hand and then tried the other side. Instinctively, Donte touched his beltline, assuring himself that his little .22 pistol was there, hidden and secure in its concealed holster. When the man didn't find anything in the second bag, he seemed to give up and started to walk away. Suddenly, he stopped, turned around, pulled a cell phone out of his pocket, and appeared to take a couple of pictures of the bike. Then he strode away—but not back to the pickup or the Honda. Rather, he walked to the street and then headed in the direction of the hotel.

Donte had been so absorbed in the man's subversive activities that he'd failed to notice someone standing a short distance behind him. Now he heard a slight scuffling of someone's feet, and he turned away from the window.

CHAPTER FIVE

THE EXPRESSION ON CHEY'S FACE was one Donte hadn't seen there in the short time he'd known her. It was fear, of that he was certain. One hand was over her mouth, and the hand shook slightly. "Donte, what was that man doing?" she asked. The fear was also in her voice.

"I guess he thought there might be something of value in my bike's saddlebags," Donte said, forcing a grin.

She didn't have a grin to return, stepping toward him and clutching his left arm. He put his arms around her and pulled her gently to him. She laid her head on his chest, and he just held her like that for a few moments. Finally, he asked, "Chey, what's the matter? Is it Jessica?"

"She's still in surgery. No, I'm worried about that man."

"Chey, he won't hurt you. It was my bike he was snooping in," Donte said, pulling her close and loving how it felt.

She pulled back and looked up at him. "I know that, Donte. It's you I'm scared for. Something's going on in your life that must be terrible. You are such a good guy. You knew exactly what was wrong with Jessica, and you gave her a beautiful and inspired blessing. I wish you'd tell me what's happening."

For a moment, he simply looked deep into those pretty blue eyes. He found his resolve weakening. But then as he thought about the man outside, a man he knew nothing about and yet seemed so familiar, Donte made a decision. "Chey," he began, "I am not a bad person, but there are people who would cause me great damage if they found me. And anyone around me could also be in danger. I can't tell you more than that, but you must forget about me. As soon as I'm sure Jessica is going to be all right, I need to get away from Tonopah."

"I don't want you to leave," Chey said softly. "I feel safe with you here."

"But you're not. No one is. I must not endanger you. But someday, if things change, I'd like to look you up, if you don't mind," he said impulsively.

"I'll write down my address and phone number," she offered, pulling back again and looking up at him with eager eyes.

"No, you can't do that. Someone could find it on me, someone like whoever that guy outside was. But you can tell me, and I'll memorize it. I won't forget. I promise."

So she gave him her Vernal address and phone number and said, "My parents can always tell you where I am. And if you don't mind, I'll tell them your name and that if you call looking for me that they can tell you how to reach me. Or you can contact me at my Gmail account." He memorized it but didn't think he'd actually ever use it.

"Okay, thanks, Chey. You're such a sweet person. I'm honored to get to know you, but I can't tell you anymore," he said. "Should we go back to the waiting room?"

***

Clive Granger was making good time and was anxious to get to Provo, where he could meet Donte's sister, Sara. Clive had many questions and hoped that she could provide him with answers. The more he thought about Donte and the horrible situation his new friend was in, the more puzzled he was. If Donte was innocent of any crime—and Clive firmly believed that to be the case—then why was his fiancée so intent on having him arrested? Did she truly believe Donte was a murderer, or did she have other, sinister and even self-serving motivations?

Some of the questions pressing on his mind were about the murder itself. Donte had said nothing about how Walker Aklen had died. Clive wondered how much Donte even knew about the details. If Donte did know, why didn't he supply that information? Clive regretted not pressing Donte for details.

Clive was a mystery writer. He loved mysteries. He also loved to solve mysteries. The facts surrounding the death of Walker Aklen were a mystery to him, and he decided it was time to get to the bottom of it. He determined that he would stop at the next rest stop and use his laptop to learn what he could. Ten minutes later, he was doing just that.

It didn't take him long to find what he was looking for. He accessed several articles about the murder, read each of them, made some notes, and finally shut down his computer. He went over his notes then began to write on a clean page. The first item on his list was the date of the murder—a little more than three months ago. It was disturbing that so much time had elapsed without the police looking for other suspects. According to the accounts he had read, they were focused only on Donte. In fact, there had been a warrant issued for his arrest.

One of the first things he intended to learn when he got to Provo was what evidence the cops had—other than what he'd read about—that made them focus so intently on Donte. Clive wanted to know if any effort had been made to verify where Donte had been when the murder occurred.

The next thing he wrote down were facts as they had been presented by the media concerning the location of the murder. Clive had been surprised to learn that the murder had occurred outside a bar in the early morning. Many murders occur in or near bars and almost always involve alcohol, but this is what surprised Clive. How could the cops think that Donte, a man who it could easily be established did not frequent such places, would be at that location? That didn't seem logical to Clive unless the murder had taken place somewhere else and then the body dumped there. But the reports made no mention of witnesses who could place Donte at the scene. Did the cops know something they hadn't revealed to the press? Clive made a note to look into that.

The news reports *had* pointed out that the body had been discovered by an employee of the bar who had been taking some garbage out to the dumpster. The reports listed the employee's name but no address or any other facts about her.

Next, Clive listed the cause of death, which was also not what he had expected. Walker hadn't died of a gunshot wound, a stabbing, a powerful blow to the back of the head, or by being beaten at all. No, the cause of death was poisoning. It was determined by the autopsy that Walker had died following an injection of Fentanyl, a painkiller normally administered in the form of a patch. To be used as an injection, the killer would have had to dissolve the drug from a patch in some sort of solution, like saline, and then inject it. The fact that Fentanyl is a controlled substance appeared to Clive to be part of the evidence that the police might use against Donte since he had worked at a hospital and might have had access to the drug.

Of course, this cause of death raised a lot of questions in Clive's inquisitive mind. For example, Clive scribbled furiously on the sheet, how would Donte have gotten close enough to Walker to administer an injection? And how exactly did Donte get a patch or patches? How long would it take for a person to die once given a lethal injection of Fentanyl?

Finally, Clive made note of the fact that Donte had surfaced as a suspect when an anonymous tip came into the police department. That bothered Clive, and it made him wonder why the police had focused on Donte with so little evidence. However, further reading had revealed the next fact that he wrote: Donte's car, a dark blue Chrysler Sebring convertible, had been found two days later, abandoned in a parking lot only a short distance from the bar where the body had been found. When the police had searched the car and the crime lab had processed it, the only prints they'd found on the steering wheel or the shifting lever, even on the driver's side door, were Donte's.

When the police had gone to Donte's home to interview him, he was nowhere to be found and he hadn't been seen since. Both the police and the media implied that Donte had absconded due to the compelling evidence of his guilt.

One final note Clive made dealt with the fact that a car had been stolen from the same parking lot where the Sebring had been found. The stolen car was later recovered in Arizona, wiped clean of any fingerprints. The only thing that had been found in it was a blank checking deposit slip that was clearly Donte's.

Clive put his notebook down, climbed out of his truck, and stretched. He took a moment to avail himself of the facilities at the rest stop and then resumed his journey to Provo, his mind mulling over what he'd learned. Contrary to what he'd told Donte, Clive had a feeling that he wouldn't be content to just try to stir the police to action. He was itching to launch his own investigation. He promised himself that if he did, he would use extreme caution.

He couldn't help but smile as ideas for a murder mystery of his own invention began to stir about in his mind. The use of Fentanyl might be part of it. His creative juices began to flow.

***

When the doctor came into the waiting area, there was a smile on his face. His report also brought a smile to the faces of Chey and Donte. Jessica's surgery had been successful. She was out of danger and should be able to leave the hospital in a few days. They were told that she was still in recovery but that as soon as she was moved to her room, they could go see her.

Donte took a deep breath as he watched Chey, her back to him, ask the doctor a few questions. He made a quick decision. It was time for him to go. She and Jessica would be okay now. He slipped unnoticed from the waiting room and hurried outside. Once on his bike, he peddled back to the hotel in the dreadful heat. There, contrary to his previous conversation, he informed the woman at the desk that he would be checking out in a few minutes. Her name tag read Estela. She was an attractive young Hispanic woman. "But we have you down as staying for another night," she said.

"I'm sorry, but something has come up, and I need to get on my way."

"There were two of you yesterday. Did your friend already leave?"

"He did," Donte said. "And now I need to."

He was anxious to leave, and that anxiety increased dramatically when she asked, "Is your friend Donte Noble? If so, his brother was in here a few minutes ago asking about him."

"No, his name was Dave Smith," Donte said, glad that he was being mistaken for Clive. It was clear that the man dressed in gray, for that was surely who had inquired, knew his name. "I still need to pack my things and load them, but if it's possible I'd like to settle the bill now and just leave my key in the room," he said.

"That will be fine, Mr. Granger," she said. "Did you want the payment made with the credit card on file?"

Donte had intended to pay cash, but he changed his mind. He didn't want this girl to think he was anyone other than Clive Granger at this point. He'd make it up to Clive later—he hoped. "That'll be fine," he said. "Thank you very much, Estela."

Estela smiled at him. "I'll have your receipt in a moment."

As soon as she handed him the receipt, he walked away, wadded it up, and threw it in a trash can in the men's restroom before going up to his room. He didn't want anything with Clive's name on it on his person.

Back in his room, Donte feverishly filled his water bottles with ice and water and packed up his things. Outside, he watered his dog and loaded his meager belongings on the bike. He attached the small trailer to the bike, and Dude got in. If it hadn't been for this suspicious stranger, he would have stayed in town a little longer, but he felt that by sticking around, he might get caught and possibly put Chey and Jessica in danger. So as much as he wanted to stay, his good sense told him to move on.

The question now was what direction to go. He studied his small map for a moment and then made his decision. He'd go back the same way he'd come, back on the highway that Clive had found him on, back toward Las Vegas. If the man in the gray clothes knew so much about him, the man might have known that Donte came from that direction and wouldn't expect him to backtrack. As a precaution, in case he was wrong, Donte kept his pistol in his waistband, something he hadn't done before while on the bike. He also kept a sharp lookout for the stranger and anyone else who might be a danger to him.

As he pulled onto the road, he looked again but saw no one resembling the man who had claimed to be his brother. He began peddling feverishly. For the first time since he'd begun his lonely bicycle wanderings, he felt vulnerable. Someone was after him. Whether it was someone from the police or someone Kasiah might have hired in her fury, he had no idea. But there was someone.

***

Chey had been alarmed to see that Donte had disappeared while she was talking to the doctor. At first she wondered if he might have gone in search of a vending machine, and she spent a couple of minutes searching for him. But then she stepped to the window where she expected to see Donte's bike, only to discover that it was gone. He'd left her. She hardly knew him, but she already felt lonely in his absence.

Feeling depressed, she walked slowly back to the waiting area. She sat there for a few minutes before she again wandered to the entrance. Her heart hammered in her chest, and she felt slightly faint. The man in the gray shirt and blue baseball cap was standing where Donte's bike had been parked.

He stomped his feet, pounded his fist in the air, and pulled out a cell phone. As he talked on the phone, he approached the hospital entrance. Fear poured over Chey, and she headed for a women's restroom, the first place that came to mind where she could stay out of the man's sight.

She spent ten minutes in there before she finally peeked out, her heart still pounding and hands sweating. She didn't see him and worked up the courage to walk out. She hurried back to the waiting area, and then when she still hadn't seen him, she went to the nurses' station and inquired concerning Jessica. Chey was told that Jessica was now in her room. Receiving the room number and the nurse's general instructions on where it was, Chey strode off. A minute later she was standing by her friend's bed.

Jessica appeared to be sleeping, so instead of disturbing her, Chey left the room and went to the front of the hospital, with every step, watching for the man in the gray clothes. When she didn't see him, she approached the receptionist. "Did a man in a gray shirt and a blue cap come in here a few minutes ago?" she inquired.

She got her answer and more. She stepped away, frightened for her new friend, who may have looked like a tramp but who she knew in her heart was far from one. The man in the gray shirt had asked the receptionist about a man by the name of Donte Noble. He had then described Donte and been told that, yes, he had been in the hospital foyer earlier. The man had then literally jogged out of the hospital.

What was it about Donte that had someone looking for him? She puzzled all the way back to Jessica's room. Had Donte known the man? Was the stranger the reason Donte had left without so much as a good-bye? Or was it her? Did he simply want to get away from her? Of the two choices, she would rather believe that he wanted to get away from her. The thought of him being in danger cut her to the core. She missed him, but again, she hadn't known him for long. But she had known him long enough to grow fond of him and not want anyone to hurt him.

Back in Jessica's room, she pulled a chair up to the bed and tried not to think about Donte or the stranger. She wasn't having a lot of success until Jessica stirred. "Chey, you're here."

"Of course I'm here," she answered. "Where else would I be?"

"With that shaggy man who gave me a blessing," she said. "Who is he?"

"Just a guy I met when I was washing our clothes last night," Chey said. "He seemed to know a little bit about medicine and offered to give me an opinion about how sick you were. He told me exactly what was wrong and helped me get you to the hospital."

"And he gave me a blessing. I felt the power of it. He's a good man, Chey. I'd like to meet him," Jessica said.

"I'm afraid that's impossible. He's gone now."

"Gone? Where?" she asked.

"I don't know." She shrugged. "He was just a good man who entered our lives long enough to save yours and then went on his way to wherever it is he was going."

"You liked him, didn't you?" Jessica asked.

"Probably too much," Chey admitted. "But we can forget about him now. We just need to get you well and then go home."

"But we aren't finished with our trip," Jessica protested.

"Oh, I think we are," Chey countered. "You need to go home and recuperate."

"What's the matter with me?" Jessica asked.

"Your appendix burst. The doctor who operated on you says you'll be fine. But you need to go home and rest. You had a close call."

"I want to thank that man. What's his name?"

"Donte."

CHAPTER SIX

WITH SWEAT POURING FROM HIS face, Donte peddled as fast as he could. He was in great shape, but the oppressive heat was draining. He kept looking over his shoulder, fearing pursuit by the stranger in gray. Every time a vehicle approached from the rear, Donte moved as far to the side of the road as he could, praying it wasn't the man.

So far, there had been no sight of him, and for that Donte was grateful. But he knew he couldn't keep up this pace. Coming to a small dirt road that led away from the highway, Donte veered off to the west. It was clearly a road that had very little use, and that was okay with Donte. He took it, followed it for a mile or so, then stopped and walked his bike over to a small outcropping of rock that offered some shade from the relentless sun.

He took a drink of water, gave some to Dude, and then pulled out a single power bar. Dude ate a couple of pieces of jerky and then made himself comfortable in the shade. Trying to relax, Donte leaned against the rock and closed his eyes. He now regretted even more that he'd given Chey his name. That had been foolish and dangerous. In the future he had to be more careful. At least Estela, the girl at the hotel desk, thought he was Clive.

He'd made two friends in the past day. One he knew he had to try to forget. But that would be hard to do. There was just something about Chey that had touched him in a way he'd never been touched before.

With his eyes still closed, he tried to picture the mysterious stranger. Donte wished he could remember where he'd seen the man before, but try as he might, he couldn't. He began to feel sleepy and eventually drifted off. He awoke to the sound of a churning motor and wheels passing over rocks and dirt. He instantly recalled where he was. Dude began to growl, so Donte put a hand on the dog's head to silence him. Then, crawling around the base of the cliff, Donte peered over a small rise toward the road. An old, rusty brown pickup was churning up dust as it made its way slowly to the west. It passed close enough that Donte was able to get a look at the driver. Donte heaved a sigh of relief when he determined that it wasn't the stranger from Tonopah.

Donte wanted to move on but decided that it might be best if he rested a little more first. Then, if he could, he would bike into the night, putting as much distance between him and his pursuer as possible.

***

It was close to six before Chey finally returned to the hotel. Jessica was doing much better and had been asleep when Chey left. She stopped at the desk and asked if Donte Noble had checked out. The young lady, whose name tag read Estela, said, "Actually, there was no one here by that name."

Chey described Donte to Estela, who instantly smiled and said, "Oh, you mean Clive Granger. His friend Dave Smith left yesterday, but Clive checked out before noon."

"Thank you, Estela," Chey said as she turned away, very confused.

Now she didn't know if the man that had befriended her was Donte Noble or Dave Smith or somebody named Clive. And sadly, she thought, shaking her head, she might never know. But that night in her prayers, she thanked the Lord for sending Donte or Clive or Dave—or whoever he was—to help her and Jessica. And she prayed that the Lord would keep him safe. And then, she asked the Lord if she could someday meet that man again.

***

All Winn wanted to talk about was their date. It had been nice, but frankly, Sara would rather just get her work done. Winn, however, was persistent. He was ready to move into a relationship, but Sara wasn't sure she was ready for that.

"Ah, come on, Sara," he said as he leaned against her desk, a mischievous look in his eye. "You know we had a good time."

"I didn't say otherwise," she said with a patient smile. "But that doesn't mean we have to go out again tonight."

"Okay, then let's make it Monday night. Will that work?" he asked plaintively.

Sara wasn't sure how to handle this. She liked Winn, but if they got to dating steadily and then it didn't work out, what would happen to their professional relationship? She liked her job and didn't want to lose it. He waited, never taking his eyes from her face. Today was Friday, so Monday was three days away. That guy that Donte wanted her to meet would be here soon. Monday should be far enough away. Finally, she smiled and said, "Okay, Winn, Monday night then."

"Great. Let's make it six. We'll make sure to finish up here in time for both of us to get ready," he said with a broad smile. Her heart fluttered ever so slightly as she realized he must like her a lot. She hoped she wasn't making a mistake.

"Now, it's back to work," she said. "We both have plenty to do."

The phone rang, and Sara picked it up, listened for a second, and then said, "It's for you, Mr. Bertram." He winked, touched her lightly on the shoulder, and went into his office, shutting the door behind him. She transferred the call.

***

Winn answered the phone in his office, the smile still on his face.

"It's me," a familiar voice on the other end said. "I seem to have lost him again."

The smile faded. "Are you sure it was Donte?" Winn asked.

"Yeah, it was him all right. He's been biking with some dog in a little trailer."

"Find him, Bo, and keep track of him. I've got to know what he's up to," Winn said, frowning and running a hand through his hair.

"Hey, Winn, I know it doesn't seem like it right now, but I'm good at this. I found him when the cops couldn't."

"That may be. But then you let him get away. How did you do that?" Winn asked, not even attempting to keep the anger from his voice. "You with a nice SUV and him on a bike! Come on, man, you can do better than that."

"There are only three ways out of Tonopah. I've been on all three of them as far as the next town," Bo said, sounding sulky now.

"I don't suppose he could have gone a fourth way?" Winn asked.

"Fourth way?" Bo asked. "You mean back to Vegas? Why would he go back there?"

"Why wouldn't he?" Winn said. "If I were in Donte's shoes, and I had even the slightest suspicion that someone was after me, I'd go back the way I came. So that's what you do. Head south, and do it now!"

"Okay, boss." Bo sighed. "But I don't think—"

Winn cut him off. "That's right, Bo, you don't think. If you'd been thinking, you wouldn't have lost him in the first place."

It was Bo's turn to be angry. "I checked back at the hotel I saw him at earlier. They said he'd never been there. So I checked at the other motels in town. While I was doing that he got away."

"What about the hospital?" Winn asked.

"I asked there. But he was already gone."

"Time's wasting, Bo. Get on the road. I'd be willing to bet he's headed south. I want to know where he goes and what he does. Sara's warming up to me now, and I don't want Donte to interfere. And be more careful that he doesn't see you in the future. Am I clear?" Winn asked, slamming the phone down before Bo could answer.

"Bo Gray," Winn muttered. "You better find him and keep track of him. I've got a lot at stake here."

***

Sara left the office late that night. She hadn't seen much of Winn after agreeing to another date with him. However, he left the office uncharacteristically early. He muttered as he passed her desk, seeming preoccupied about something. He'd had several phone calls, and she guessed that one of them had upset him. She didn't give it much thought since she had more work to do than she could complete by five. So it was almost six when she stepped off of the elevator on the first floor.

A very attractive man who looked about thirty stood near the doors, trying to look inconspicuous as he watched the elevators. When he saw her, his eyes lit up, and he smiled, moving toward her. "Sara Noble?" he said as he drew near.

"Yes?" she replied.

"Clive," he said. "I promised to look you up."

"Oh, yes." This was the man her brother had told her about. He certainly looked like a nice man.

"I don't suppose you've eaten yet," he said. "And I know I haven't. Would you like to?"

Assuming that he meant that he would like her to go to dinner with him so they could talk, she agreed. "Sure. Would you like to follow me?"

He gave her a friendly smile, and they walked side by side out the door. Once outside she suggested a restaurant, and ten minutes later they were waiting to be seated. "We'd like as private a table as you have," Clive said to the hostess.

The waitress did well, Sara thought after the two of them were seated. It was a table in a far corner with no one very near. If they talked softly, their conversation would be private. "It's nice to meet you, Sara," he said with a pleasant smile.

"The same here." She favored him with a smile. Then she became instantly sober. Dropping her voice, she asked, "How's my brother?"

"Scruffy, dirty, lonely, but healthy as a horse," Clive answered.

"He's totally innocent."

"I know that," Clive said. "That's why I'm here. He wants the two of us to convince the police to look elsewhere for a suspect."

"As if I haven't tried," she said, unable to keep the frustration from her voice.

"Well, I can be persuasive," he said. "I really believe I can help Donte. He's a good man—despite how he looks." He grinned at her. "His dog's a bit scruffy too."

A waitress appeared, left menus and water, and then disappeared. "What do you mean, he looks scruffy? And what dog?" Sara asked. Apparently there was a lot she didn't know about what Donte was doing. Pretty much all they communicated about was each other's well-being and any possible progress on the case.

"Let me tell you about that first, then I'll tell you why I think I can help," Clive said.

"Does he look just awful?" Sara asked sadly.

"Well, let me just say this," Clive began. "He probably doesn't look like you're used to seeing him. He had a full beard—as full as a beard can get in three months. His hair is over his collar, and when I met him, it was greasy. And he smelled pretty bad. He was wearing dark glasses, a floppy felt hat, and sitting beside the road with this gray dog. According to the temperature gage on my truck, it was around 115 degrees outside. I felt sorry for the two of them, so I stopped and offered them a ride."

"I knew he was on a bike. The police took his car—after someone else left it in a parking lot. He could buy a new one, but apparently he prefers to bike," Sara said.

"He told me it is because he looks like a homeless man, and as a rule people seem to ignore him," Clive explained. "In fact, Donte said that most of the time, even though people look right at him, it's like they don't even see him. He's hiding in plain sight."

"What's this about a dog?" she pressed, leaning forward so she could keep her voice low.

"Like I said, it's just this gray mutt, gentle, housebroke, and seems quite attached to Donte. He pulls a little two-wheel cart behind the bike so the dog can ride most of the time."

"Where did he find the dog?" Sara asked in surprise.

"He didn't. It found him. So he pulls the dog, and he carries food and water for both of them. But when I stopped and offered him a ride, he was almost out of water, and what he had was warm. He didn't hesitate in accepting the ride," Clive explained. "He put the dog, the bike and the little trailer in the back of the truck. Then he got in with me."

"And he smelled bad," Sara said. "It breaks my heart. I can't believe this is happening to him. He was just about to start medical school. He's so smart and motivated. He would make a great doctor."

"I can see that. He was worried about how he smelled and how he looked. I decided to offer him a copy of the Book of Mormon that I carry in my truck just in case. I was hoping he'd want to read it, but then he told me he carries his scriptures with him and reads them every day. I think my jaw must have dropped right into my lap," he said with a chuckle.

"He's done that faithfully since he was a deacon," Sara said, fighting back the tears in vain.

"He's lucky to have someone like you," Clive said as he reached across the table and tenderly wiped the tears from her cheeks.

She felt a tingle run through her, but she didn't even know the guy. It was time to get on with whatever it was he wanted to tell her about himself. She said, "Thanks for wanting to help. I pray that you can. Now, please, tell me about yourself."

"Where to start," he said as he leaned back.

Just then they both spotted their waitress, so nothing more was said until they'd ordered. Then he began again. "I'm an author. I write mysteries. I'm currently doing much like your brother—only I'm in a nice, air-conditioned truck, and he's on his bike exposed to whatever the weather happens to throw at him. I'm driving around the West looking for places I want to set my stories in—meeting people and getting ideas. Anyway, I'm into mysteries—and not just writing them. I also like to solve them."

"What does your family think about you being gone like this?" she asked, sincerely wondering.

"My wife died several years ago, and we didn't have any children, so I'm on my own."

"Oh, Clive. I'm so sorry."

"Me too, but it's been six years now. It's been hard, but I'm trying to get on with my life. I'm doing pretty well."

Sara wanted to ask him what had happened. But she didn't dare, as it seemed insensitive, so instead she said, "Sometimes life can deliver pretty hard blows."

"That's for sure," he said.

"Are you sure you want to help us?"

"Positive," he said, "especially considering the connection I have with Donte." Before she could even ask, Clive went on. "Donte served his mission where my wife and I lived. He was in a mall there when a gunman came in. My wife was one of the innocent bystanders killed that day."

"Oh, Clive!" she exclaimed. "She was murdered?"

"Yes, and it was horrible. They got the guy that did it, but even that didn't help me much in dealing with it. But like I said, I'm moving ahead with my life right now, and writing is my life. Well, mystery is also my life. I want to help you and your brother solve the mystery that has turned your lives so upside down."

"Thank you," she said. "But it may be dangerous."

"I can take care of myself. Don't worry about me," he said with a smile. "I want you to tell me all you know about the murder and the evidence the police have. I've read up on it, but I suspect there's more that the press doesn't have. But right now I see our food coming, so let's eat."

CHAPTER SEVEN

"HEY, I HEAR YOU HAVE a girlfriend." The remark was snide, even biting, and it was not what Winn Bertram needed right now. Of all the people he didn't want to hear from, his ex-wife, Mara Bertram, was at the top of that list. She'd gotten more than a fair settlement from their divorce, and he wanted nothing more to do with her. Every so often she surfaced, though, and caused him trouble.

"What I do or don't have is none of your business, Mara. You left me, remember? We're through, over, done. Now don't call again."

"I'll call you whenever I like," she countered.

"Then I'll quit answering your calls."

"No you won't," she said. "I know things that you might not want anyone else to hear."

"Mara, what's the matter with you? You didn't used to be like this," he said, trying to keep his hand from shaking. She did have power over him, and he hated her for it.

"Nobody messes with me," she said. "If they do, I can deal with them. Now, let's talk about the girlfriend. Do you really think it's smart to date your own employee? I don't think so. I'd watch my step if I were you." Not for a moment since the conversation had started did Mara lose the nastiness in her voice.

"We're just friends, Mara," he said. "There's nothing for you to worry about."

"I know you, Winn," she snapped. "You're after something, and that's fine with me, just as long as you share." With that his ex-wife terminated the call. Winn rubbed his temples. He couldn't believe her. She thought she could smell money. Despite the settlement she had received, she was always trying to get more money from him. Sara had some money, but his interest in her was about something far more important than money. Someday, if Mara didn't back off, he would find a way to put an end to it.

***

"What is the name of the officer in charge of the investigation?" Clive asked as he set his fork down and prepared to add to his notes.

"Detective Jaren Fields," she said. "I have his card here in my purse."

She handed it to Clive and watched as he copied down the officer's contact information. When he handed it back, he asked, "How does he seem to be to work with?"

She shook her head. "He's stubborn," she said. "His mind's made up. He's even been trying to pressure Winn Bertram, my boss, to get me to tell him where Donte is. Of course, I can't do that because I don't know."

"I gathered from what Donte told me that he's careful to never give you that kind of information." He chuckled. "You didn't even know he was pretending to be a homeless, nearly penniless man. And of course, you haven't asked me where I saw him."

"I don't intend to either. I think it's best if I don't know; that way no one can force me to say. Not that Winn would do that. He's a good man," she said.

"It doesn't sound like I can expect to get much cooperation from the officer, but I'll try anyway. I promised Donte I would."

They ate in silence for a while, and then Clive said, "Let me tell you what I've learned from the articles I found, and you can correct anything that's wrong. After that, you can answer a few questions for me and fill in any gaps."

They both continued to eat as he recited the facts as he had gleaned them from his research. She mostly listened and agreed with what he'd concluded.

"I really don't know much, I'm afraid," she said after a few minutes.

"Do you have any idea how his car got to the parking lot where it was found?" he asked.

She shook her head. "I'm not really sure how it got there." She hoped he couldn't see on her face that she wasn't telling him all that she knew.

"Can you tell me where he was when the murder took place?" he asked, tapping his pencil on the notebook.

Sara's face fell. She looked down at her food and stirred with her fork for a moment. She didn't know how to tell him this, but she decided she simply had to tell it like it was. "Donte went out of town for several days of hiking, snowshoeing, and camping around Mirror Lake. He went alone and left his car at a trailhead. According to what the detective told me, no one could verify having seen him or his car. I'm really not sure how hard they tried. Donte returned the day after Walker's body was found behind the Provo bar."

"That does present a problem," Clive said. "But I would guess that more can still be done that hasn't been."

"Like what?" Sara asked.

"You and I can try to convince Detective Fields to check such things as the use of Donte's credit cards at places near Mirror Lake. And people that work in some of the nearby towns could still be interviewed."

"What if he won't do it?" Sara asked.

"Then I guess I will." Clive thought about what he'd told Donte—that he wouldn't get too personally involved. But he was determined now. If no one else would do the necessary footwork, then he'd do it himself.

"We can't ask you to do that," Sara said, almost on the verge of tears again.

"You're not asking; I'm volunteering. Besides, it'll be good experience for me. It'll help me write more realistically," he said. He was suddenly very excited to get started.

"Our parents left us plenty of money," Sara said. "I'll pay your expenses. And if I can, I'll help you do the footwork you were talking about."

"We'll see," Clive said. "Now, I need to clear something else up in my mind."

"What's that?" she asked.

"If Donte didn't get back until the day after Walker's body was discovered, how did his car get to where it was found?"

Sara rubbed her eyes and smoothed her hair behind her ears. Clive seemed like someone she could trust. And knowing Donte had trusted him, she decided she would as well. She decided then and there not to hold anything back from him. "I don't know how his car got to where it was, but I do know that he didn't leave it there. Actually, I'm not sure where he left it. I warned him on the phone about what was happening and that Kasiah was blaming him. I suggested that he might not want to come back to town. But he did anyway. He left his car somewhere and came home in a taxi. He snuck in the back door and put some things together."

"Did you talk to him then?" Clive asked.

"Yes, and while he was there, Kasiah came by. She asked if I'd seen Donte yet. She knew he was supposed to be back that day." Sara ducked her head and picked at her food again. Finally, without looking up, she continued. "I lied to Kasiah. I said that I hadn't seen him, that maybe he was staying an extra day. She said the police were looking for him, that they knew he had killed her brother. I wanted to scream at her and scratch her eyes out because I knew Donte hadn't done it. But for Donte's sake, I was able to keep my anger in check. When Kasiah left, Donte told me he'd heard what she'd said."

"That must have really hurt him," Clive said.

"I'll say," Sara responded. "I asked him what he was going to do, and he told me that he figured he'd have to get out of town, but he didn't want me to know how he left or where he went. In five minutes, he was out the back door and gone. I haven't seen him since, but as you already know, he contacts me by e-mail once in a while. He never uses his name, and he keeps the messages short and simple." She took a deep breath but said nothing more.

"Sara, do you have any idea who actually killed Walker?" Clive asked after they had both eaten a few more bites.

She looked up at him earnestly. "I've thought about that for the past three months. I've thought of little else. I don't have any idea."

"Tell me what kind of man Walker was. I know you and Kasiah were friends, so she must be a decent person. Was he a good man?"

Sara scowled. "I thought Kasiah was a good person, but now I'm convinced that's just what she wanted me and Donte to believe. As for Walker, no, he wasn't a good man. In fact, he was a terrible man. He was lazy and always trying to find a way to cheat people out of their money. He drank a lot and was into drugs. Kasiah even admitted that. But now she says he was changing and that if Donte hadn't poisoned him, Walker could have become very successful and respected. I don't believe that for a minute."

Sara watched Clive put down his fork and make some notes. Then he appeared to read through what he'd written. At last, he looked up, caught her eyes, and asked, "Are you convinced Kasiah truly believes Donte killed her brother?"

She nodded her head. "I'm afraid so. She wants him caught. So does her brother, or at least I thought he did. Now I'm not sure."

"She has another brother?"

"She had two brothers," Sara responded. "She's the youngest. Walker was a few years older than Kasiah. Sawyer is the other brother. He's several years older than Walker was."

Clive's brow was furrowed. "So why do you think Sawyer changed his mind?"

"He e-mailed me and said he would be in town soon and that he wanted to have dinner with me and explain why he now believes Donte is innocent," she said. "He told me that he thinks he can help clear Donte."

Clive's back stiffened. "What kind of a man is Sawyer?"

"I've only ever met him a couple of times, and I don't really know much about him. They're all from Grand Junction, Colorado," she explained. "Sawyer still lives there. Walker and Kasiah have been here in Utah for two or three years."

"Sara, I don't like the sound of this," Clive said. "I don't think you should meet with him."

"I have to, Clive," she said. "What if he really can help and I miss that opportunity?"

Clive slowly shook his head. Finally, he said, "Okay, but I'm going to have you do something that some of the characters in my books do. I'll check around and see if I can buy some kind of little recording affair that you can wear and I can monitor. Would you be okay with that?"

"Oh, yes, that would be great," she said as a wave of relief swept over her.

"You still can't think of anyone else who might be the real killer?" Clive asked.

"No. But I don't know Walker's crowd." She frowned. "That's what makes me so angry. The kind of guy he was, he could have lots of enemies. And I've told Detective Fields that, but his response was that those kind of people wouldn't be sophisticated enough or have the means to poison him the way he was." She shook her head angrily. "Just because Donte worked in a hospital isn't a reason to blame him for murder."

"Sara, I've got to think that whoever did it wants Donte blamed," he said. "So what we've got to do—if the cops won't—is find out who that could be. It looks like I've got my work cut out for me."

"Are you sure, Clive? You're a writer, not an investigator," she said with a look of concern.

"I can do it, Sara. At least, I can give it my best shot. Donte might not agree, but I feel like it's something I can do and, therefore, should do," he said. "And no one is going to talk me out of it."

"You have to be careful. Donte would feel terrible if you were hurt trying to help him," Sara said, concern in her eyes.

"I'll be careful; I promise. Would you like some dessert now?"

***

Donte wanted badly to get to a computer somewhere so he could see if Sara had heard from Clive yet. But he couldn't do that now. The soonest he could would be in the morning. He was using the cover of darkness to try to get back to Las Vegas. Knowing that he'd been found once was extremely disturbing. He couldn't let it happen again. Every car that passed him could be the man in gray, and that thought was a constant worry. Donte prayed that he'd be able to get away from the guy, whoever he was.

At least it wasn't so hot this late at night. He was able to travel much faster. But he still had to take an occasional break to drink some water, eat a power bar, and rest for a few minutes. He came to a rest area as he neared Las Vegas and stopped for a restroom break. He parked his bike out of sight behind the building and left Dude with it. A couple minutes later, as he walked out of the building, a burly trucker with a ruddy face and thin crew cut hair spoke to him. "Was that you on the bike?" he asked.

"Yeah, that was me," Donte said as he glanced around, searching for any sign of the man in gray. If he was there, Donte couldn't see him.

"Pretty hot weather for biking," the fellow continued. "I'm running empty right now. I could give you a lift if you'd like. Where you bound for?"

"That'd be great. I'll go wherever you are," Donte said gratefully.

"Where's the bike and the dog?" the fellow asked.

"Behind the building," Donte said. "I've learned a man can't be too careful."

"Ain't that the truth? Well, I'm in the truck right over there, the one with a shiny green tractor. Get your stuff, and we'll be on our way."

The bike and trailer went in the back of the semi, and the dog got to ride in the cab with the men. It wasn't until they were ready to roll that the man turned to Donte. "I'm Carl Judd."

"Dave Smith," Donte said. "I sure do appreciate this. The heat, even at night, is oppressive."

"I'm bound for Phoenix to get a load. You can ride all the way or get off anywhere in between," Carl said.

"As a matter of fact, Phoenix would be perfect. And I'd be glad to pay for the lift," Donte volunteered.

Carl waved a beefy hand and said, "No need for that. I guess you got money for grub, huh?"

"I do," Donte agreed. "In fact, it would be an honor to buy you breakfast in a few hours."

The big fellow chuckled. "I'm a big eater. Are you sure of that?"

"I'm sure," Donte said. "It's the least I can do for a chance to be out of that awful heat."

"It's hot in Phoenix too," Carl reminded him.

"I suppose, but it's not in your truck. At least Dude and me can get cooled down while we're riding with you."

Carl put the big diesel in gear and slowly pulled forward. A man, dressed all in gray, was standing beneath a tree near the exit. Donte sucked in a breath. He got a good look at the man's face and knew that it was the man he'd seen in Tonopah. Donte shivered when he realized that the man apparently knew Donte was in the rest area and was waiting for him. After they passed him, Donte leaned forward and looked in the truck's right mirror. His pursuer was still watching the restrooms. Donte slowly let out his breath. That was close, he thought as he offered a quick prayer of gratitude.

Suddenly, even as he was silently praying, Donte remembered where he had seen the man before. It had been about a month before the murder. Donte had dropped a sandwich off to Sara at her office. She'd been especially busy that day, and when he offered to buy her lunch, she had asked him to bring it to her.

That same man, dressed in gray, had stepped into the elevator as Donte had stepped out. Donte had turned and watched the elevator, noticing that it had stopped at the second floor, the one Sara worked on. He'd hoped the man wasn't heading for her office—he'd given Donte a creepy vibe—and Donte remembered asking Sara about it that evening.

"Yes, he came to see my boss," she had said. "He comes in every once in a while. It's always personal business, the guy says. And as long as there's no client in his office, Mr. Bertram always has him come right in. I guess they must be friends. But you know what's strange," she had added, "he always wears gray, except for his hat if he's wearing one. I think of him as the man in gray. And I don't really like him. There's just something about him . . ."

As that all came back to Donte, a shiver ran up his spine. What in the world was a friend of Winn Bertram's doing following him? The thought was so disturbing that Donte couldn't get it off his mind all night long as the truck rumbled toward Phoenix. Winn seemed like a nice fellow, but a burning in the pit of Donte's stomach caused him to doubt that assumption now. How he wished he could talk to Sara and warn her that things might not be good at her office.

CHAPTER EIGHT

AFTER EATING A GOOD BREAKFAST at a truck stop the next morning, Carl suggested that they both might want to take a shower. Donte was all for that. He made his a quick one and then sat down at a bank of computers as he waited for Carl to finish. It was seven thirty. Since it was Saturday, he was pretty sure Sara wouldn't be going to work. But he wasn't sure if she'd be home or not. If not, at least she would have her phone, he thought, and she could read a message from him and respond to it. He composed a short e-mail and sent it, hoping she would get it right away. He hoped she would understand the entire message, not just the first two sentences. It was the only way he could think to warn her.

***

Sara heard the beep on her iPhone. She got lots of e-mails, and when she could, she checked them as they came in, hoping it was Donte and not wanting to miss him if it was. She knew this one was from him when she saw it, and her hands began to shake as she opened it. She smiled as she read the short message. It simply said: *Scrunch: Did you hear from the salesman yet? I like the stuff he had. Oh, and don't buy anything from the man in gray. Slurpee.*

Sara read the message over several times. The first two sentences were very clear. Clive was the salesman, and Donte trusted him. The third sentence was the puzzler. For the life of her, she couldn't make sense of it.

She finally typed a short reply: *Slurpee: he had some good product. I'll be getting some of it right away. What? Scrunch.*

She hit Send and sat back on her sofa. She bowed her head and thanked the Lord that Donte was still safe and prayed that the meaning of his message would become clear.

Suddenly, like a flash of light, it did. Months ago, she had called some friend of Winn's "the man in gray" when Donte had seen him in her office building. She felt sick to her stomach. She quickly typed another response to Donte. It read: *Slurpee: I got it. Scrunch.*

Within seconds another message came back from Donte. Her head was reeling. His message simply said: *Seriously, Scrunch. He's a bad salesman. I've watched him sell. Tell the other salesman. Love you. Slurpee.*

Her response back was one word: *Okay.* He wanted her to tell Clive, and she would.

It was the first thing that Sara said to Clive when she saw him later that morning in the parking lot of the police station. "I heard from Donte. And I'm scared to death now. I don't know what to do."

"Why? Is he in some kind of trouble?"

"I'm not sure, but I think it was a warning. In fact, I know it was a warning."

"Do you have the messages?" Clive asked.

"I usually delete anything from him as soon as I've read it, but I kept these so you could see them," she answered. "Read them, and then I'll delete them before we go inside to talk with Detective Fields. I'm Scrunch, and he's Slurpee. Those are nicknames our father gave us when we were kids."

They stood beside Clive's truck, with Clive leaning against the pickup bed. She handed her iPhone to him with the first e-mail opened. He read it, and then she scrolled to the next one. Sara watched his face as he read. His brows were furrowed, and he seemed to be thinking deeply. Finally, he handed her back the phone and said, "Tell me about this mysterious man."

The furrows in his brow deepened as she told him about the man who often visited her boss and how all Winn would say is that he was a friend. "Winn is a good boss and a friend," she said after finishing. "Yet, I can't help but worry about him now, even though I have no idea why Donte is suddenly warning me about this guy, this friend of Winn's."

Clive suddenly took a deep breath and pushed away from the truck. "He said he'd seen the salesman work. I wonder if—"

Sara finished his sentence. "He's seen the man."

"Yes, that was my thought exactly," Clive agreed. "I'm guessing that the man has spotted him somewhere. I'm also guessing that Donte managed to evade him or we wouldn't have gotten this message."

Sara deleted the e-mails as she thought about what Clive had said, and then she murmured, "I have a date with him Monday night."

Clive leaned toward her. "Did you just say you had a date Monday?"

Sara nodded, her eyes studying her white running shoes as first one and then the other scuffed at the blacktop. "Yeah, I'm afraid so," she said without looking up.

"Sara, who do you have a date with?" he asked urgently.

"Winn," she said quietly.

"Your boss?" he asked, putting his hands on her shoulders.

"Yes, Mr. Bertram." Her eyes finally met his. "We went out earlier this week too. He's been pressuring me. I thought it was because he was attracted to me, but now I'm wondering."

"Sara, he could be attracted to you. You're a very pretty girl. But if there *is* something more sinister going on, then we need to figure out what it is." Clive paused for a moment before continuing. "We need to talk this over before we go inside and talk to Detective Fields. We have a few minutes. I told him I'd be there by eleven. He said he'd be in his office until at least noon. So let's go for a ride."

They drove a short distance away, sticking to residential streets. Clive drove slowly as they talked. "When was the last time this friend of Winn's came into the office?" Clive asked.

"It's been a couple of months or more. That's why it took me a minute to figure out what Donte meant. Since it's been that long, I wonder if they aren't such good friends after all," Sara reasoned.

"Unless . . ." Clive began, his brows furrowed in thought. She waited to see what he might say. "Unless," he finally went on, "the guy's been looking for your brother, or even following him."

Bile rose in Sara's throat at that thought. "Why?" she asked, a tremor in her voice. "Why would he do that? Are you suggesting that maybe he's doing it for Winn?"

"That's exactly what I'm suggesting," Clive said.

"If that's true, then it might . . . might . . . Oh my goodness!" she stuttered. "Could Winn have something to do with Donte being accused of murder?"

"We need to keep an open mind about that," Clive said calmly.

"It could also mean—I hate to think this, but could it mean—Winn is a murderer?" she asked, forcing the words out.

"We need to keep an open mind about that too," Clive answered, his voice still calm. But then he added, his tone more worried now, "You could be in danger if he has done either of those things."

"But why?" she asked. "He didn't even know Kasiah's brother."

"At least, you don't think he did. But can you be sure?" Clive stole a glance at her.

She hesitated but finally said, "No, I'm not sure at all. Right now I'm not sure of anything."

"I have an idea. Let's go talk to Detective Fields, and then we can see if we can find out about this gray-dressed fellow," he suggested.

"Okay," she said slowly, rubbing her chin. "But how will we go about doing that?"

"Leave it to me," he said. "I'll think of something. That's what I do, you know. I think of things." He grinned at her. "And I'm pretty good at it."

She gave him a wan smile and then asked, "Should we tell the detective about the man in gray?"

"Not unless we can think of a way to do it without letting on that we've been in contact with Donte," he said as he again turned into the parking lot. "Let me take the lead and see where it goes," Clive suggested.

Detective Jaren Fields was a stocky man who stood about five eight. When Clive and Sara entered his cubicle, he stood up, brushing a hand across his short, dark, graying hair. He extended the hand to Clive. "Jaren Fields," he said.

"I'm Clive Granger. Of course you know Sara Noble."

"Sure do," he said. "What brings you in today?"

"It was my idea," Clive said.

Detective Fields waved them to seats in front of his desk and then sat down himself. "And what is your relationship to Miss Noble?"

"I'm a friend of her brother. Donte served a mission in Omaha when my late wife and I were living there," he said, implying that he'd known Donte since then.

"I see. And you keep in touch?" the detective asked slyly.

"Not as much as we should," Clive answered. "My wife was murdered in a mall shooting along with several other people. Donte was there when it happened."

"In Omaha?" the detective asked.

"Yes, but also in the mall. I'm a writer, and I'm doing research on a future book," Clive said. "When I learned that Donte had been accused of murder, I was shocked. I know him well enough to know he could never do such a thing. I would like to try to help him, but I have no way to get in touch with him."

"A lot of us would like to find him," Detective Fields said with a frown. "There's a warrant out for his arrest."

Sara was staying out of the conversation. She was impressed with the way Clive was leading the officer without actually lying. He was very good with words. She hoped someday she could read his books. She suspected they'd be pretty good.

Clive spoke again. "I know you're looking for him, but honestly, Detective, I don't believe he's the man you should be looking for."

The detective frowned. "His fiancée does. I would think that if anyone were to believe him innocent, it would be her."

"I understand why you would think that way, but I don't understand why she feels that way. I think more focus should be put on looking for other possible suspects," Clive said.

Detective Fields's face darkened. He leaned forward in his desk. "Such as whom?" he asked.

"Well, I don't actually know. That's why I'm here asking you to look beyond Donte." Clive shifted in his chair. "I know a little about the victim. He was the kind of man who could have lots of enemies. You know that."

The detective sat back, and his face relaxed a little bit. "That much I must admit is true. But you must admit, if you know anything at all about this case, all the evidence points directly at Mr. Noble."

"I beg to disagree with that," Clive said. "For example, he was in the mountains on snowshoes and camping when your victim died."

"We have nothing to substantiate that," the detective argued.

"Sara told you that. She's certainly a trustworthy witness."

"And she is also Donte's sister. No offense, Miss Noble," he said, glancing briefly at her. "She has a reason to cover for him."

"And that reason is?" Clive pressed.

"They are a loving brother and sister," Detective Fields responded, his face going dark again. "Other than her word, there's no one who can back up the purported alibi. Not one soul."

"Kasiah Aklen knew where he'd gone," Clive pointed out.

"She knew where he *told her* he was going, but she doesn't know that he actually went there or that he may not have returned early. Miss Aklen loves the guy but is willing to admit he did something she hates," the detective countered. "And remember, his car, full of his fingerprints, was found just a short distance from where the body was found."

"That's another reason I think you should be looking for someone else. Donte's a smart man. He'd been accepted into medical school, had perfect grades, and so on. He would never be so stupid as to leave his car near the crime scene. If he'd killed Walker, I would have expected the car to be a long ways from there."

"Another car was stolen from that same parking lot and then found a long ways from here," the officer said. "And in it we found one of Donte's checking deposit slips. That's pretty good evidence."

"What about fingerprints in the stolen car. Did you find Donte's prints?" Clive asked.

"No. It had been carefully wiped clean of any prints," the detective said smugly. "Don't you find that quite interesting?"

"As a matter of fact, I do," Clive agreed. "But not in the way you are thinking. Let me ask you to consider this: why would Donte be so thorough in making sure he didn't leave a single fingerprint in the car and then leave a deposit slip where it could easily be found? That's what I find interesting."

Detective Fields cleared his throat and drummed his fingers on his desk. To Sara, he seemed nervous, something she had not seen in her previous encounters with him. He cleared his throat a second time, ceased the drumming, and said, "There is also the matter of the manner of death. He was poisoned using a pain killer called Fentanyl. It is typically used by applying a patch onto the skin of the person being treated. It's a controlled substance but available in hospitals. It appears that one or more patches were soaked in something, probably saline solution, then the solution was apparently sucked into a syringe and injected into the victim's left arm, killing him within minutes. This is all in the medical examiner's report."

"Are you saying that only Donte would know how to do that or have access to the drug?" Clive asked, shaking his head as if in disbelief.

"That's exactly what I'm saying," Detective Fields confirmed. "He had access, and he had knowledge, even expertise." He again sat back smugly.

"I again beg to disagree with you. Not that he wouldn't have the access or the knowledge, but that no one else would," Clive said, a touch of anger in his voice now.

"Disagree all you want," the detective said. "Of course, if you can name someone who might have that knowledge and had a reason to kill Walker, then I'd be glad to look into that person's whereabouts at the time of the murder. But we both know that someone who associated with Walker isn't likely to have that kind of knowledge."

"Ah, Detective," Clive said with a glint in his eye. "You mention motive. Would you care to state for me a motive in the case against my good friend Donte Noble?"

The detective squirmed, rubbed his hair, and then began to drum his fingers on the desk again. He said nothing, and Clive pressed his advantage. "There is where your case falls apart. In fact, the lack of motive is strengthened by the fact that Donte was engaged to marry the victim's sister. It makes no sense, and you and I both know a jury wouldn't buy it, that he would, for no articulable reason, kill the brother of the girl he loved! Come on, Detective. You can do better than that."

Detective Fields's face was mottled in anger. He came to his feet, as did Clive. "I'm working on the motive. It's not like I'm sitting around doing nothing on this case," he practically shouted.

"Then why, after three months, haven't you found one?" Clive demanded. "I'll tell you why. It's because there isn't one! And it's about time you admitted that. And one more thing you need to consider is why Walker would let Donte stick a syringe in his arm? It seems to me that either someone else was holding the victim—an accomplice—or else he'd been knocked out and then injected."

The officer's mouth opened then closed. He sat back down. "Sit down, Mr. Granger," he said through gritted teeth. Clive did so. "If you can give me any names I could focus on, I'll give it my best shot," he said.

"Do I have your word on that?" Clive asked.

"Yes, you have my word."

"Thank you. I'll do that. Just give me a few days."

"I'm not suggesting that you go digging around, Mr. Granger." There was a warning tone in the officer's voice.

"You want names, I'll find names, but to do that, someone has to dig. When a beautiful young woman with not a lot of brains accuses someone, that doesn't take any digging around. Kasiah doesn't know why Donte would have killed her brother, but she thinks he did. That's pretty weak. Yes, I'll do some digging, and when I find names, I'll bring them to you."

"Don't get yourself killed in the process," the officer said in a low voice.

"If Donte is the killer, who would want to kill me besides him? Of course, I know he would never do that," Clive pointed out as he came to his feet and pushed his chair aside. He pointed a finger at the officer. "By giving me that caution, you as much as admitted that the real killer could very well be someone else, someone who doesn't want his or her name brought up and looked into. Good day, Detective."

With that, Clive motioned for Sara to follow him. At the door, he stopped, pulled out his wallet, and extracted a business card. He walked back over to the desk and dropped the card in front of Detective Fields. "Call me if you want to talk. I'll make sure my cell phone is always on."

CHAPTER NINE

"THAT WAS PRETTY AMAZING IN there," Sara said as they walked out of the police station. "If I *had* believed that Donte was the killer, you certainly would have filled me with second thoughts."

"But does Detective Fields doubt his own case now? I'm afraid not," Clive said with a shake of his head. "He's as determined as ever that Donte is guilty, and I don't see him backing down. So it looks like I've got some detecting, some *digging,* to do."

"I'll help if you'll let me," Sara said softly.

"It could be dangerous. If anything should have Fields thinking this whole thing through again, it's that he told me to be careful," Clive said, walking swiftly toward his truck.

"Yeah, I like the way you handled that," Sara said, almost jogging to keep up. "And I think maybe that did set him back a little. Who knows, maybe you'll get a call from him."

"Maybe, but I doubt it. I'm hungry," Clive said suddenly. "Would you like to get some lunch somewhere?"

"With you?" she asked with a tiny little smile.

"Yes," he said. "You and I need to brainstorm some more."

"Then the answer is yes, I would. But I'm buying."

***

The burley trucker was dozing in the sleeping unit of his truck. Donte had also slept for a little while, though it hadn't been easy in the uncomfortable seat. Anyway, Carl had told him that he could use the sleeper when they hit the road again in a few hours. They'd stopped at another truck stop, and Donte thought maybe he'd use a computer while he was waiting for Carl to wake up. He left Dude tied to the grill in the front of the truck in the shade. Walking inside he was on constant alert for the man who seemed to prefer wearing gray. Vigilance had become second nature. Inside, Donte did the same thing but was once again reasonably satisfied that the man hadn't found him.

As he'd hoped, the rest stop had computers available for the use of customers. Donte sat down at one and read the latest news for a few minutes. The world was still the same: unemployment was high, crime was high, wars raged in the Middle East, and politicians spent all of their time pointing fingers at one another instead of solving any problems. Tiring of the monotony, he opened one of his several generic e-mail accounts. He very much wanted to make contact with someone. It was a strong temptation.

For a moment, he held his fingers suspended over the keyboard, but he pushed his concerns aside and let his emotions take over. He made several key strokes, entering an e-mail address that had been on his mind ever since he had first memorized it. Then he began to type a message. He wrote a couple of things and then erased them. He wrote some more, changed a few words, and studied what he'd written.

Doubts again flooded his mind, but he didn't discard the message. Then, almost recklessly, he succumbed entirely to the temptation and hit Send. At that point the message was beyond stopping. That done, he sat and looked at the computer for a minute, hoping he hadn't made a terrible mistake. Logging off the computer, he went in search of a snack and a book to read. The name of his new friend, Clive Granger, came to mind, and Donte searched the book shelves for something Clive had written. To his delight, he found one. He immediately took it from the rack and read the summary on the back cover. It grabbed his interest immediately. Next, he picked up a cold soda, a candy bar, a small bag of nuts, and a little bag of jerky. The jerky was for his faithful dog, everything else for himself. At the checkout stand, he paid for his purchase.

Donte wandered outside and returned to the idling truck. He freed his dog, and the two climbed back into the cool interior, where Donte began to snack, feed his dog a treat, and read the book by Clive Granger.

***

"You're awake," Chey Beckett said as she stepped into Jessica's room after a light lunch at the hospital cafeteria. "It looks like they brought your lunch while I was gone. But you didn't eat much of it." She pointed to Jessica's tray.

"I ate all I could. I'm afraid I'm not hungry," Jessica said.

"I didn't eat much myself," Chey admitted.

"Worrying about a certain homeless man?" Jessica asked with a tiny smile on her pale face.

"Yes, as a matter of fact, I am," Chey said. "I just wish I knew who he really is. I do know that he's not who he looks like."

"He did me a huge favor," Jessica agreed. "In fact, according to what you and the doctor told me, he saved my life."

"Him and the Lord," Chey reminded her.

"That's why he showed up when he did. The Lord sent him to save my life. Then He let him move on. I know you don't want to hear this, but you'll probably never hear from him again."

"I can hope, and I can dream," Chey said wistfully.

Her phone was on silent in her purse. She pulled it out to check it.

"Check my e-mail, would you, Chey? I hope there's something from my parents."

Chey did as her friend asked and discovered that Jessica had a dozen e-mails from not only her parents but her siblings and some friends. The messages were all pretty much the same, wishing her a speedy recovery.

"Thanks, Chey," Jessica said.

Next, Chey checked her own e-mail account. The most recent message was not from an address she recognized. With a suddenly accelerated heartbeat, she opened that one without even checking to see who the others were from.

She felt the blood drain from her face as she began to read. The message said: *C. Sorry to leave so fast. I'm fine. Miss you. Is J. okay? Did you see the man in gray again? Please delete this when you have read it. D.*

"Chey, you look like you've seen a ghost," Jessica said. "Are you okay?"

"Yes, I'm fine, I think."

"Is that from who I think it is?"

Chey didn't even bother asking who that would be. She just nodded. "Yes."

"What did he say? Is he okay? Where is he? Why did he take off like he did?" Jessica asked quickly. Her face, though pale, was almost radiant in expectation.

"I don't know where he is," she said. "But he's okay, or he says he is. Jessica, he says he misses me. I miss him too. This is crazy. He looks like a bum, but he is the kindest man I've ever met." As she spoke she was smiling and looking wistfully at the screen on her phone.

"What else did he say?" Jessica begged. "Tell me. And how did he sign his name. Is it Donte or Clive?"

"Neither, but I think he meant Donte, although he might have meant Dave. He only typed initials. Here, read it."

Jessica took the phone, read the message, then handed it back to Chey. "That man, the guy you said had gray clothes and a blue ball cap. He's after Donte, isn't he?"

"I think so," Chey answered. "I need to send him back a message. I hope he gets my reply."

She typed a quick response, hit Send, and deleted the message. She opened her other messages one at a time, but she was barely aware of what she was reading. Her mind was focused on the message from Donte. She was thrilled by it, and she was also frightened. She silently prayed that Donte was safe and would continue to be so.

***

After about thirty minutes, Donte again tied his dog up and walked back inside. He went directly to the small bank of computers. They were all in use, and all three customers seemed very intent on whatever they were doing. He paced back and forth for a moment then gave up and walked outside.

When he got back to the truck, Carl was awake and petting Dude's head. "This is a good dog you have here, Dave," he said. "I'll bet he's good company."

"He is at that," Donte agreed. "Are you getting ready to hit the road again?"

"In a bit, but I need to go inside for a minute. Then we'll go," Carl told him.

"I've been waiting for an e-mail," Donte said. "If you don't mind, maybe I'll check once more before we go?"

"Not a problem, but don't be long," Carl said.

Just as Donte was approaching the computers, one fellow stood up and walked off. Donte hurriedly sat down, and a moment later he was opening a message from Chey. It read: *D., I haven't seen him since you left. J.'s doing well. Miss you too. C.*

He hurriedly typed: *C., I'll ask again later. Take care. D. Oh, and delete this for sure.*

He hurried back to the truck, feeling a warm glow at the few words from Chey. He wished he could have met her under other circumstances—before he ever met Kasiah. Even though he'd only known Chey briefly, he felt the goodness that emanated from her. She was not a raving beauty like Kasiah, but she was much, much more attractive to him. But, he thought as he untied Dude and watched Carl striding toward them, it was foolish even thinking about her. After all, his life was no longer his own, and maybe it never would be again.

As they settled back and Carl started driving out of the parking lot, Donte started to think about Sara and Clive. He wondered what was happening in Provo and if they had been successful in getting Detective Fields to broaden his investigation. Donte hoped so, but he also couldn't help but feel that their attempts were probably futile. From everything he'd read and all Sara had told him, it seemed that Fields was totally convinced that Donte was the guilty party and it was a waste of time to look for other suspects. The thought was depressing.

He opened his book and began to read again. "What are you reading?" Carl asked.

Donte waved the book in the driver's direction. "It's a mystery. Pretty good, actually."

"Oh, it's by Clive Granger," Carl observed. "It's got to be more than pretty good. I've read a couple books by Granger, and I even have one on CD. He's an excellent writer."

"When I'm through, you can have this one," Donte offered.

"Thanks, that'd be great," Carl said. He pointed over his shoulder toward the sleeper unit. "Mine are back there. We'll trade, if that's okay."

"That would be great," Donte agreed.

"If you get sleepy, just crawl back there and get some shut eye," Carl told him. "It's not hot back there. Dude can just curl on the seat here and take a nap, if he wants."

Donte smiled. The dog had already curled up between the two men, his nap well underway.

***

Winn Bertram was not a happy man. He was on the golf course with three buddies, and they had a good game going. But Bertram's game had been spoiled. He'd received a call that was not what he wanted to hear. Bo had said, "I can't find him, Winn." That was all he'd needed to ruin his day.

"Don't you know how important this is to me?" Winn had asked. "You have got to find him. It's extremely important that I know where he is and what he's doing. When you do find him, you know what to do."

"Yes, I do. And I'm giving it my best, Winn. But as you said yourself, Donte is a very smart man. He could be anywhere now."

Winn had tried to control his temper. He'd let Bo bluster on for a couple of minutes about how hard he'd looked. Then, tiring of the excuses, Winn had sent Bo back to Tonopah. "Go to the hospital there and that hotel you think he might have stayed in. Find out what he was doing there, who he might have talked to, why he'd been at the hospital."

"He'd been at the hospital, but they didn't tell me why." Bo was whining.

"Go back and find out why he was there," Winn snapped. "His bike was at the hospital. I doubt he was there just to get a bite to eat at the cafeteria. He went to see someone. Find out who, locate whoever that is, and put some pressure on them. You had better find him and soon."

As his golf game plummeted, he worried about Donte, where he was and what he was doing. If Bo didn't find him, Winn didn't know what he'd do. Bo just had to, that was all there was to it. It was imperative.

***

With their lunch over, Clive and Sara walked out into the bright sunlight. Clive had mapped out an itinerary for the afternoon. Now he simply had to follow it. "Why don't you go home, Sara?" he suggested. "I'll get to work."

"I want to help if I can," she said. "After talking to Detective Fields, I am restless. He's not doing his job."

"You're right, he's not, so I'll do it for him. If you want to go with me, that's okay, at least for now. Do you want to take your car home and ride with me?" Clive asked.

"If that's okay, or we can take my car," she suggested.

"Okay, let's do that," he said, "if you don't mind. I can leave my truck at the hotel, and then you can drop me off back there when we've finished for the day."

That agreed to, they drove to the hotel. "Why don't you come in for a minute?" he suggested. "We can begin here. The first thing we need to do is follow a hunch. You use the phone book, and I'll use my laptop."

"You didn't mention a hunch," she said. "What hunch?"

"The man who wears gray. I'm wondering if his name, by any chance, might be Gray."

"That's kind of a long shot," she said dubiously, as they entered the hotel and approached the elevators.

Clive nodded in agreement and punched the up button. "Yes, it is, but it's a starting place. I think we need to find out who that guy is."

"Okay, whatever you say," she agreed.

In his room, Clive started his laptop, and Sara got out the phone books. "What do I look for?" she asked. "There'll be lots of Grays."

"Look for a private investigator by that name. I may be wrong, but if so, we can try something else," he said.

Clive wasn't wrong. They both found a Bo Gray Investigations within minutes. His office was in Salt Lake, but he also had a Provo phone number. "I wonder what color of clothing he wears," Sara said with a hopeful smile. "At least if he's an investigator, he's not likely a murderer."

"We can't count on that," Clive cautioned. "Killers can come from all walks of life. I've never actually known of a PI who is a murderer, but I'd be willing to bet there have been some. Even cops can be murderers— and nannies, babysitters, doctors, nurses, lawyers—you name it."

Her stomach rolled uncomfortably. "Or lawyers and PIs working together," she said.

"Exactly. Let's begin making a list of persons of interest, as the cops say. I know you like your boss, but we need to list him and this Bo Gray. If we find that Bo Gray is not in any way connected to Winn Bertram, then we'll remove Winn's name. But for now, they're both on the list."

"Are you going to give Detective Fields those names?" she asked as she pictured her boss, a man she enjoyed working for.

"No, I won't give him any names until I have more information. If I gave this to our detective friend, he'd just laugh at me. I'm pretty sure he'd do nothing at this point," Clive explained. "No, we've got to have something concrete for him, someone we can show had both motive and opportunity. Right now, all I'm doing is guessing."

Sara walked over to where Clive sat at the desk on the far side of the room. He looked up at her from where he'd just typed the names of Winn and Bo. She was looking down at him with furrowed brows. "What's the matter, Sara?" he asked.

"I thought we were just going to get some possible suspects," she said, "and then give those names to the officer to work on. Isn't that what we talked about at lunch?"

"Well, yes, it is, and I will give him the names we come up with but not without anything to substantiate why I consider them worthy of his time," Clive explained. "Like I said, I'm not giving him my guesses."

"In other words, you intend to solve the crime," she said sternly. "Clive, I'm sorry, but I don't think that's a good idea. It could be dangerous. In fact, it almost certainly will be. I don't want you to risk your life."

Clive stood up and studied her face for a moment. "Sara, your brother's innocent. We both know that. I haven't been totally open with you, I admit. But in my opinion, the only way we'll ever get the real killer is for me to do it myself."

"Clive, you don't have to do that," she said.

He reached out and placed a hand on her shoulder, giving it a gentle squeeze. "Yes, I do. I lost my wife to a killer. I wasn't able to do anything for her. I've felt guilty all these years that I wasn't there to help when that man went on his rampage. I've mostly been able to put it behind me, but not totally. I feel like finding and bringing this person or persons to justice would finally bring me closure so that I can get on with my life."

He paused, removed his hand from her shoulder, and stared across the room, deep in thought. This time, it was Sara that reached out and touched Clive. She laid a hand on his arm. He drew his eyes slowly back from where they had been staring, and she said, "Please, I'd be devastated—and so would Donte—if anything happened to you."

The smile that Clive favored her with was a sad one. "If I were to die trying to help someone else, I'd die knowing my sweetheart would welcome me with pride," he said.

Sara felt like her heart might burst. Clive was so unselfish and caring. She removed her hand from his arm and turned away, walking hesitantly toward the door, and he sat back down at his computer. She stopped at the door and stood there for a moment with her hand on the knob.

Finally, she turned back and looked at him. She was full of pain over what her brother was going through, but this good man, one she and Donte scarcely knew, was willing to put himself in harm's way if that's what it took to save them from the kind of pain he had suffered for so many years.

CHAPTER TEN

WHEN SHE FIRST HEADED FOR the door, Sara had planned to go home, but she didn't want to. Dangerous or not, for Donte's sake she wanted to be involved in whatever Clive was going to do next. "What now, Clive?"

"I'm just going to do a little more digging the rest of the day. Then tomorrow—"

Sara gently cut him off. "Tomorrow, you and I will go to church together."

"I'm not very good company," he said.

"I think you're rather nice to be with," she countered. "I know you'll want to go to church somewhere, so it just as well be with someone you know."

Their eyes met, and then a smile crossed his face. "I'd be honored to go with you."

"Okay, so that's settled," she said with a smile. "Now let's talk about the rest of today. I'd be more than willing to help dig." Clive looked uncertain for a moment, and Sara said, "If you don't want me to help, then say so, please."

"It's not that," Clive said as a shadow passed over his face. "It's just that . . . well, I'm used to being alone, to working alone."

"So does that mean . . ." she began.

He shook his head, got up from the desk, and moved toward her. Sara stood still and watched him approach. He came right up to her, put his hand on her shoulder again, and said, "It's like this, Sara. I haven't dated another woman since . . . since she died. I feel awkward around you. And yet," he said, looking deep into her eyes, "I also enjoy your company. You're the first woman I've had dinner alone with in six years. Does that seem strange?"

"No, I think I understand. If I make you uncomfortable, then . . ." She let her voice trail off again.

"That's not the problem. The problem is just the opposite. I feel awkward, and in a way, unfaithful, but I also find being with you comforting and enjoyable," he admitted.

"Then let's work together on this . . . this, ah . . . case," she stuttered.

"But if I got you hurt, I don't know if I could live with myself," he said softly.

"You won't get me hurt. I want to do this. I want to do this for my brother." She stopped, her eyes searching his. They were hazel, clear, intelligent, and full of emotion. She liked his eyes a lot. They were quite spellbinding. She shook her head as if trying to escape from a trance. "And I'd also like to do this to help you find the closure you seek. Please, can we be a team until Donte's safe again?"

Clive slowly nodded his head, and then he held out his hand. She took it, enjoying the strength she felt there. "It's a deal—on one condition," he said as they slowly shook hands.

Still holding his hand, she asked, "What's that?"

"If it gets really dangerous and I ask you to step aside, you'll do it. Agreed?"

She nodded, not saying a word. Apparently that was enough to satisfy him, and he said, "Then let's get to work."

They left the hotel together in her car, as they had previously discussed. She drove to the Salt Lake address they had found for Bo Gray, the man they both hoped was "the man in gray," the man who had found Donte. When they arrived at the large office building, it was closed, the door locked, and no one responded to Clive's knock—as they'd feared.

"Now what?" she asked.

"We need to see what we can learn about Kasiah and her family. There may be something that will help us get on the right path," he mused. "Is she in town?"

"She was in Grand Junction—that's where they're from—but I don't know if she's still there or if she's back," Sara responded.

"How can we find out?"

"I can call her, or we can go to her apartment," Sara said. "But she and I aren't exactly friends anymore, as you can imagine."

"Let's go there."

***

It hadn't taken Bo long to get back to Tonopah. He'd berated himself all the way back for not asking why Donte had been at the hospital. He was upset with himself that he hadn't thought to find out who might have been in the hospital that Donte would have a reason to visit. He'd done something he knew better than; he'd *assumed* Donte had gone to the hospital seeking some kind of help for himself. Bo promised himself that he wouldn't make such an egregious error again. He knew that it was important to Winn to find and keep track of Donte. Winn hadn't told Bo why he wanted Donte followed, only that there was a lot at stake. Why Winn didn't just let the cops know when Bo had first located Donte was a mystery. Bo wasn't beyond using unscrupulous means to accomplish his work, but he also wasn't about to do something that was likely to get him arrested. He trod a thin line.

Bo was also concerned about damaging his already shaky relationship with the cops in Salt Lake and Utah counties, where he did most of his work. That was especially true when it came to Detective Fields. He'd crossed paths with Fields before and had learned that the detective did not take kindly to someone interfering in his cases. Right now, by searching for and having actually had Donte in sight, Bo knew that Fields would consider that interfering. Bo had familiarized himself with the evidence against Donte, and it was pretty compelling. Yes, he was definitely putting his professional reputation on the line, and he hated doing that, but on the other hand, Winn Bertram paid very well.

He drove to the hospital first. Bo knew all about the confidentiality laws that guided what hospitals could and couldn't—mostly couldn't—divulge about a patient. Therefore he needed to devise a plan that would allow him into the area where patients were being treated. He parked and watched the hospital for a few minutes, thinking and scheming. Suddenly, an idea hit him. He started his car and drove to the hotel where Donte had been staying. He checked in and then did something he seldom did. He dressed in his blue shirt and blue pants. That was as far from gray as he ever strayed, but right now, he felt the need to do it. He combed his hair and, leaving his hat in the room, went back to his car.

He again drove to the hospital, parking as far away from the main entrance as he could. Then he got out and strode toward the building, still not entirely sure what he'd do once he got inside. He hadn't yet reached the door when an attractive young woman came out. She looked familiar. Bo was good with faces—when he saw one, he usually remembered it—and he had seen this girl somewhere in town. He searched his memory as he stopped near the entrance and turned to watch her climb into a silver car. He nodded to himself. He knew where he'd seen her. Quickly, he headed back to his own car and started it up. The silver car pulled out of the parking lot, but Bo kept it in sight and followed.

He pumped his fist when it turned into the very hotel where he now had a room, the hotel where he was certain Donte had stayed. "You are the means to finding Donte," he said softly to himself as the young woman parked and headed for the front entrance. Not all of Bo's connections with the police were as strained as his relationship with Fields, and he intended to take advantage of that now. He parked his car where he had a good view of the license plate on the silver Chevy Malibu. Then he called a number that was stored in his phone.

He made a request, thanked the officer, and sat back to wait. Ten minutes later his phone buzzed. Bo wrote down the information, again thanked the officer, and terminated the call. Chey Beckett was the registered owner of the Malibu. She had a Vernal, Utah, address. Now all he had to do was find out if she knew Donte Noble.

He went to his room, carrying his laptop and briefcase. For the next few minutes, he worked on his computer, doing a series of searches. He learned very little about Chey Beckett, and there was nothing there that seemed to indicate any connection between her and Donte. They went to school in different parts of the state, had grown up far apart, and didn't appear to have anything in common.

But he still had a feeling that they knew one another. Perhaps he needed to take the direct approach. He didn't have her room number, but he was reasonably sure he could get it from the front desk now that he knew her name. He went downstairs and directly to the counter. He remembered the pretty little Hispanic girl who was on duty there. She was on the phone, so he leaned against the counter and waited.

"Hi, Estela," he said when she hung up. "Would you leave a message for a friend of mine, Chey Beckett?"

"Certainly, Mr. Gray," she said. "What's the message?"

"Just tell her that Bo Gray is back and that we can finish our business when she gets a few free moments," he said. "She should be back from the hospital soon."

"Oh, she's already back," Estela said brightly. "I saw her come in a few minutes ago. I'm sure glad her friend is going to be okay. She sure had close call."

"Yeah, pretty serious. I'm glad she's okay too." He had no idea what was wrong with Chey's friend, but that was beside the point.

"Would you like me to call her room and see if she'll come down and meet you?" Estela asked.

"Sure, I guess that would work," he said. The girl was playing right into his hands.

Estela picked up the phone and punched in the room number, which he quickly memorized. Before the phone had time to ring, Bo said, "Never mind. I don't want to disturb her now."

Estela put the receiver down. "Are you sure?" she asked.

"Yes, I suspect she's tired. She's probably been at the hospital for a while and came back to rest," he said in a caring tone. "I'll contact her later. It's nothing pressing. You've been a big help, Estela."

"Thank you, but I really didn't do anything," she said.

"But you were willing," he replied with his most charming smile. He turned away and headed outside, thinking that she had helped more than she had any idea. He now knew Chey's room number, and he could contact her at his leisure. Right now, he was hungry, and he didn't like to be hungry. He headed on foot to a nearby café. He selected a table where he could keep an eye on the hotel parking lot just in case Miss Beckett decided to leave.

***

Chey tried to rest, but she couldn't. She had too much on her mind. She was worried about Jessica. Her friend was running a fever today, and although the doctor said not to worry about it—that they would get it under control—Chey worried anyway. And she couldn't get the man dressed in gray out of her head. She finally got up. Perhaps she should go back to the hospital. She hated leaving Jessica there too long at a time, and she could rest about as well in the soft chair in the hospital room as she could on the hotel bed.

As Chey passed the front counter, Estela, the sweet girl on duty there, called her by name. "Chey," she said, "are you leaving already?"

Chey turned and walked over to the counter. "I'm just so worried about Jessica," she said.

"I thought she was doing better," Estela said.

"She was, but now she has a fever. I came back to rest, but I'm too worried, so I guess I just as well be over there," Chey said.

"I guess you haven't talked to your friend yet?"

Chey felt a sudden chill. "What friend?" she asked in concern. She didn't have any friends here unless Donte had come back, and she was pretty sure that wasn't the case.

"A really nice man was just here asking about you. He first asked me to give you a message, to tell you that he was back," Estela said.

Chey felt a surge of hope. "Was he dressed kind of like a bum and with long hair and a beard?" she asked.

"Oh no, I remember that guy. He didn't look like much but was sure nice. Was he your friend?"

"Yes," Chey said. "But if it wasn't him, what *did* the guy look like?"

"He was probably about forty. He wasn't too tall but not short either," she said as she twisted a long strand of shiny black hair. "He had short hair and a really nice smile."

With her heart almost in her throat, Chey asked, "Was he dressed in a gray shirt and pants?"

"No, his shirt was blue. I think his pants were too," Estela responded.

"Did he have a hat on?" Chey asked.

"No, not this time. But when he checked in he did," Estela said, and then her dark eyes suddenly grew wide. "Oh, I just remembered, he *was* dressed in gray earlier. But the cap was blue, I think."

Chey felt faint. She grabbed the edge of the counter for support.

"Chey, are you okay?" Estela asked in alarm.

Chey nodded her head. "He's after me. I think he's dangerous. I don't know what to do."

"Call the police," Estela said. "Here, I'll dial for you."

"No, that won't do any good. There's nothing they can arrest him for. He hasn't done anything—yet," she said as tears filled her eyes.

"Here, come back into the office so that if he comes in again, he won't see you," Estela suggested. "And then we can talk about it. I'll help you if I can."

Chey did as directed and stepped through a door Estela opened. Estela directed her to a private room where she'd be just out of sight of the hotel lobby. Finally, when the phone was quiet and no one was at the counter, Estela joined Chey and asked, "What do you want to do? How can I help?"

"Do you know if he's in his room now?" Chey asked.

"I don't think so. He left out the front door and was walking toward the café down the street," Estela said.

"You can see the hotel parking lot from there, can't you?"

"The front, yes," Estela responded.

"I'm parked in front, so if he's in the café, he could be watching my car?" Chey's voice trembled.

"I'm afraid so."

Chey rubbed her eyes, trying to keep the tears in check. "Then I can't leave," she said. "I'm trapped."

Estela twisted her black hair for a moment, and then she said, "I have an idea. My car is parked in back. You can take it if you want."

"Oh, I hate to put you out," Chey said. "Then you won't have anything to drive."

"Maybe I could borrow your keys," Estela suggested with a smile. "We could pull a switch on that awful man."

"But I would still need to come back here, and he could see me come in, no matter what car I'm driving."

Once again Estela thoughtfully pulled at her hair. Just as she was about to speak, the phone rang. "Excuse me while I get that. But I think I know what we can do."

Chey was sweating even though the air was cool in the little office. She was frightened. Donte wouldn't have warned her about the man in gray if there wasn't a good reason.

When Estela came back, she began, "Okay, I have a plan. Let's check you out of the hotel, and you can take your things and your friend's things out the back way to my car. I'll give you directions to my place. I live alone in a small apartment, two bedrooms, just a few blocks from here. Of course, anyplace in Tonopah is just a few blocks from anywhere else in town. Anyway, you can stay there while your friend gets well."

"That's so sweet of you, but my car—he'll follow you when you leave in it," Chey said. "I don't want to cause you any trouble."

"My brother works at a garage in town. He can take your car and hide it. He also has two cars, a Dodge pickup and a little green Subaru. He usually drives his pickup, so I'll use his Subaru and you use my little yellow Neon," she suggested.

"Okay, that might work, but I still hate to do this to you." Chey hesitated. "I might be putting you in danger."

"No, that man won't know where to look for me or even have a reason to," she said with more confidence than Chey was feeling.

"No matter who takes my car from here, that man will see it. By the way, did he say what his name was?" Chey asked.

"Yes, he did. It was an easy name to remember. He said he was Bo Gray."

"Who is he? What does he want from me?" Chey mused.

"I don't think you want to find out," Estela said, shaking her head. "Now, you let me and my brother worry about your car. We'll figure out a way to move it without Mr. Gray knowing."

"But how?" Chey wanted to know.

"That's easy," Estela said with a grin. "We'll distract him. Now, let me check you out, and then we can get you out of here before he comes back. You drive to this address." She jotted it down on a slip of paper and handed it to Chey. "My apartment key is on the car key ring. In case you need to go to the hospital before I get off, just leave the apartment key in the little flower pot at the side of my door. I'll do the same for you. Just shove it beneath the dirt. It won't hurt it. Now let me tell you how to get there without passing the café."

Twenty minutes later, Chey was in Estela's very clean but quite small apartment. She had managed to calm down, but she was still worried about what she was going to do next. She wished that Jessica was better so they could just leave town. But she wasn't, so Chey would just have to deal with it. She prayed, and then she called Jessica to explain that she wouldn't be able to come back to see her for a few hours. That done, she typed a short message on her iPhone and sent it off, praying that Donte would get it before too long.

CHAPTER ELEVEN

DONTE WOKE UP FROM HIS nap feeling much refreshed. He crawled from the sleeper, scooted Dude aside, and sat back down on the seat. He was thinking about Chey again and hoping that the man in gray hadn't gone back to Tonopah. If their roles were reversed, that's exactly what he would do, and then he'd try to find someone who knew the man. Since that's what he would do, it was likely that his stalker would do the same; he might go to the hospital or the hotel or both, find out about Chey and Jessica, and then use them to try to locate him.

Carl said, "Something's bothering you, Dave. Is there anything I can do?"

"You could magically make a computer appear," Donte joked.

"Why do you need a computer?"

"I have a friend who's sick, and I'm worried about her. The only way I can make contact is through e-mail," Donte explained.

"I can't make a computer appear, but I do have an iPad. Will that help? It has the Internet, and it has whatever they call it that allows it to work off a phone tower. I don't understand much about technology. I don't really even know how to use it, but my wife gave it to me for Christmas, so I carry it around in my truck and plug it in once in a while. That way she'll think I'm getting a lot of use out of it."

"Carl, you're a lifesaver. Does your cell phone also have Internet?"

"I don't know, but it doesn't have very good reception. The iPad would be best. You're more than welcome to use it if you can figure out how."

"I know how to use it," Donte said.

"You are a surprising man, Dave. You aren't what you appear to be." Carl eyed Donte for a minute. "The iPad's in the sleeper in my suitcase. I keep it in a side pocket. Help yourself."

"Thanks," Donte said and began to climb back into the sleeper.

"Use it back there if you like, or you can bring it up here. Whatever suits you," Carl said.

Donte chose to use it in the sleeper. He probably didn't have any messages, but he wanted to be sure. The first thing he noticed when he turned it on was that the iPad only had a small charge left. He shoved his hand back in the pocket of Carl's suitcase and found a charger. He'd use the iPad for a minute now, he decided, and then take it up front and plug it in.

There were two messages. He opened the first one. It was from Sara. *Slurpee, the man in gray could be a PI working for my boss. Name's Bo Gray. I'll let you know more when I can. Scrunch.*

Donte hit Reply, typed a quick message, sent it, and then deleted both Sara's message and his own reply. Then he opened the second one. It read: *D, that man is in town asking for me. His name is Bo Gray. I'm hiding but scared. C.* Donte felt a shiver travel all the way down his spine.

With shaking hands he replied to Chey, sent it off, and again deleted both the message and the reply. Then he sent another message to Sara. If this Bo Gray was working for Winn Bertram—and that appeared to be the case—then Sara needed to be very careful what she said around Winn. For all Donte knew, Winn could be the source of all their troubles. That was a very frightening thought. Donte warned her, praying that she would understand. He felt so helpless. Two women he cared about were both in danger, and he didn't know what he could do beyond warning them. He also thought about Jessica. She could also be in danger. He typed yet another message to Chey warning her that Jessica might be in danger too. He felt so helpless. He had to do something, but what? An idea came to him—a desperate idea—but the more he thought about it, the more he realized it was probably his only choice.

***

Sara and Clive, after failing to make contact with Kasiah, were back in his hotel room. Clive was on his phone, making a call to the police in Grand Junction, hoping to learn a little bit more about Kasiah's brothers. She could hear him explain, "Yes, I'm a private investigator from Utah. I'm trying to get some information on the background of a murder victim by the name of Walker Aklen and his brother, Sawyer. A typical background check would probably be sufficient."

A minute later, Sara tuned him out and checked her e-mails. She could hardly believe it when she found that this latest one was from Donte. She couldn't imagine how he could have gotten to a computer so fast, but she guessed that didn't matter. What was important was what he had to say. She opened his message: *Scrunch, thanks for the info. Keep me informed. Will have frequent access for a while. Slurpee.*

She was about to send her reply when another e-mail came in. She opened it and read: *Scrunch, I just learned that Bo Gray is the man. You know what that means. Be careful around W. B. Slurpee.*

Clive's call to Grand Junction ended while Sara was finishing her reply to Donte. "I talked to a detective," Clive told her. "He said he knew about Walker's death and that no one there felt too bad about it. He also says that both Walker and Sawyer are pretty bad characters. The detective will call with some specific information later." Clive was looking closely at Sara. "You look like you've seen a ghost," he added.

"I heard from Donte. Bo Gray *is* the man who's after him. He says to be careful around Winn. Clive, what's going on?"

"That's what we're going to find out," he said. "And I think we are making progress."

***

Chey was reading a reply from Donte, surprised but grateful that he had responded so quickly. She read: *C, don't let him find you. Sorry you're mixed up in my troubles. Will get back to you. D.*

He wasn't kidding, she thought as she opened a second e-mail from him. *C, J's in danger too. Trying to think of something. Wish I could put the guy out of commission for a while. D.*

She replied and then sat back, rubbing her eyes and thinking. She called Jessica at the hospital. "I don't want to scare you, but something's come up. Tell the nurses that you don't want any visitors but me. And I mean no one. The man in gray that I told you about, the guy who seemed to be looking for Donte, is in town. His name is Bo Gray. You mustn't let him into your room."

"Chey, what's going on?" Jessica asked in alarm. "Why is anyone after Donte? He's a good guy."

"I know. Now listen. I checked out of the hotel, and I'm staying somewhere safe. I can't come over right now. Please," Chey begged, "tell the nurses to keep people away from you. We don't know what this Bo Gray guy might do."

"But we don't know where Donte is, do we?"

"No, but Gray probably won't believe that. I'm sorry, Jessica, to scare you like this. I'm trying to think of something. When I do, I'll call again. Love you, girl. Hang in there," Chey said, ending the call.

She then made another call. This one to the hotel. She was relieved that Estela answered. "Estela, it's Chey, I'm at your apartment. Thanks so much. I was just warned that Bo might try to get to Jessica, my friend in the hospital. I told her on the phone not to let visitors in—no one but me, anyway. But I don't dare go there right now. Have you seen Mr. Gray?"

"Not yet. I'm pretty sure he's still in the café. My brother and his friend will get your car soon," she said.

"Thank you, Estela. You are such a wonderful person."

"And so are you. I'm glad I met you. I'll talk to my brother about Mr. Gray. He might be able to think of something. I'll let you know," Estela said in a secretive voice. "Just don't worry, Sara."

***

Estela had to handle a couple of hotel matters before she could make another call, but when she had a minute, she went into the privacy of the little office and called her brother. "I don't want you to get in any trouble," she said when he answered, "but this man who is causing so much trouble might hurt a girl in the hospital. I think he's dangerous. If we can, we need to do something to keep Chey and Jessica safe."

She listened to her brother's reply, then she continued. "Please, don't get in trouble. But thank you." She listened again. "Are you sure?" Once again she was quiet. Then she said, "You won't hurt him, will you?" His reply satisfied her, and she hung up the phone.

A customer was at the counter, so she had to hurry out. Then the hotel phone rang, and Estela got very busy. For the next half hour, she didn't have time to even think about what her brother had said. Finally, another employee came in, as was always the case this busy time of day. "I need a short break," she told him, and she stepped outside. To her relief, Chey's car was gone. She looked for Bo Gray's vehicle. On his check-in sheet, Bo had written that his vehicle was a white Ford Expedition. There was a vehicle meeting that description close to the street.

Satisfied, she went back inside, her mind never far from Chey and the man who was stalking her.

Estela looked up once about a half hour later as she was checking a customer in and spotted Bo stride by. He was dressed in gray again. He stopped at the door and, to Estela's dismay, turned and walked over to the counter and stood in line.

"Have you seen Miss Beckett?" he asked when the other person had finished his business.

"She checked out. She said she needed to go home," Estela lied smoothly. "I would have given her your message, but you said not to."

"But her friend is still in the hospital," he said. "There's no way she'd leave without her friend."

"I wouldn't know about that, Mr. Gray," she said politely, trying to keep her voice from giving away her extreme anxiety.

"Well, I would," he said, his face suddenly going dark. He turned and strode angrily from the hotel.

Another customer was waiting for Estela's help. The lady made a comment about how rude the man in gray had been. Estela nodded and said, "How may I help you?"

***

Chey was surprised when she got another e-mail from Donte. She quickly opened it and read: *C, I've decided what has to be done. Get a message to Mr. Gray. Tell him I'll be in Phoenix in the morning. Tell him to send me an e-mail at this e-mail address. But don't contact him personally. Have someone take him a note, leave it on his car, or slip it under his door. And do it as soon as you can. I miss you. I won't let him hurt you. This should get him out of town. D.*

***

When Estela's shift ended, she went outside and immediately saw that the white Expedition was gone. She circled around to the back of the hotel. Her brother's green Subaru was there, key beneath the floor mat, as he'd promised. She started the car and drove straight home, keeping a sharp lookout for the white SUV. At her apartment, she parked next to her own car and went inside. Chey was sitting on the sofa, reading something on her iPhone. Her face was long, and it looked like she'd been crying.

"I'm home," Estela said in a chipper voice, hoping to cheer Chey up. "Are you doing okay?"

Chey stood up. "I think so, thanks to you. This is a really nice apartment."

"Thanks. I like it," Estela responded. "Did you put your things and your friend's in the spare bedroom?"

"I did. I don't know how to thank you," Chey said.

"It will be nice to have a roommate for a few days. Have you talked to your friend at the hospital?"

"Not for a little while. I wish I could get over there to see her."

"Maybe we can both go over in a little while," Estela said. "I need to make a phone call, and then we can decide. But first, tell me what you are so upset about. I can see something's wrong. You're not all right."

"I need your help again," Chey said, "if it's not too much trouble."

"Of course. What do you need?"

"I have to write a note to Bo Gray and tell him where Donte is. Donte insists, even though it will put him in an impossible situation. If I write the note, will you go slip it either under his windshield wiper or under the door of his hotel room? Please."

"Let me make that phone call first and see if you need to," Estela said.

"But I must get the message to him," Chey stressed.

Estela held up a finger. "Give me a minute, and you sit down and relax if you can."

Chey sat back on the sofa while Estela made her call. Chey could only hear Estela's half of the conversation. "So are my friends safe yet?" Then, a moment later, "Are you sure, Marcos?" Another pause and then, "You won't get in trouble, will you?" She laughed at whatever her brother said next, then she responded, "Thank you. I owe you big time." There was another long pause, and then she said, "Okay, I'll do that. I promise. And tell Jose he's invited too."

The conversation ended on that note, and Estela was smiling. "It's safe to go to the hospital now. We'll go in my car, if it's okay with you."

Chey was not sure and she said so.

"Hey, girl, Mr. Gray is not going to be looking for you. I promise. Come on, we can go visit Jessica, and then we'll go out and eat."

"Are you sure?" Chey asked. "Has something happened?"

"Don't you worry about that, Chey. Believe me, I'm positive he won't bother you now," Estela said.

"I hope your brother didn't do something terrible," Chey said, still worried.

"Don't worry, he's a smart man," Estela said. "He can take care of himself. Should we go now?"

"Okay, but first let me send a message to Donte."

***

Donte looked up from the screen. "Sorry I'm using your iPad so much, Carl."

"Don't worry about it. I hardly use it at all. I'm glad it's getting some use. And my wife would be glad too," Carl said.

"Thanks," he said, opening another e-mail that had just come in from Chey. He read it, puzzled and then reread it. *D, Mr. Gray has already left town. I won't be able to get a note to him, but he won't be coming back. J. and I are no longer in danger. That's all I can tell you. Miss you too. C.*

Donte looked at the message once more. What could have happened? He hoped that Chey hadn't done something that could get her in trouble. He wished he was back there. He made a sudden decision. He turned to Carl, "I need to go back to Nevada," he said. "I'll get out anywhere you can stop."

"We've come a long way. Are you sure that's what you want to do?" the burly man asked in surprise.

"It's what I have to do, Carl. Someone in Nevada needs me."

"Okay." The big man shrugged. "There's a rest area up ahead. We truckers kind of stick together. Let me see if I can get you a ride with someone going that way," Carl offered.

"That'd be great, but if not, I'll take old Dude here and do what I've been doing."

Donte addressed an e-mail to Sara and sent it off. He told her he was pretty sure Bo Gray wouldn't be a problem for a while but that later he might be even a bigger problem. He didn't know what had happened in Nevada, but whatever it was, at some point, Bo Gray could be more dangerous than ever. That was why he needed to get back to Tonopah, and that was why he was warning Sara.

He sent one more message to Chey, and a few minutes later, good to his word, Carl had found a trucker who was headed for Las Vegas and was more than willing to have some company. Donte reluctantly gave up the iPad and loaded his bike, trailer, and meager belongings on another truck. With Dude in tow, Donte was going back the way he'd just come, a feeling of urgency pressing down on him.

CHAPTER TWELVE

CHEY OPENED THE MESSAGE FROM Donte as she and Estela sat in Jessica's hospital room. The fever was bad, and Jessica was miserable. "Are you sure we're safe now?" she asked Chey.

Chey looked over at Estela, who just said, "Yes, you're safe."

Chey's phone indicated that she had another e-mail. She opened it, saw it was from Donte, and began to read. He'd written: *C, I am coming back. It might take me a couple of days, but I'll be back. I won't be able to contact you again for a few hours, at the best, but I will when I can. Be careful. Give my regards to J. See you in a few. D.*

"What are you smiling about?" Jessica asked in a weak voice.

"Donte's coming back. It may be a couple of days, but he's coming back!"

"Why?" Jessica asked.

"He's worried about us," Chey replied. "And I'm worried about him. I can't wait to see him."

***

First his golf game and now his bowling. This was supposed to be a day of relaxation for Winn. It had been a busy and stressful week, and he didn't need this. "What do you mean you can't find Donte or the girl in Tonopah? Of course you can. That's what you do, Bo! You said yourself that you're good at that kind of thing. Now get at it. I have got to know where Donte is and what he's doing."

"But I ran into a little trouble with some guys," Bo whined.

"What kind of trouble? Can't you just find the girl, whoever she is, and make her tell you where Donte is? What could be easier for a man of your experience?" Winn was trying to keep his temper under control and his voice down. He was right in the middle of a game and had been forced to step away to have this private conversation with a man who was making him increasingly angry. Stalling the game wasn't making his friends happy, either.

"Okay, Bo, calm down and tell me exactly where you are and what you are doing right now," Winn said as calmly as he could.

"I don't know," Bo said, the whine still in his voice. This was not like Bo. Winn felt a tremor run through him.

"What don't you know, where you are or what you're doing?" Winn asked, keeping his anger in check.

"Both."

Winn took a deep breath. "Let me get this straight, Bo. You don't know where you are?"

"Yeah, that's what I said."

"And you don't know what you're doing?"

"Well, other than talking to you, I'm not doing anything. I can't."

"Okay. Let's take this from the top, but we need to do it quickly." Winn rubbed his temples, trying to stave off the threatening headache. "You had a run-in with some guys. Who were the guys, and how many were there?"

"There were three. Two were Hispanic; one was white," Bo said, sounding like he was near tears.

"And what did they do to you?"

"They made me get in my Expedition, and they drove me way out into the desert," he said.

"Then drive back from the desert," Winn interrupted angrily, "and get your job done."

"They did something to my car. I can't move it. The engine runs, but I can't put it in gear, and all four tires are flat. They left me here alone," Bo said.

"Okay, so call for help—call a tow truck."

"I can't. I don't know where I am. That's what I'm trying to tell you," Bo said, his poutiness turning to anger. "They put something in my water, and I fell asleep."

"So you don't know how long they drove before they left you." Winn paused, thinking. "Okay, do you know what time they picked you up, or kidnapped you, or whatever it is they did to you?"

"I don't know for sure. It was sometime this afternoon, several hours ago. But I don't even know how long I was unconscious after they got me here."

"Let me get this straight, you can't drive your car but you can run the engine?" Winn asked.

"That's right."

"How much gas do you have?"

"It looks like it's full. They must have refilled it before they left me here."

"But you don't know?"

"I was unconscious." Bo emphasized each word.

"Okay, do you have food and water?" Winn asked.

"Yes. The note they left says I have enough food and water for over a week," Bo said.

"Well, that being the case, I guess you can take the food and water and hike back to civilization. And I would suggest you do it quickly," Winn said in exasperation.

"I can't do that."

"Because you don't know which way to go?" Winn rolled his eyes.

"That's true. But even if I did, I can't walk."

"They injured you?" Winn asked.

"No, they took my shoes and all my clothes but my boxers and a t-shirt," he whined.

"Bo, what a fool you are. I can't believe you let this happen."

"They caught me by surprise."

"Well, we have no choice but to call the cops. They can trace your location through your cell phone. Just don't tell them what you were doing in Tonopah."

"I'm not that big a fool, Winn. I never betray a client. But we can't call the cops."

Winn heaved a sigh. "Okay, and would you like to explain *why*?"

"Winn, they left me with a bunch of drugs. Bad stuff. Felony stuff. If the cops come, I'll end up in jail."

"And if you don't, you'll die in the desert," Winn told him.

"They said they'll come back for me before that happens," Bo said.

"And you believe them?"

"What choice do I have?"

"Maybe someone will come along and find you," Winn suggested.

"That won't happen. I'm nowhere near a road, as far as I can tell," Bo told him.

"In that case, Bo, I guess I'll have to replace you. I can't afford to lose track of Donte."

"You do that, Winn. I quit! I don't know what kind of connections Donte has, but I have better cases I can work on. I'm lucky to be alive. That man is a killer, as you well know."

"*If* you survive," Winn said, not responding to the comments about Donte. "*If* you can trust your abductors to come get you."

"I think I can," Bo said.

"But are you willing to bet your life on it?"

Bo was silent for a long moment, and then he said, "Probably not. You can't let me die here, Winn." The statement came out as a long and plaintiff wail.

"I can make an anonymous call to the cops," Winn said.

"No, don't do that. I'll get arrested."

"Then what do I do?" Winn asked. "Technically, I'm not obligated to do anything since you just quit."

"No, you fired me."

"I said that maybe I'd have to replace you. That's not the same."

"Then I don't quit," Bo said. "You've got to figure something out."

"I won't let you die, Bo. So here's the plan. If you haven't made contact with me within nine days, I'll call the cops. So keep your phone charged. They'll need it to find you. In the meantime, get rid of the drugs. Bury them or whatever you have to do, but get rid of them."

"They told me not to do that, that the cops would know."

"Do it anyway. Bury them deep."

"I'll try," Bo said. "But I don't have any tools."

"You have a jack handle and lots of time to dig."

"No, they took it."

"Then you think of something," Winn snapped. His patience was gone. "But whatever you do, keep your phone charged."

"They took my charger," Winn said.

"Then shut your phone off. Turn it on briefly once or twice a day to check for messages. You will hear from me in a week at about this time of day unless I hear from you first. Got that?"

"Yes, but—" Bo began.

"No buts, Bo. Let's hope Donte's friends come get you. Otherwise, you know the plan." With that, Winn ended the call and rejoined the others. "Sorry about that. That was a client. He needed advice and couldn't wait. Is it my turn?"

***

"What's next, Clive?" Sara asked as the writer shut down his computer.

They had received an e-mail from the officer in Grand Junction. They were at the hotel again and had just finished going over the report. Both Walker and Sawyer had criminal records. Kasiah, on the other hand, had no record at all. In fact, the report stated that she was, by all accounts, a law-abiding, decent young woman. The officer wrote that he'd known her in high school. She'd been very popular, got good grades, and was active in extracurricular activities. She had been a cheerleader, acted in school plays, and so on. In contrast, he didn't think that either of her brothers had even graduated from high school.

"I want to check out the bar where Walker's body was found," Clive said thoughtfully. "But I'm not sure that's a place you would want to go. Why don't you take the evening off, and I'll call you later if I learn anything."

"We're partners, remember?" she said. "I'll go with you. But I was wondering, since we've been reading about Kasiah and her brothers, if we should go to her place again and see if she's home yet."

"Okay," Clive said. "But I'm sure you've never been in a bar before. I'm really not sure that—"

Sara cut him off midsentence. "Have you?" she challenged.

"Have I what?"

"Have you ever been in a bar?"

Clive grinned sheepishly. "No, I haven't, but I—"

Once more she interrupted. "I guess we'll both have our first experience, then, won't we?"

"You are a stubborn girl, Sara," he said, but there was a twinkle in his eye.

"I love my brother. He's all the close family I have in the world. I am not going to lose him. If that makes me a stubborn girl, then I guess I am. Should we go now?"

Clive looked at his watch. "We haven't had dinner. Let's do that first. And it's my turn to pay."

"No, we aren't taking turns," Sara said. "You're helping Donte and me. We can afford it, so the expenses are on us."

Clive shrugged. "If you insist. Like I said, you're stubborn."

She chuckled, punched him lightly on the shoulder, and said, "Let's go then."

After they were seated in the restaurant and looking at menus, Sara said, "So tell me more about yourself, Clive."

He looked up. "There's not much to tell."

She grinned at him. "Sure there is. I don't know how old you are, but I'd guess around thirty," she said. "In that many years, you have to have done a lot. If we are going to be partners on this investigation, I think it might be good for me to know a little more about my partner. All I know is the tragic part . . . and that you write mystery novels."

"That's right," he said, again looking down at the menu.

"So what got you started writing mysteries?" she asked.

"You're right," he said.

"Huh? That doesn't answer my question. What am I right about?"

"I'm thirty," he said. "But I don't know your age."

"And being the gentleman you are, you won't ask," she said with a grin.

"I guess not, if you put it that way."

"I'm twenty-three, just a kid, you could say," she said as she laid her menu on the table.

He was still studying his. Without looking up, he said, "A stubborn kid, but a pretty one."

Her face flushed. He still didn't look up, but he spoke again. "I think I've decided."

"To tell me about yourself?" she asked hopefully.

"No, I've decided what to order," he replied. Then he looked up and folded his menu. "I have a degree in journalism and worked for a news-paper. I spent a couple of years covering crime, writing about it. I learned a lot during that time. After my wife was killed, I couldn't take the crime beat anymore, so I quit the paper. For a few months, I drifted from job to job, menial stuff. Then I decided to write. It worked for me. I found an agent, she got me a publisher, and I've made a living at it for the past four years."

"I can't wait to read your books. I bet they're good," she said.

Just then the waiter came. The two gave their orders. After the waiter had wandered off, Clive said, "Some of them are a bit sad. People tell me they're good, and I've had a lot of positive reviews. Anyway, they must be okay or they wouldn't sell. But I'm afraid they're heavy on sadness and trag-edy. But I want to move away from that now. I'll try to put a little more humor in my work." He paused, taking a sip of water. "Now, you aren't old like I am so you may not have as much to tell, but I'd like to know a little more about you too, partner."

"Okay, I don't have a college degree. But I was trained as a legal secretary, and as you know, that's what I do," she said.

The smile that had been on his face for the past several minutes faded. "And you work for a man I think we both agree should be considered a suspect."

She nodded gravely. "But he's such a nice guy," she said. "I can't believe he would do such a thing."

"Sara, working the crime beat taught me some things. I worked a lot with the cops. Some of them became good friends," he said. For a moment, he looked Sara right in the eye. "One of the things I learned is that you can't always tell what a person's really like. Many people have secrets that are dark and ominous. How well do you really know Winn Bertram?"

"I've worked for him for more than two years. He's treated me really well," she said.

"Has he ever been married?" Clive asked.

"He's divorced. His wife was a piece of work, as they say."

"So you know her," he stated.

"Well, not exactly. I just know what he's told me about her," she admitted. She paused for a moment, and all Clive did was look at her. Finally, she said, "I see your point."

"Then with that in mind, tell me what you're going to do about your date with him on Monday evening," Clive said.

Sara stared at him for a moment, and then she moved her gaze to the salad the waiter was placing in front of her. After he'd given Clive a salad and moved away, Sara looked up, rubbed her forehead for a moment, and finally said, "Will you be able to get something I can wear, like you said you'd do for my meeting with Sawyer Aklen? You know, some kind of recording device so that you can listen in on my conversation with Winn."

"Yes. In fact, maybe before we go to meet with Kasiah we could find an electronics store and see what we can come up with," he suggested. "We'll get something that can be used remotely with you wearing a wire, as they call it in police circles, and me listening and recording. But we'll also get a digital recorder that we can have in a pocket to record people we talk to."

"That'll be great," she said. "I know it will make you feel better, and I guess, in all honesty, it will make me a little more at ease too."

"Yeah, and we won't have to rely on our memories when we conduct interviews."

With that matter settled, they ate their dinner with a little companionable conversation from time to time.

Near the end of the meal, Clive said, "Sara, I could be wrong, you know."

"About what?" she asked.

"About Winn," he responded. "Donte and I could both be wrong. He might be perfectly innocent."

"Then how do we explain Bo Gray?" she asked.

"I'm just saying we need to keep an open mind while also exercising caution. We may have the whole Gray and Bertram thing figured wrong."

"Thank you, Clive. I needed to hear that," she said, her eyes watering. "But you could also be right."

"You like him a lot, don't you?"

She nodded. "I do, but I'm not in love with him, if that's what you're asking. He's a great boss, and we're good friends."

He smiled. "I hope he realizes what a good friend he has in you."

She felt her face go just a little bit red. "I just hope he really is the decent man I've known the past two years."

A little while later, they found what they needed at an electronics store. "It's not the quality that the cops use, but it should work okay if I'm not too far away."

"Like how far away?" Sara asked.

"Close enough to come to the rescue of a damsel in distress," Clive said with a grin. "Let's get over to Kasiah's."

There was a light on in the apartment when they pulled up outside. "Okay, now how did you say we should do this?" Sara asked.

"Just introduce me as a friend," Clive reminded her. "Ask how she's doing. Mention that you'll be meeting with Sawyer. I won't say a lot unless I feel the need." He grinned. "I suppose at some point I'll probably feel the need, but I'll try to be careful what I say. Mostly, I'll listen and watch. I want to see how she reacts, listen for inflections in her voice, watch her body language—that sort of thing."

"Okay, I'll do my best," Sara promised.

Kasiah answered the door wearing a pair of tight jeans and a Western-cut blouse. That was not Sara's usual manner of dress, but she had to admit Kasiah looked absolutely stunning. "Hi, Kasiah. How are you doing?" Sara asked.

"I'm okay, considering. I miss your friendship and your brother," she said. "This whole affair is just horrid."

"Yes, it is, but I wanted to come by and say hi and introduce a friend. We went to dinner tonight, and I was telling him about you and Donte and all," she said. "I wanted to come see you, so I asked Clive if he'd mind. This is Clive Granger. Clive, Kasiah Aklen. Was I right? Isn't she the most gorgeous girl you've ever seen?"

Sara glanced over at Clive and couldn't help but chuckle to herself. The look on his face told her that he, like every other man, was struck by Kasiah's stunning physical appearance. "It's nice to meet you, Kasiah," he said. Then he turned to Sara. "I feel honored to be in the presence of two very gorgeous women." He followed that statement with a wink and a smile that made her flush.

Kasiah grinned. "Smart man," she said. "Why don't you guys come in? I was thinking about calling you anyway, Sara. We need to talk."

CHAPTER THIRTEEN

"I'VE BEEN HARD ON DONTE," Kasiah began after they were all seated and sipping on sodas. "I'm afraid I may have been wrong. That's why Sawyer wants to meet with you, Sara. He's told me a little bit about what he's learned, and I believe him."

"What's that?" Sara looked very hopeful, but Clive didn't like Kasiah's body language. He didn't like it at all. He could see that Sara believed every word the girl spoke. He simply sat and observed, keeping his thoughts to himself for the time being, grateful for the little digital recorder dutifully keeping track of every word that was spoken.

Kasiah averted her eyes for just a moment and then looked back again. "It would be best if you hear it from Sawyer. I wouldn't want to mix anything up, and you know how I am, Sara. I'm a bit of an airhead at times."

A very intelligent and deceitful airhead, Clive thought to himself.

"I just don't want to have to wait for good news," Sara said.

"You already have the good news," Kasiah replied. "I'm thinking he is not guilty. That's the good news." She smiled. "You'll just have to wait for the details."

"So does this mean—" Sara began.

Clive, knowing instinctively what she was about to ask, cut in right then. "This *is* good news, Kasiah. And Sara will wait patiently for the details, won't you Sara?" he said, looking directly into her eyes.

He saw understanding dawn there. Sara was an intelligent woman. She gave the slightest nod of her head and again spoke to Kasiah. "Like I was asking, does this mean I'll be getting a call from Sawyer soon?"

"Fairly soon," Kasiah said. "He doesn't like to be rushed. I've pushed a little, but he says he wants to tell you in person, and he can't do that for a few days because of his work. I hope you understand."

Sara smiled, took a sip of her soda, and then said, "I appreciate what you've told me. You've lifted a great burden from my mind. I just wish I knew where Donte was so I could tell him."

"Yeah, me too," Kasiah said, a look of longing on her picture-perfect face. A look of longing that Clive was almost positive was as counterfeit as the story she was telling. He wanted to get out of there—and now.

He downed the rest of his soda quickly and said, "Sara, we need to get going. Thanks, Kasiah, for giving Sara such good news. She needed it."

Taking his cue, Sara sipped a little more soda and then placed the can on an end table as she stood up. Walking out the door, Sara paused. "Thanks again, Kasiah. You are a good friend."

"So are you," Kasiah said.

Neither Sara nor Clive said a word until they were back in the car and a block from Kasiah's apartment. Clive was waiting to hear what Sara thought about their meeting with Kasiah. He didn't want to speak first and taint her impressions in any way.

She did speak first. "Clive, I believed her at first, but now that I've had a few minutes to think, I know she's lying." She sighed. "She still thinks Donte killed her brother. She just sounded so sincere. I'm so glad you stopped me from asking if Donte would be safe if he came home now." She rubbed her eyes but kept them on the road. "I wanted so badly to believe her."

"She was pretty smooth," Clive agreed. "Now what I wonder is what she and Sawyer are trying to accomplish by their little ruse."

"I think we both know," Sara said.

"They want you to get Donte to come back or at least find out where he is so Detective Fields can arrest him," Clive said. "Is that what you're thinking?"

"Yes, but I don't know where he is," she said. "And you don't anymore."

"But Kasiah, Sawyer, and Detective Fields don't know that. They're convinced you do and want to find a way to get you to tell," he reminded her. "I wouldn't be surprised if Detective Fields is either behind what

Sawyer and Kasiah are up to or at least knows about it. After all, he tried to get Winn to weasel it out of you, didn't he?"

"Yes. Speaking of Detective Fields, do we have anything to tell him yet?"

"I don't think so, but maybe we could talk to him on Monday. It wouldn't hurt to tell him that we suspect Bo Gray and suggest his name as one that Fields might investigate," Clive suggested. "But that's all we can tell him, and I'm not even sure if it'll do any good. It sure seemed to me like he is focused on Donte and isn't interested in looking at anyone else."

"Yeah, that's what has me worried," Sara agreed. "Unless the cops start looking for whoever did it, this could go on forever."

"We won't let that happen," Clive said, trying to strike a positive tone in his voice. "Let's get on with the one other thing we can do today. Let's go to that bar and see what we can learn."

Clive was way out of his element when he and Sara entered the bar, the little recorder in his pocket, waiting to be turned on. The smell of tobacco and booze was almost overpowering. Clive glanced at Sara with concern, but she just gave him a wan smile. He led her across the floor to the bar. He asked for the manager, and the bartender, a muscular tattooed man with a shaved head, immediately wanted to know who was asking. "Clive Granger and Sara Noble," Clive said as he pushed the button on the recorder and pulled his hand from the pocket of his sports coat.

The man wiped his hands on his apron. "I'm Louie, and I'm in charge here," the fellow said. "I own this place."

"Great, then you're who we're looking for. Do you have a minute that we can talk to you?" Clive asked. "We won't take much of your time."

"Sara Noble," the man said slowly. "Are you related to the guy who killed a man behind the building a few months ago? It got us a lot of bad publicity."

"I'm his sister," she said. "And for your information, my brother didn't kill anyone."

Clive jumped right in. "That's right, and we are here to see what we can learn about the guy who was killed, what he was doing in here that night."

Louie shook his head as he signaled them to follow him. He spoke to another bartender, telling him to keep things going and that he'd be back in a minute. They were soon in a cluttered little office in the back of the building. Louie asked them to sit down, and then he said, "I've been over all of this with the cops. Why don't you just talk to them?"

"We've tried," Clive said. "And they won't tell us anything."

"I'm not too surprised," Louie told them with a scowl. "The officer in charge of the investigation, a Detective . . ." He paused for a moment and then said, "I think it was a Detective Farm or something like that."

"Detective Fields," Clive said.

"Yeah, that's it. I knew it had something to do with farming," he said with a sheepish grin that looked quite out of place on a muscular, tattooed man like him. The grin faded, and he continued. "Anyway, this Detective Fields didn't seem to believe me, my employees, or any of our regular customers when we told him we'd never heard of the dead guy. What was his name again?"

"Walker Aklen," Clive said.

"Yeah, Walker Aklen. Fields showed us pictures of him, and I can tell you for sure, like I tried to tell the cops, that guy had never set foot in this bar. That Fields guy, he laughed right in my face and told me I was lying. If he hadn't been a cop, I'd of punched him out right then."

"Did he say why he didn't believe you?" Clive asked.

"Oh yeah, he said that it was impossible to believe that the guy was killed right behind this place and hadn't even been in here." Louie scratched at his shaved head. "I can see why he would think that, but I know for a fact I'd never seen the guy before. He'd never been in here."

"Okay, that was what we wanted to know," Clive said, standing up. Sara did the same, and they started for the door. "Oh," Clive said, turning back. "Did they actually tell you he'd been murdered out behind your bar?"

"Yes, that's what Detective Fields said," Louie answered. "Is that not the case?"

"I was under the impression that the body was dumped there, but who knows," Clive said. "Maybe they're not sure, and maybe I misunderstood."

The muscular barman's face darkened. "They made people think it happened here, and like I told you, it hasn't been good for business. I guarantee that he wasn't in this bar, not that night, not ever. If he was just dumped here, then I think the cops should see that it says so in the press.

Even if he was killed out back, they need to make sure people know it had nothing to do with my business. Why don't you two tell them to make sure the press has it right?"

Clive snorted. "Us tell them? I don't think so. They accused Sara's brother, and he wasn't even in this part of the state at the time. They won't listen to a thing we say."

"What's your interest in the case?" Louie asked Clive. "Are you a relative or something?"

"I'm a family friend," Clive said and left it at that. "Thanks for speaking with us. Let's go, Sara."

"Now what?" she asked after they were back in her car.

"I'm not sure there's anything else we can do tonight, unless you can think of someone we can talk to who might have known Walker."

"Like a friend or something?"

"Yeah. Somebody killed Walker. It seems that no one, especially not Detective Fields, knows who did it."

Sara responded quickly to that. "Someone does. Whoever killed him does."

"And more than likely it was either someone he knew or worked with or was even related to," Clive said thoughtfully. "But we don't even know who those people might be. I guess we have a lot of digging to do." He looked at his watch. "If we knew where he lived, we might start there, but I don't know how we would find that out short of asking Kasiah, and I don't think we should do that right now."

"I agree," Sara said as her face brightened. "But I think I know where he lived. One time Kasiah took me by what I assumed was his place. It was down around Spanish Fork. I'm sure I can find it."

"Then drive, partner," Clive said with a smile.

***

Winn was at home, trying to unwind from the tensions of the day. Bo getting into such a jam had Winn on edge. Who knew where Donte was or what he was up to. Winn had thought about trying to hire another investigator, but that idea didn't appeal to him. Bo had succeeded in locating Donte when the cops had failed. Bo had a network of contacts throughout the western United States. It had been through a couple of those contacts that the investigator had finally discovered that Donte was traveling on a bike, occasionally catching a ride.

But something had happened in Tonopah that had tipped things upside down. Winn had no idea what it was, but he figured Donte was behind it. Winn could send someone else to Tonopah, but he didn't want to have to explain what had happened so far. Yet he felt like Tonopah was somehow the key to finding Donte again.

Suddenly, Winn knew what he had to do. He wished he'd thought of it earlier, but it wasn't too late. He didn't have anything so pressing in the office Monday that he couldn't call Sara and have her reschedule. He would do what he had to and be back in time for their dinner date Monday night. That was also important. Winn was determined to win the love of his bright and attractive legal secretary.

He hurriedly packed an overnight bag, grabbed a couple of bottles of water and an unopened package of cookies in his pantry, and put them all in his car. At the last minute, he ran back inside and grabbed a few more items. He put his laptop in the backseat, but he put the little snub nose .38 caliber pistol in a shoulder holster, and for now, stuck it inside the console beside him. He was licensed to carry it but didn't often do so. On this trip, however, he thought it might be advisable to have it with him. After Bo's problems, he couldn't be too careful. Winn hung his sports jacket and a spare pair of slacks in the back next to the left window. Finally, he entered the address of the Nye Regional Medical Center in Tonopah, Nevada, into his GPS. Then he started the engine and backed out of the garage.

Once he was out of the city and on the freeway, Winn called Sara's cell phone. When she answered, he said, "Hi, Sara. How are things tonight?"

"Fine. Is something the matter, Winn?" she asked.

He chuckled. "Sara, my dear, I can't get you off my mind. I just wanted to hear your voice."

"That's sweet, Winn," she said. "I'm fine, and how are you?"

"Doing great, but something's come up, and I have to make a short trip out of town, out of state actually. I need to have you reschedule my Monday appointments."

"Including our date?" she asked.

"Oh no, my dear, I'll be back for that. I wouldn't miss it for the world. This is a family emergency. I'm needed in Denver," he said, knowing that she knew that was where he was from. "It'll just be a quick trip. Will you do that for me?"

"Of course I will, Winn. And I'll be thinking of you. Drive safe, and call me when you get back," she said.

That made his heart race. "Sure thing, my dear, I'll do that. Thanks, you're the best."

***

"I gather that was your boss," Clive said.

"Yeah, and he sounded stressed. He says he has a family emergency in Denver—that's where he's from—and he needs me to reschedule his appointments for Monday. But he says he can be back in time for our date," Sara explained.

"Is this something he does often?" Clive asked. "I mean, having you reschedule his appointments."

"Not often but sometimes. I'll have to go in to the office tomorrow afternoon and make some calls," she said. "Off hand, I can't think of anyone that should be too put out."

"Did he say what the emergency was?" Clive asked.

"No. His dad does some kind of work for the federal government. I think Winn said that he's getting close to retirement."

"I see," Clive said.

"I hope it's nothing too serious." After a couple of minutes of silence she instructed, "Okay, I think we need to get off the freeway at the next exit."

Sara's memory was good, and she found the apartments where Walker had been living. She parked across the street and pointed. "It's that apartment right over there. I don't know the number, but I know that's the place. It looks like there are lights on. What do we do now?"

"We knock on the door and play it by ear," Clive said.

It sounded like the TV was turned up quite loud as Clive first rang the doorbell and then knocked on the door. He repeated the same actions a minute later. At first, Sara didn't think anyone was going to come to the door, but suddenly, a man shouted from inside, "Hang on, I'm coming."

When the door opened, a man of around thirty was standing there in a robe and slippers. His hair was disheveled, and the odor of alcohol was strong on his breath. "What do you want?" he asked in a slur. His face was flushed, and his eyes were bloodshot.

"I'm Clive, and this is Sara. We'd like to talk to you for just a moment."

"Okay, come in," the guy said. "Place is a mess, but I've been awful busy."

Clive ushered Sara in ahead of him as he once again activated the small recorder in his pocket. The guy might be a busy man, but from the smell that assaulted Clive's nose, Clive knew what he'd been busy at most recently. Clive had spent enough time with the cops that he knew the smell of freshly smoked marijuana. As the two of them stepped in, Clive shut the door behind them. He looked quickly around the small living room. A TV was still turned on, but the sound was muted. A bottle of beer was on an end table next to a blue recliner, which was facing the TV. Next to it was an ashtray, the contents of which were not just from tobacco cigarettes.

Across the small room and at a slight angle from the recliner was a badly worn sofa. The man waved at it and said, "Go ahead and sit down. What did you say your names were?"

"We missed yours." Clive momentarily sidestepped the question.

"Trevor Wells," the guy offered as Clive sized him up. He was a short, thin man. His messy hair was sort of a mousy color. Clive couldn't tell the color on the eyes—other than that they were bloodshot and glazed. "Again, who are you two?"

"My name is Clive Granger, and this is Sara Noble," Clive said slowly and distinctly.

"Noble," he said as he rubbed a hand through the greasy mop on his head. "I've heard that name somewhere. Noble."

"We just need to ask you a few questions," Clive said.

"What kind of questions? What are you doing here, anyway?"

"I'm conducting an investigation," Clive said. "Sara is my partner."

"Wait a minute," Trevor said as something seemed to click in his foggy brain. "Noble. That's the name of the guy that killed my roommate. Donte Noble, it was. You two better leave. I don't want to talk to nobody about that." He stood up. "Go on, get out of here. You ain't welcome."

CHAPTER FOURTEEN

CLIVE GOT QUICKLY TO HIS feet, but he didn't step toward the door. Instead, he stepped closer to Trevor, pointed a finger at him, and said, "We came to talk to you, and that's exactly what we plan to do."

"I don't have to talk to you," Trevor said, bunching up his fists. "I said get out of here, and I mean it."

"And if we don't?" Clive asked.

"Then I'll . . . I'll . . . call the cops," he stammered.

"Go ahead. I'm sure they'll be interested in the pot you've been smoking. They'll arrest you, and then Sara and I will visit you at the jail," Clive told him. "Or if you'd rather, we can leave and call the cops ourselves. Either way, you'll be in jail before the night is over. Is that what you want, or would you like to speak with us instead?"

For a moment, those glazed eyes stared at Clive. Then they moved to Sara. "You related to Donte the killer?" he asked.

"I'm Donte's sister," she said. "But he's no killer, and I think you know that. Please, sit down; we just want to talk to you."

Trevor stood there for a minute, swaying; then he backed up to his recliner and dropped into it. "Okay, so what do you want to know?"

Clive exchanged a quick glance with Sara and then said, "We're just trying to figure out who might have wanted to hurt your roommate. Nothing we've heard adds up."

"The cops and Noble's fiancée say it was Donte. I thought it was all settled and they was just trying to find him." Trevor's slur was getting worse and his eyes even more glazed.

"They've got it wrong. Donte was camping up around Mirror Lake," Clive said. "He couldn't have done it. Plus, he had no reason to. Why would a guy want to do something to turn a hot gal like Kasiah against him?"

Trevor nodded his head and said with a lascivious grin, "Yeah, good point, man. She's a knockout."

"What we'd like, Trevor, is for you to tell us about Walker. I'm sure you weren't his only friend," Clive said.

"Walker couldn't keep friends." The man reached for his beer and took a long swig.

"He couldn't keep friends. What do you mean by that?"

"He was always bumming money and stuff off guys and then not paying it back. You know . . ." Trevor stopped and belched. He wiped his face with the back of the hand not holding the beer, and then he took another swig. Finally, he spoke again, his words getting more difficult to understand with each swallow. "He was always bumming cigarettes, beer, pot, even the hard stuff, or a few bucks for this or that."

Trevor took another drink from his beer and then looked at it with a longing in his bleary eyes. "It's empty," he said. "Need another."

"Is it in your refrigerator?" Sara asked. "I'll get you one."

"Yes, perty lady. You do that," he said, swinging a hand in the general direction of his kitchen.

As Sara left the room, Clive continued, "So you're saying he didn't pay people back?"

"Yeah, that's right. Just kept their stuff and their money."

"Who are some of the friends he owed money to?" Clive asked.

"Bunch of us," Trevor said. "Where's the perty lady with my beer?"

"I'm right here." Sara walked into the room with a brown bottle in her hand. "Where do you keep your bottle opener?"

Trevor reached up, and she let him take the bottle. "Right here," he said, and he popped off the lid with his teeth. Sara grimaced, but she recovered quickly and again took her seat beside Clive.

"Okay," Clive began again as Trevor began to guzzle the beer. "Walker was indebted to a lot of people. Were you one of them?"

Trevor slammed the beer onto the end table. "Yeah, he owes me for rent. Wouldn't pay his share. I figured I'd kick him out if he didn't pay, but he kept saying he had some money coming."

Once more he reached for the bottle of beer. He missed, and it tipped over and rolled off of the coffee table. Sara was pale as she watched the beer soak the carpet. Clive took hold of her hand and squeezed. "Hang in there," he said very softly.

She smiled and said, "I'm okay," equally softly. He kept his eyes on her for a moment. She didn't look okay. He needed to move this interview along.

Clive turned back to Trevor. "How much did he owe you?"

"Couple grand," he said, again reaching for his beer. "Hey, where'd my beer go?"

"It's on the floor," Clive told him. "We can get you another one before we go. But first, tell me what you did to get Walker to pay you his share of the rent."

"And the grub . . . and the beer . . . and the . . . oh, everything. He didn't have no job," Trevor rambled.

Clive could see that pretty soon Trevor wouldn't be able to respond to any questions, but Clive pressed on, hoping to learn a little more. "Did it make you angry?" Clive asked.

"Yeah." Trevor spat out a bunch of vulgar expletives. "Me and a lot of others. We hated the guy."

"But you still let him live here?" Clive asked.

"Yeah."

"I see. So when you didn't get your money, you decided to kill him?" Clive asked, watching the man's eyes.

"Nope. Donte did it first."

"Donte didn't kill him," Sara said angrily.

Clive squeezed her hand again. "I've got this," he said softly to her. Then to Trevor he said, "Give me the names of some of the other guys he owed."

Trevor rubbed his eyes, belched again, leaned back in his recliner, and passed out. "I guess we just as well go." Clive shook his head. "But we'll come back. We need to talk to this guy when he's sober."

"That was a waste of time. We still don't have any names to give to Detective Fields, do we?" Sara asked after they had closed Trevor's door behind them.

"Yes, we have one. We have Trevor's name, but I think we'll save it until Monday," Clive suggested. "I'd like to talk to this guy after church tomorrow and see if we can catch him sober enough to give us some more names. For right now, let's talk to some of the other people in these apartments. See if we can learn anything more that will be helpful.

For the next hour, they had conversations with the neighbors. They didn't learn much more than what they already knew, that the two men were a couple of drunks and druggies. However, the very closest neighbor, an elderly widow by the name of Brenda Finn, told them that she'd heard the two men arguing one night. "The walls in this place are paper thin," she said. "When those two would raise their voices and argue, I could hear every word. I've complained to the manager, but he says he can't do anything about the walls. Anyway, this one night several months ago, not long before Walker was murdered, I heard them arguing. It was an ugly argument, and they were both cursing something awful."

"What did they argue about?" Clive asked, "Or could you hear them well enough to tell?"

"Oh, I could hear them all right. They were fighting over money. Trevor told Walker he owed back rent. Walker said something about he'd catch up later, that he was a little short right then. Then Trevor, he said to Walker, and I remember the exact words. He said, 'If you don't pay tomorrow, I'm going to kill you.'"

"Are you sure that's what you heard?" Clive asked urgently.

"Oh, yes, that's what he said word for word," the elderly lady said. "And then after that, they argued some more and Walker left. I never saw him again. It was maybe two or three days later that I saw on the news that he'd been murdered."

Back in the car, Sara slipped the key into the ignition. "Clive, did you have the recorder on when that woman said she heard Trevor tell Walker he'd kill him if he didn't pay up?"

"Yeah. I got it," he said. "But even sober, does he have the knowledge to poison someone the way Walker was poisoned? Of course, I suppose he could know someone that did. My biggest question is, did she say that to Detective Fields, or did any of the cops even talk to her?"

"I think Fields has done a sloppy job of police work," Sara said in sudden anger. "We need to go over his head and talk to one of his superiors."

"You read my mind, partner," Clive said. "That will be one of the first things I do Monday while you're at work."

"Oh, I didn't think about that." She sounded disappointed. "I can't help you when I'm working."

"I'll record everything that's relevant and let you hear it," he promised. "But for now, I think we can call it a day. You look beat."

"That's for sure. But at least the evening hasn't been a waste," Sara said, a hopeful note in her voice. "You're good at this."

Clive chuckled. "I'm just feeling my way. I'm doing what I have characters in my books do. I guess in a way it sort of comes naturally.

Listen, why don't you drop me off at the hotel and go on home and get some rest. I'll make some notes on my laptop of what we've done today and type all the notes from my notebook. And maybe I'll listen to some of the recordings we made and type them up too."

"I'd be glad to help." Sara's words were undermined by her yawn.

"I know you would, but I can do this. You've got to be ready for a shower and some sleep. I'm afraid you got dragged through some pretty awful scenes tonight."

"I'll say," she agreed. "How can people live the way they do? It sure makes me grateful for my faith. Which reminds me, I'll pick you up at the hotel at eight thirty and you can go with me to my ward. If you don't mind, that is."

"That would be nice," he agreed. "But if people ask about me, just tell them I'm a friend of Donte's who is helping you try to figure out what really happened to Walker Aklen."

"That's good," she said. "After all, it's the truth."

***

It was close to ten that night when Chey got another e-mail from Donte. She was back at Estela's apartment, getting ready for bed when the message came in. At nine she'd left Jessica sleeping soundly at the hospital. Then she and Estela had visited for over a half hour. She'd tried to get Estela to tell her more about why the girl was so sure that Bo wouldn't be a problem, but her new friend just grinned, her white teeth flashing and her dark eyes sparkling. "My brother is a smart guy," was all she would say.

Chey opened the message, her hands trembling. She read: *C. I'm on my way. I wish I was already there. Is J. still okay? Are you sure about B.? Are you okay? So sorry I got you in this mess. Miss you. D.*

She quickly replied to him and then sat for a moment with her head in her hands. Then she prayed. Finally, she got into bed and tried to sleep.

***

Sara's phone indicated a new e-mail when she pulled into her garage. She shut the garage door and hurried into the house and to her computer. She wanted to read Donte's message—if it was even from him—on the computer. It only took a minute to bring the computer out of sleep mode, and a little bit longer to connect with the Internet. The message was from Donte: *Scrunch. I'm doing okay. How are you and C. doing? Is the officer making any progress, or will he even listen? C's a nice guy, isn't he? Don't worry about B. for now, but be very, very careful what you say around W. I'm restless. Surely someone can help us. Maybe you should hire a PI. I've been thinking about B and that's why I'm suggesting you hire someone. But get someone good, someone from Salt Lake maybe. I'll bet C. will help you find someone. Love and miss you. Slurpee.*

Sara's eyes were watering. She wanted to tell him about what she and Clive were doing, but she wasn't sure how he would react. She was afraid that he might be so worried that he'd simply come home, and she didn't want that, at least not until his name had been cleared.

She hit Reply and began to type. Midway through the message, she stopped and called Clive's hotel, using her house phone and asking to be put through to his room. "Clive," she said as soon as he'd answered. "I'm intentionally not using the cell phones so I can feel like talking a little more freely. Let me read the latest e-mail from Donte."

"Okay, I'm listening," he said.

Sara read the entire message and then asked, "What should I do?"

He told her what he thought, and since it mirrored her own idea, she said, "Thanks, Clive. That's what I'll do then."

She finished typing and sent her message. She waited up, hoping to hear back from him before she went to bed.

***

Donte was still sitting at a computer in a truck stop while his latest truck driving benefactor was taking a shower. He read Chey's e-mail first, and then, when it came in, he read the one from Sara. She had written: *Slurpee. The officer is not very helpful. His mind is made up. A private investigation sounds like a good idea. I talked to C. about it, and he agrees. We'll get someone good. But we haven't given up on the cops. We still might get some help from them. You take care. Love and miss you too. Scrunch.*

***

Sara went through and carefully deleted any messages connected to Donte from both her phone and her computer. Then she sat at the computer desk and thought about what she'd just done. She had just misled a man she both loved and admired, a brother who had always been there for her when she needed him. She hoped someday he would forgive her and that God would too. Of course, she reminded herself, as Clive pointed out, it wasn't a complete lie. There *was* going to be a private investigation, exactly like she'd told Donte. And they would have a good person conducting it, for she was convinced, after working with Clive today, that he would do an outstanding job—that together they would solve this crime, with or without the help of the cops. However, she did hold out hope that the cops would yet do more.

CHAPTER FIFTEEN

As Sara stepped into the meetinghouse beside Clive, she felt much better than she had for several days. The environment was familiar, and she finally felt like Donte was going to be vindicated, thanks to Clive. They stayed for all three meetings, constantly buffeted with questions. She answered the same way to every curious inquiry: Clive was a friend of Donte's who had come to help clear his name.

After church, Clive said, "I'm going to go find some lunch, and then it's back to work. I don't want to let this thing drag on longer than it has to."

"Why don't you come to my house?" she offered. "I can whip us up something quickly while we plan the rest of the day."

"Are you sure?" he said. "I don't want to put you out."

"Put me out," she huffed with a smile on her face. "You're the one being put out. It's the least I can do."

Since they both agreed that the first thing they would do after lunch was visit Trevor Wells again, Clive parked his truck in Sara's spacious garage. He wanted it out of sight. After eating, they headed south in Sara's car.

Once again they knocked on Trevor's door and pressed long and hard on his doorbell. No response. They repeated their actions. Still no response. They both put their ears to the door. They couldn't hear the TV or any other noise inside.

As they turned away, Trevor's next-door neighbor opened her door. "Good afternoon. Trevor isn't home. He and some friend left about two hours ago."

"Oh, thank you, Mrs. Finn," Clive said. "Do you have any idea who the friend was?"

"Just some guy about forty-five or so. I don't think I've seen him here before," she said, shaking a flabby arm. "But I'm not sure."

"Can you describe him to us?" Clive pressed.

She was very thoughtful for a moment. "The guy seemed nice enough. I heard them talking while they were still in the house. It sounded like the guy said that he was going to see to it that Trevor quit drinking and smoking dope. I could hear them, but they weren't shouting, so I couldn't be positive about every word they said. But he must be a good friend to want to help Trevor like that."

"Must be," Clive agreed. "Did Trevor ever call his friend by name?"

"I think so, but like I said, they weren't shouting so I'm not sure of every word I heard."

"But you did hear his name?" Clive pressed.

"I think it was George or Jared or something like that," Mrs. Finn said. "Or it might have been Jimmy. I'm pretty sure it started with a g or a j," she said.

Clive looked at Sara and shrugged. Then he said to Mrs. Finn, "So what does he look like? You did see him when they left the apartment, didn't you?"

"Well, yes, I wasn't trying to be snoopy or anything, but I wanted to see what such a nice man looked like. There aren't very many nice people ever coming to visit with Trevor."

Sara was getting impatient. "So please describe him," she said.

"Yes, well, he was maybe 45 or 50," she said. She glanced at Clive and then added, "He wasn't as tall as you but was quite stocky."

"What color was his hair, and how did he wear it?" Clive asked.

"He had a ball cap on, but I could see that his hair was sort of black but going gray. He had his arm around Trevor's shoulder as they walked to the parking lot," she said. "He was being so nice." She scowled. "I don't know why he was being so nice; Trevor is not a very nice guy. He and that roommate who was murdered were not the kind of people I would choose as neighbors if I had my choice—but I don't have a choice."

"Did you see the car that this friend was driving?"

"No, I didn't."

"Would you do us a favor?" Clive asked.

"Yes, of course," she said. "What favor do you need?"

Clive handed her a card, one that had his cell phone number on it. "When Trevor comes home, would you call me at this number?" he asked, pointing to it on the card.

"Certainly," she said.

Sara pulled a card from her purse. "My home phone number, my office number, and my cell phone number are all on this card. If for any reason you can't get ahold of Clive, you can call me," she said.

Mrs. Finn studied the two cards for a moment, then she gasped. "Oh my, a mystery writer. Are you working on a book, Mr. Granger?"

He smiled at her. "Oh yes, I'm always working on a book."

Clive and Sara were both disappointed that Trevor wasn't at home. "I wonder who the friend is that Mrs. Finn thinks is going to get him off drugs and alcohol," Sara mused as she started her car.

"That's a very good question," Clive said. "I wish we had more names to give to Detective Fields, but it does appear that not all of his friends are total losers. Maybe there *is* someone among his acquaintances who is smart enough to kill someone using Fentanyl. I just wish we knew who the guy is. I'm afraid Mrs. Finn wasn't much help in that regard. When we see Trevor again, we definitely want that man's name."

"It would probably be more effective to go up to the Mirror Lake area on a weekday," Clive said a few minutes later as they headed north on the interstate. "But I feel like we need to be doing something, and I'm not sure what else to do right now."

"If we need to, we can go again another day, but I agree about going today. I think the most critical thing that will help us convince the cops to look at other suspects is a solid alibi for Donte," Sara said.

Clive looked over at her. "Don't get your hopes up too high," he said. "The police have already done this, and we're three months behind when it actually occurred. People are likely to have forgotten a lot."

"I know," she said. "But I have to be hopeful."

"Of course you do," he agreed. "So do I. And who knows, maybe the passage of time will work in our favor rather than against us."

"Now that's a positive outlook," Sara said. "I like that about you. You're a very positive person."

"That just goes to show that you hardly know me," he said with a grin.

They rode a few miles in silence, and suddenly, Sara had a worrisome thought that just came out of nowhere, it seemed. But she was glad it had. They were near Heber City, with their first stop planned for Kamas, a place Donte was likely to have stopped as he passed through on his trip to Mirror Lake more than three months ago. She pulled to the side of the road.

"Is something the matter?" Clive asked.

"Will you drive for a little while? I want to make some phone calls," she said.

"Sure, if you want me to. Who do you need to call?"

"I just remembered that I was supposed to call and reschedule Winn's appointments for tomorrow. I can't believe I forgot," she said, disgusted at herself.

"I didn't think about it either," Clive consoled. "I guess we're both caught up in this investigation. Do you have the numbers with you?"

"No, but I do remember some of the clients. I'm going to try to see if I can find their numbers." As soon as they had changed places and Clive had started to drive, Sara pulled out her iPhone and began searching the Internet for numbers. She found a couple and made the necessary calls, but she couldn't remember who else had appointments. Suddenly, she knew what she needed to do. "I have my laptop in the backseat," she said. "If we can get Wi-Fi somewhere in Heber, I'll see if I can connect to my computer at work. Winn insisted that I have a program on my computer to do just that."

"Okay, we'll find a place," Clive said.

Sara was thoughtful for a moment, and then she again accessed her phone and searched for another number. She remembered Winn's father's name and was able to find a number for him. She dialed it and waited while it rang. Finally, there was an answer, a gruff voice who said, "Hello, who is this?"

"Hi, this is Sara Noble. Are you John Bertram?" she asked.

"I am," he said. "Do I know you?"

"I work for your son, Winn," she said. "I was just canceling some of his appointments for tomorrow, and I thought I'd call and see how things are."

"Why would you cancel his appointments, and why would you call me to see how things are?" Winn's father asked.

"He asked me to cancel them when he told me he was going to Denver."

"He's coming here?" Mr. Bertram sounded quite surprised. "Why would he be coming here?"

"He told me there was a family emergency. He left last night." Sara felt a twist developing in her gut.

"Nope, no problem here," he said. "Must be some misunderstanding."

"I'm sorry. I'm sure you're right," she said and ended the call.

"Sara, are you thinking what I'm thinking?" Clive asked. "If your boss isn't headed for Colorado . . ."

"He's not," she said. "Clive, he lied to me. If he's not going there, where is he going?"

"Perhaps he's headed for Nevada," Clive said.

"That's what I was just thinking," Sara told him. "But why? Donte's not there."

"But he was there. And Bo Gray was there. Maybe Winn is hoping to find something there that will help him find Donte again," Clive said.

"Oh, Clive, you might be right. I need to warn Donte, to tell him not to go back to Nevada no matter what," she said urgently.

***

Donte got out of the semi and stretched his legs. With the help of the driver, he unloaded the bike and trailer. He thanked his benefactor and then pushed his bike and trailer toward the store. He locked his bike with the chain around a lamppost then tied Dude to the bike and went in search of a computer. He'd learned that he could almost always find a computer in the convenience store, café, or motel that were parts of the bigger truck stops. He sat down at a computer in the store and pulled up his e-mail.

He drafted a message to Sara. He hoped that she might have something positive to report. Even though it was Sunday, maybe she and Clive had been able to locate an investigator. Once he left Vegas on his bike, it might be a long time before he could contact her again. He typed, reviewed his message, and then sent it. Next he sent one to Chey, telling her that he planned to be in Tonopah by the next day sometime. Then he sat and waited. He hoped that Sara would get right back to him.

***

Sara caught herself dozing as Clive drove. Suddenly, her phone brought her fully awake as an e-mail came in. It was from Donte. She whispered a silent prayer of thanks and opened the e-mail. *Scrunch. Doing fine. How are things? Have you had time to find an investigator? I know it's Sunday, but I won't be at a computer for quite a while. Love and miss you. Slurpee.*

"What did he say?" Clive asked, looking over at her.

"He's wondering if we've found a PI yet."

"Sara, when you warn him about Winn possibly going to Tonopah, tell him that just this once it would be helpful to both of us to know where he is right now," Clive suggested.

"Okay." She began typing a reply on her iPhone.

***

Donte felt like it had been hours before he received an answer from Sara, yet it had been only a few minutes. Her response read: *Slurpee. Something strange is going on with W. I have reason to believe he is headed for Tonopah. Make sure you're nowhere near there. C. suggests that you let us know where you are. I know we have avoided doing that in the past, but please, just this once, let us know. We are together right now, so we will both know as soon as you respond. Love, Scrunch.*

Telling his sister where he was went against everything he had been doing these past three months. He didn't want to do that. And yet, he told himself, maybe he needed to trust her—and to trust Clive. Donte debated back and forth for a couple of minutes, but before he had made up his mind another message came into his in-box. It was from Chey.

D. Be careful. I look forward to seeing you. J. is doing better today. C.

Be careful, she had said. Did that mean he shouldn't tell Sara where he was or that he should? Or was his mind playing games with him? He finally decided and typed a reply to Sara. Hoping he had done the right thing, he sent the e-mail and got up from the computer. He decided to wander around the store for a bit, maybe go outside and check on his dog, then see if Sara had a response for him.

***

Clive and Sara had pulled into Heber by the time they received a response from Donte. When it came, they pulled into the parking lot of a store there and read the message together. It read: *Scrunch. This is hard. I've been so careful not to let anyone know where I am, but I know I have to trust you. I am in LV. I have a new plan. I'll let you know what it is later. Love you. Slurpee.*

"What does he mean by a new plan?" The question was directed as much to herself as to Clive.

"He's in Las Vegas," Clive said. "I hope he isn't going to Tonopah. And why would he? Maybe he's just going to stay in Vegas for a bit."

They discussed things for a minute. Finally, Sara said, "I'll just send him a message saying thanks and that we'll be back in touch with him. Then I better find someplace to use my laptop and hope I can connect with my office computer. The thing I worry most about is remembering the passwords we used when we set the program up."

"As soon as we can get that done, we'll get on our way again," Clive said.

"Okay, I'll get this sent."

"Wait, Sara. I have an idea. Ask Donte if he made any stops in Kamas, and if so, where. And ask him if he can remember anyone he might have talked to in Mirror Lake or even on the trail when he went camping. You can tell him his new investigator needs it."

"That's a good idea," she said. She typed the message as fast as she could on the iPhone and sent it. "I told him that we'd wait for his reply. I just hope he's still by a computer."

While they were waiting, they went to a hotel and got permission to use the Wi-Fi.

***

Donte checked back at the computer a few minutes later. He had to wait for a moment while another fellow finished something, and then Donte sat back down. A message from Sara was waiting. Eagerly he read the message and then sat back for a moment, arms folded. They had apparently found someone to look into his case. For that he was grateful. He sent a message back telling Sara of a little convenience store and a grocery store he had shopped at. At Mirror Lake, he had visited with several people. He explained that the place hadn't been as busy as it usually was later in the year and that the snow hadn't melted yet, although it had been an early thaw up there and the lodge had been open for limited business.

After sending that message, he decided to act on what he'd been thinking about while he was walking around. He sent another e-mail to Chey: *C. I need a ride. Can you come and get me if I tell you where I am? That way I can be there tonight. A new danger has come up, and I need to be with you and J. I'll leave my bike someplace and just bring Dude. Let me know right away. D.*

Chey must have been sitting right by her laptop or holding her phone, for her reply was very quick. Her message read: *I'll come as soon as*

I can get some of the stuff out of my car. Where can I find you? Are you far? I'll be waiting to hear from you. Can't wait to see you. C.

Donte gave her directions and sent the message off through cyberspace. Then he found a place to shower and did so. He bought some new pants and a new shirt and washed his dirty ones. He also bought a blue duffle bag and put everything in it that he wanted to take with him. The next thing he did was make arrangements with the hotel that was part of the truck stop to store his bike and trailer, giving the employee some money and promising to come back for his things in a few days.

There was a barber in the big complex, and he took a chance, having his beard trimmed and his hair cut a bit. When he was done, he felt like he looked quite presentable. A new pair of dark glasses, and he was ready to meet Chey.

CHAPTER SIXTEEN

With just one exception, Sara had been able to reschedule. She was satisfied with that, and she and Clive headed again for Kamas. They talked to every employee they could in both the Foodtown grocery store and the convenience store. As they feared, no one remembered Donte. The farther north they drove, the prettier the scenery became.

"Donte has always loved the Uintahs. It has been his tradition to come up here once or twice a year since he was old enough to drive," Sara said as they drove. "It's rugged country with miles of wilderness area. I've known him to be gone for as much as two weeks at a time before. He even took me a couple of times for shorter trips."

"So being alone and wandering isn't something new to him?" Clive asked, looking over at Sara, who was driving again.

"Oh, no, not at all," Sara answered.

"Do you know how Kasiah reacted to his trip?" Clive asked.

"Donte told me about it the night before he left. I was helping him organize his backpack and tie his snowshoes onto it. I asked him that very question. I remember how he stopped what he was doing and looked at me. He said, 'Sara, we had our first fight when I told her what I was planning.' He went on to explain that she told him it was a stupid thing to do and that he must not care much for her if he would leave her for a week."

"That's too bad, but it makes me wonder about her motivation in accusing him of murder," Clive said.

"Don't think I haven't thought a lot about that, and yet, it seems absurd that she would do something so drastic over her fiancé wanting to go camping."

"This is gorgeous country," Clive said. "I think I might take a trip back in there sometime. It might inspire a good novel."

"Donte will take you," Sara said. Then her face dropped. "If he ever gets out from under this black cloud, that is."

"Sara, chin up, girl. We are going to succeed, and he'll be coming home soon."

A few minutes later, they turned into the parking area of the lodge at Mirror Lake. They got out of the car and stretched their legs. Clive looked around. "That's a pretty lake."

"Yes, and Donte says there are hundreds even prettier than that one up in the mountains."

"Some pretty impressive peaks up here too." He gestured to the north.

"That tallest one, that one right there," she said, pointing, "is called Mount Agassi. They say there used to be a plane a little ways down on the face of the mountain. It was a Twin Baron, a fast twin engine plane. A guy was flying it by himself late at night and simply went too low— drove straight into the cliff at around 200 miles per hour. Of course, the plane exploded and burned. Donte told me that the Duchesne County Sheriff and some of his deputies went up with a helicopter and then worked their way down to the wreckage. They recovered what little was left of the pilot. The plane was apparently there for several years before it was finally removed."

"Another idea for a book," Clive said. "I am definitely going to come up here sometime. But right now, we have work to do. Let's go inside."

The place was very busy. Customers were coming and going, many wearing their fishing gear. Others looked like they had either just returned or were preparing to leave for the mountain trails. Clive and Sara worked their way to the front and began to talk to employees. None of them had been working here that early in the spring. Discouraged, the pair decided to order a couple cheeseburgers and eat before they left for Provo.

They had barely sat down when a tall older gentleman approached their table. He had white hair and wore a matching white beard. His leather pants were complemented by a leather shirt with long fringes and even some beadwork. "Mind if I sit for a minute?" he asked.

"Of course not," Sara said, surprised but intrigued. She judged him to be about 65 or 70, probably at least six-foot-five, with dark, leathery skin, and eyes as blue and clear as the deep waters of Mirror Lake. There couldn't have been an ounce of fat on him.

"I couldn't help hearing you young 'uns talking to some of the employees here," he began. Then he grinned, revealing a set of teeth that looked like they could use a little repair work. "Sorry, I should introduce myself proper-like. Name's Jacob Hickman. Folks call me Hick."

"I'm Clive Granger," Clive said with a broad smile, reaching his hand across the table. "And this pretty girl is Sara Noble."

Sara also offered her hand. His hands were calloused and sinewy, but she was surprised at the strength of the man's grip. He looked deep into her eyes, making her squirm. His head began to nod, and as his right one continued to hold hers, he reached up with his free hand and removed his leather hat. "You favor Donte," he said, sending shockwaves up her arm. "Same eyes, same cut of the jaw, same mouth. He talked about you. Sara Noble, the sister he told me was the best sister a man could have."

He turned his piercing gaze on Clive and released Sara's hand. "This young woman yours, Mr. Granger?" he asked.

Clive grinned uncomfortably. "Not exactly. I'm a friend of Donte's. I'm helping him and his sister here out of a bit of a jam," he said.

"What do you do, young fella?" the old mountain man asked.

"I write novels, mysteries."

"He's a best-selling author," Sara added with a touch of pride in her voice. "And he's a good friend."

The old man looked from one to the other, and then, studying Clive's face, he said, "If she's not your girl, she should be. Don't let her get away." He chuckled heartily at their reactions. "I don't mean to make the two of you uncomfortable. No, sir. There be something else I want to talk to you about."

He looked from one to the other, his eyes finally holding Sara's gaze. "It's a lie," he said.

"What's a lie?" Sara asked in a shaky voice.

"What they say about your brother, Donte," he said. "He didn't kill nobody. He couldn't hurt a flea, that young fella couldn't. He told me on that last trip of his up here that he was going to be going to medical school. Said he wanted to help people."

"You saw him when he was up here three months ago?" Sara's heart began to pound.

"Sure did. Me and him, we're good friends. I've eaten with him around a campfire a time or two. We share the love of them mountains," Hick said, waving a hand toward the towering peaks outside.

Clive said, "Hick, Sara and I are trying to prove that the accusation against Donte is a lie. Maybe you could help us."

"I will if I can. I overheard you asking a couple of those young 'uns over there if they'd seen him up here. They weren't here then, but I met Donte up the trail a piece. We was both out on snowshoes. I'd swear to that in a court of law," Hick said.

Clive had already activated his small recorder, but he pulled it out of the pocket of his sports coat. "Do you mind if we record our conversation?"

"Not if it'll help young Donte," Hick said without hesitation. "Where is he now?"

"He's out wandering somewhere by himself, trying to keep from getting arrested. He doesn't dare let anyone know where he is until the cops quit looking for *him* and go after the real killer," Sara said.

Clive chuckled. "He claims he has a beard and long hair now."

The old man guffawed for a moment, and then he said, "Good for him. Okay, young 'uns, let's get down to business."

When they had finished, Clive shut off the recorder and leaned back in his chair. Sara put one of her hands on the old mountain man's and said, "God sent you to us. With your sworn testimony, we can prove he wasn't in Provo when Walker Aklen was killed."

"He couldn't a been, 'cause he was with me, like I said to that little silver thing there," he said, pointing at the recorder. "Anyways, that's the least I can do for the kid," the old mountain man added, his eyes watering up. "He's one in a million, that guy."

A minute later, Hick eased his long frame from the chair and said, "You know how to reach me. I'll tell them lazy cops exactly what I told you. If they'd a done their job, they'da found me and this woulda all been settled months ago."

Sara and Clive had cold cheeseburgers, but they had warm hearts. They both wanted to shout with joy. Instead, they ate their cold cheeseburgers and fries and drank warm root beer.

***

Chey threw herself into Donte's arms when he came walking toward her in the large truck-stop parking lot. "You look—" she began, and then her face went red.

"I hope I look a little better. I can't cut it all off yet, but new clothes help."

"You look really good," she said.

"And so do you. Do you want something to eat before we head for Tonopah?"

"Sure, but can we get something we can eat on the road?"

"Of course," he agreed. "And I'll get something for Dude too."

"Where is your bike and trailer?" she asked as he put his new duffle bag in her backseat.

"The motel's storing it for me," he said.

"I'm so glad you let me come get you," Chey told him. "Jessica's glad too and so is Estela."

"Estela?"

"The girl who works at the front desk of the motel. She's so sweet," Chey said. "I'm staying with her right now. It's thanks to her brother that Bo Gray isn't pursuing you anymore."

"Now that worries me. What did her brother do?"

"Estela won't tell me. All she'll say is that I shouldn't worry about it, that her brother is a smart man. What I do know," Chey continued, "is that Estela's brother helped switch cars around so that I was able to leave the motel without Bo knowing."

***

As soon as they got back to Provo, Sara and Clive tried Trevor's apartment again. He still wasn't home, and when they knocked on Brenda Finn's door, the neighbor told him that Trevor hadn't been back since that morning. Clive looked at his watch. It was almost eight o'clock. "Is he usually out this time of day?" he asked Brenda.

"Not on the weekends. He usually stays in and drinks," she reported. "Maybe that nice man who was helping him this morning has taken him to a hospital or something where he can get help."

"Maybe," Clive said, but when his eyes met Sara's, he could see that she was as skeptical as he was.

They thanked Brenda and left. "I guess that's about all we can do until morning," Clive said.

"In that case, I think I'll go into the office and make sure there aren't any appointments on my desk that I didn't get onto the computer. I think there might have been," she said.

"I'll go with you, if you don't mind," Clive said.

"Oh, you don't need to do that," she protested mildly. "It shouldn't take long."

"Sara, I'd like to. We've done quite a bit of poking around, and we may have stirred someone up by now. The whole thing with the *nice* friend taking Trevor from his apartment this morning is bothering me," he said.

Sara scrunched her eyebrows, and a worried look filled her eyes. "Are you suggesting that whoever Trevor went with might not be doing it to help him?"

"The thought crossed my mind. Trevor might know something that someone doesn't want us to know," he said.

"Oh," she responded with wide eyes. "Are we being followed or something?"

"It's possible," Clive said. "I want to make sure you're safe, so I would really like to go to the office with you."

"Then yes, please do come," she said. Back in her car, she asked, "Clive, did you tell me you have a permit to carry a concealed weapon?"

"Yes," he said. "Why?"

"I was just wondering if you have a weapon on you right now?"

"I do," he said. "I'm sorry, Sara, I don't mean to worry you. We just need to be cautious."

"Yes, we do," she agreed. "Thanks for reminding me."

When they entered the office, Sara shut the door behind them. "That's usually open when I'm working," she said. "Winn's private office is always closed."

She approached her desk and sat down. Clive was watching her face as she looked at her desk. Sara was slowly shaking her head; then she rustled through some papers in the inbox on her desk, then the outbox, and then she looked up at Clive. "Somebody's been at my desk," she said. "Nobody ever messes with things on my desk, not even Winn."

"Do you have custodians that come in and clean?"

"Well, yes," she said. "But they're under strict orders to never touch *any* papers on *any* desk in *any* office. And they're pretty good about that. They've never touched mine before."

"Is something missing?" he asked.

"Yes, there is. I had a legal pad right here on my desk." She pointed at a spot right in the very center. "As you can see, it's not here." She leaned to the side and checked her trash. Next, she looked in all of her unlocked drawers. After that she pulled out her keys and checked the locked ones. Finally, she unlocked and checked her filing cabinets. "It's gone," she said at last.

"Do you have any idea what you had written on it? And was it just on the top sheet? Was the rest of the pad blank?" Clive asked.

"Yes, I had a call just before I left Friday. I'd already shut my computer down. It was some guy that wanted to talk to Winn, and I think I told him to come in first thing Monday, before the first client was scheduled to arrive," she said. "It sounded like it was quite urgent. I guess I'll just have to tell him Winn isn't here when he comes in—whoever he was."

"Why would someone have taken your legal pad?" Clive was concerned. Anything out of the norm was a worry since they had started their own investigation into the murder.

"I don't know," she said. Then she suddenly brightened. "Maybe Winn took it. He might have come in for something before he left for—wherever he went—and noticed my note. He doesn't usually mess with my desk, but he might have seen what I'd written, recognized the name, and taken the pad into his office to call the guy." She was already on her feet and approaching Winn's private office, keys in her hand. She unlocked his door and stepped inside, flipping on the light switch as she did so.

"There it is," she called out to Clive, who had stayed in the outer office. "Come here, Clive."

He came in. The legal pad was on the desk. "The page I wrote on is gone," she said. "He must have called the guy and taken the page. That's a huge relief. I was worried."

She left the pad where it was and turned toward the door. Just then the phone on her desk began to ring. She hurried past Clive and answered the phone. "Law office of Winn Bertram."

She listened for a minute, her face getting red, the fingers of her left hand drumming her desk top. "I work here," she finally said. "I have every right to come in."

Sara listened for a moment again, and then she said, "You'll just have to take that up with Winn when he gets back. It's not any of my concern."

She listened for a moment longer, and then she suddenly slammed the phone down with a resounding crack, muttering something under her breath. Clive, who was standing back beside Winn's door, said with a grin, "I take it that wasn't a call from someone you care much for."

"That's for sure," she said. "It was Winn's ex-wife, Mara. She wanted to know what I was doing in here on a Sunday night."

"How did she know you were here?" he asked, suddenly concerned.

"I don't know, unless . . ." Sara began and trailed off, rubbing her forehead.

Clive finished for her. "Unless she's watching us."

Sara slumped back in her chair. "Why would she do that?" she asked softly.

"That's a very good question," Clive answered. "Is she somehow involved in the murder, I wonder?"

"She's the kind of person that would kill someone, that's for sure. She's awful."

"Winn told you that?" he prodded gently.

"Well, yes, but after that phone call, I learned it first hand," she said. "She sounded really mean."

"What else did she say to you?" Clive asked.

"She said she wanted to know where Winn had gone. Apparently she's keeping track of him."

"Was that all she said?" Clive pressed.

"No, there was more. She told me to keep my relationship with him on a strictly professional basis. She told me I better not continue to date him or I would lose my job. That's when I slammed the phone down."

"My, a jealous ex-wife, it sounds like," Clive said. "Or one who knows something she shouldn't."

"Like something about Walker's murder?" Sara asked.

"Yeah, something like that."

For a minute or more, Sara sat at her desk, lost in thought. She'd picked up a pencil from her desk and was chewing on it. Finally, she put the pencil back and stood up. "Could it have been Mara that was in here rather than Winn?" she asked.

"Actually, Sara, you might be onto something there. Maybe she still has keys from when she and Winn were married," Clive suggested.

"Yes, and maybe she is holding something over his head, something completely separate from the murder," she suggested, walking purposefully back into Winn's office. "We're here now; I think I'll snoop around a little."

"Is that a good idea, Sara?" Clive cautioned.

"Winn gave me the key to his office. I have access to his files. He trusts me."

"What if he finds out and takes exception to what you're about to do?"

Sara stopped beside Winn's huge oak desk and said, "Then I guess he could fire me, but I don't think he would. He likes me, Clive, and apparently Mara knows that." She paused then finished, saying, "I just wish I knew how I feel about him. One thing's for sure, I don't trust him like I did. He lied to me about going to Denver."

"And he hired a man to find your brother," Clive reminded her.

"At least, we think he did, but we don't know that for sure," she said.

That made Clive think for a moment. "Okay, you got me on that one. I've just been assuming," he admitted.

"We both have," she agreed. "Maybe there's something in here that will either prove or disprove our assumptions. You can watch, Clive, but don't help. I have the right to be in here; you don't. I don't want to get you in trouble."

"Maybe I'll sit in your office while you look," he said, knowing she had a valid point. "I'll be checking my e-mail on my phone."

About a half hour passed. Then suddenly Sara shouted, "I found something, Clive. You've got to see this."

CHAPTER SEVENTEEN

"Hi, Jessica. You look a lot better than the last time I saw you." Donte smiled at her.

"Yeah, they tell me I could have died," she said. "I have you to thank that I didn't."

"No, you have the Lord and a good surgeon to thank," he countered.

"Okay, the Lord and the doctor and you," she said with a smile. "How did you know what was wrong with me?"

"I was a pre-med student," he said. "And I've worked at hospitals a lot. I've seen people come in with the exact symptoms you had. It was a pretty safe guess."

"Are you going to be a doctor?" Chey asked from where she was standing next to him at the foot of Jessica's bed.

"That was my plan at one time," he admitted. "But I don't know now if that'll ever happen."

"Why, Donte? You're such a good man and so smart. You've got to continue your studies," Chey said earnestly.

"That may never happen," he said softly, turning away from Jessica's bed.

"Donte." Chey reached out and touched his shoulder. "What's going on?"

"I can't tell you that," he said. "I've already put you two in way too much danger. I only came back to make sure you were safe and that you can get on your way home soon."

Chey's eyes filled with tears, and she stepped around in front of him. "Who's Bo Gray?" she asked.

His shoulders slumped. "He's someone who's after me. Please, don't ask for more than that."

"Okay," Chey said as she stepped close to him and put her arms around his waist.

He pulled himself free and stepped back. "Don't, Chey. This is hard enough for me as it is. I've never met anyone quite like you before. But I can't pull you deeper into my troubles. The last thing in the world that I want is for you to get hurt."

"And the last thing I want is for you to walk out of my life," she said, her hands folded in front of her, but her eyes never leaving his face.

"I'm sorry, Chey," Donte said as he turned toward the girl in the bed. "You get well fast, Jessica. It really is good to see you feeling so much better. I need to get a room now. It's getting late."

***

The phone rang again before Sara and Clive had left the office. She looked at it dubiously, then picked it up, and answered. "You again!" she said angrily when she recognized the voice of Winn's ex-wife.

"Yes, it's me," Mara said loudly. "Why are you still in Winn's office?"

"This is *my* office," Sara reminded her. "Why do you care anyway? You two are divorced. I thought that meant he was out of your life."

"Not hardly," Mara said angrily. "But you better be or you'll pay. Mark my word."

Sara was going to slam the phone down, but Mara beat her to it. Sara looked up at Clive, who was watching her with concern. "Mara again?" he asked.

"Yes, I'm afraid so."

"Not unexpected," he told Sara gently. "Not after what you just found."

"Let's get out of here," she said. She stood with a photocopy of a single sheet of paper. The original had been placed back where she'd found it, where Winn would find it eventually.

She held the paper up and read it one more time: *Winn, darling, we'll be getting back together soon. You know you still love me. Get rid of that annoying girl that works for you. I don't just mean to quit dating her, Winn. I mean get rid of her. I want her completely out of your life. I won't have her messing up our future. I found the note on her desk and called your friend, Ron. I told him to stay out of our lives or I would find a way to destroy both of you. And you know I can. And one more thing, my darling. Fire Bo. Let the cops take care of Donte like they plan to, that will keep you safe from them. And yes, I do know what you did. But it's okay. We'll see you through it together. I'll see that you aren't arrested. Do as I say, Winn. I'm the only one who will ever love you, and don't you forget it. Mara.*

"This is unbelievable," she said for the third or fourth time since finding it. "This has got to have something to do with the murder. Why else would she mention Donte?"

"I think she's convinced that Winn killed Walker, and that makes me lean in that direction too. If that's not it, then Winn has done something else pretty serious," Clive said. "She obviously wants Donte to take the fall for the murder. And you're in danger. She's watching you."

Sara shivered. "What can I do?"

"We—both of us—will go talk to anyone above Detective Fields and see if they can get him moving. Surely, with what we've learned, the cops will see that Donte is innocent and start looking for more suspects."

"The main one being my boss." Sara rubbed at her eyes. She liked Winn, and even now, with all that she'd learned, she didn't want to think that he was in any way involved. And yet it was looking more like that all the time. It didn't make sense to her.

"That is likely," Clive said gently. "At least now we *know* that he hired Bo Gray."

"Am I safe at my house?" Sara asked, trying to keep herself from trembling. "I have a good burglar alarm system."

"That's not enough. Unless someone's there with you, I'd say we should move you somewhere else," he suggested.

"Would you stay at my house?" she asked. "It's a big house, and I would feel safer with you there."

"If that's what you want, then yes, I will, at least until the danger is past," he said.

"Thank you, Clive," she said in relief. "I can see why Donte trusts you. You're a good man."

***

Estela was on duty at the hotel when Chey and Donte arrived. "Mr. Noble," she said with a pretty smile. "It's good to see you again."

"And it's good to see you," Donte replied. "I need to thank you for what you and your brother did for me."

"Oh, it was nothing," she said modestly. "Anyway, I have a new friend. Chey and I have had some really fun talks."

"Estela," Donte said as she was checking him in, "I'd like to meet your brother and thank him personally."

"He'd like that," she replied with her ever-present smile. "I'll call him and have him come over. I think he's at his place right now, and I know he'll want to talk to you."

Donte had an idea. It had been rolling around in his head since he'd first begun to wait for Chey at the truck stop in Las Vegas. He planned to act on that idea if he could. Chey walked him to his room, and they talked for a minute or two before she left for Estela's house. "You don't have a way to get around," she said as they stood in the hallway just outside his door.

"Don't worry about that," he said with a chuckle. "Me and Dude, we can walk. This isn't a big town, you know."

"I'll come over in the morning," Chey volunteered. "We could have breakfast."

"Sure, I enjoy your company, but you've got to remember what I said at the hospital. You and I need to, you know, not let ourselves get involved," he said awkwardly.

She nodded. "Breakfast then." He watched as she walked quickly down the hallway.

***

Sara's home had an excellent alarm system, but even with that, she felt better knowing that Clive—and his gun—would be in the house. She showed him to a room, one of six bedrooms in the large house. Then they went back into the kitchen, where Sara began to prepare some sandwiches and hot chocolate. The doorbell rang.

Sara's heart jumped. Clive looked at her and said, "I'll be out of sight, just in case. Be careful opening the door."

"I can see who's out there by looking through the little peephole." And she did just that. Suddenly, she squealed and unlocked the door, swinging it open. "Mr. Hickman," she said. "What are you doing here?"

"I had your address. Donte gave it to me and told me I needed to come by someday. Well, here I am," he said with a big grin as he swept his hat off and stepped inside.

"Thanks for coming. I just wish Donte was here to see that you came."
She smiled as Clive walked over and shook the old mountain man's hand.

"I'm not here to bum a bed," Hick said. "I sleep just fine in the
camper on my truck. But I wanted you to know I'm in town. Tomorrow,
I'm going to the cops who are working on this case of Donte's. I'll set
them straight once and fer all."

"Sara has to work tomorrow, but I'm going to the police department
in the morning," Clive said. "Why don't you come with me?"

"That would be great," Hick said. "I won't keep you. I suppose you'll
be heading for your place, Clive?"

"Actually, there has been a threat against Sara tonight, so I'll be
staying in the house to make sure she's not bothered," Clive explained.
"I'll escort her to her office in the morning."

"You got a firearm, young fella?" Hick asked.

"Yes, I do," Clive responded.

"Well, I have several in my truck, and with your permission, Miss
Sara, I'll sleep in my truck right outside your house," Hick offered.

"There's no need for that; this is a big house." Sara gestured at their
surroundings. "You can sleep in one of the bedrooms like Clive is going
to do, and that way, I'll sleep even better."

"If you're sure, Miss Sara, I'll sure enough do that, and me and the
young fella here will keep you safe as a bear in his cave."

So it was settled. Sara went to bed feeling reasonably safe, grateful for
Donte's good friends and wishing that she had met them weeks before.
She lay in her comfortable bed, feeling quite confident that Donte would
soon be able to come home and resume his life. She just wished he would
e-mail her so she would know that he was okay. She very much feared
that Winn was somewhere in Tonopah by now, or at least close by. She
fell asleep with mixed emotions.

***

It was late, but despite the hour, Donte was sitting in the front room of
the home of Marcos, Estela's twenty-nine-year-old brother. Chey had
gone back to check on Jessica at the hospital one more time before turning in for the night. Marcos offered Donte a bed, but Donte had other
plans for the night. "Thanks for doing whatever it is you did to keep Bo
Gray from bothering Chey and Jessica."

Marcos grinned. "I'm glad to have been of service, and I'm glad you're all safe now."

Donte shook his head. "I hate to tell you this, but there are some real bad people after me. One of them is the man who hired Bo, a lawyer by the name of Winn Bertram. I have reason to believe he is here in town looking for Chey and Jessica. I'm sure Chey will be fine at your sister's place, but I am worried about Jessica," Donte explained.

A hard, determined look crossed the Hispanic man's face. He shook his head. "No one is going to bother her," he said. "Me and my friends will sleep outside the hospital if we have to."

"Actually, I didn't want to worry Jessica and Chey too much, but I actually plan to spend the night, with Dude here," he said, patting his dog on the head, "watching out for Mr. Bertram at the hospital."

"You'll have help," Marcos promised. "Any friend of Estela's is a friend of mine. Is that what you wanted to talk to me about, this lawyer?"

"No, not entirely," Donte said. "I was hoping you would help me with something else."

Marcos grinned. "I'll do whatever I can," he agreed.

"I'd like to talk to Bo Gray. Is that possible?"

"Of course. We didn't hurt him, just made it so he couldn't bother anybody for a while."

"Does he have his cell phone?" Donte asked.

"Yes, but not his charger. I took his number so I could call him once a day to check on him," Marcos said. "I warned him in a note about running his battery down and suggested he only turn his phone on about the time I'd be calling."

"Have you checked on him?" Donte asked

"Yes. He isn't in a very pleasant mood." Marcos grinned.

"Tell me about him."

"Okay, but not until me and you check by the hospital to make sure the lawyer isn't bothering anyone," Marcos said. "You can ride with me."

"Glad to," Donte agreed. "Let's go."

Donte knew Winn's car by sight, a sleek black Cadillac. He searched the parking lot, eventually satisfied that it wasn't there. He and Marcos watched in silence from the shadows at the rear of the lot as Chey came out, got in her silver Malibu, and left. A few minutes later, Donte said to Marcos, "Okay, tell me about Bo."

Marcos did, and Donte wasn't sure if he was mostly horrified or amused. He decided amusement, under the circumstances, was the more appropriate emotion, and he chuckled. After a moment, he asked, "Will you take me out there tomorrow? I have some questions for the guy, and I suspect that under his present circumstances he might find it in his best interest to talk to me."

"I think you might be right," Marcos agreed with a grin. "But there's one problem. I have a job to do at the garage that can't wait. We could go at around five o'clock, if that's okay."

"That'd be great," Donte said. "I'll keep an eye out for Winn in the meantime. I sure appreciate your help. I hope someday I can repay you."

"There's no need for that, my friend."

"But still . . ." Donte didn't have words to express his gratitude. He cleared his throat. "Now, I think you should go ahead and go home. I'll stick around here for a while."

"Would you like me to take your dog for now?" he asked, patting Dude on the head. "I have a large fenced yard, and my dog would like the company, I'm sure. And your duffle bag is already there."

"That'd be great," Donte told him. A minute later, Marcos drove off with Dude in the back of the truck.

Donte kept a vigilant watch out for Winn, but after a couple of hours, he began to seriously consider that either Sara had been wrong—which he hoped—or something had come up that changed Winn's mind. That would be okay too, Donte decided. As long as the guy wasn't around.

Eventually, Donte wandered inside, went to the nurses' station, told them of his concerns, and asked permission to keep watch in Jessica's room. Permission was gladly granted, under the circumstances. When Donte asked how she was doing, he was told that she was actually doing great and that there was a good chance that she could be released the next day.

That took a great weight off Donte's shoulders. That meant that by the time he and Marcos went out into the desert to confront Bo, the girls could be headed home. He stepped into Jessica's room. She stirred, so he stepped to her bedside and told her quietly that he was going to wait there during the night, if it was okay with her. She smiled and mumbled that it was and then drifted into slumber again. He then sat in the large, soft chair not far from the door.

CHAPTER EIGHTEEN

WINN WAS IN A JAM, and he knew it. What he couldn't figure out was how to get out of it. He paced the small jail cell where he had been sitting since he'd fallen asleep in the wee hours of Sunday morning and wrecked his luxurious Cadillac. As if that wasn't bad enough, the cops had arrested him. He'd known that his driver's license was suspended because of too many speeding tickets, but he hadn't worried about it. He'd just tried to drive slower, hoping he'd get his license back soon.

Driving slower had not been an option as he was approaching Wendover. He needed to get to Tonopah as soon as possible, and he'd been driving fast. He'd have been okay if he hadn't fallen asleep. But he did, and he'd drifted off the road and destroyed his car. He hadn't been hurt badly, but they took him to a hospital just to make sure, and then, when they decided his injuries weren't bad, they'd informed him he was going to jail. He shouldn't have panicked, but he did and had tried to make a break for it, running right out the front door of the hospital.

That had been a mistake. He knew that now. For his freedom had been short lived, and it had only brought more charges. He'd figured that at least he could get out on bail, rent a car, and go on his way. But that plan fizzled out when he realized he'd left his wallet at home. He always kept a little cash in his car, but he didn't have access to his car. And anyway, it wasn't nearly enough to make bail.

He thought about calling one of his law partners, but he didn't because of the implications it could have on his job. This needed to be kept as quiet as possible. He thought of a couple of friends, but he didn't have their phone numbers since he'd lost his phone in the wreck. The cops claimed they hadn't seen the phone. All the arguing in the world about who he was failed to convince them, and thus he found himself, early Monday morning, taking up residence in a jail cell.

There *was* one number he knew by heart, although he'd tried to forget it. The person would, he was almost certain, help, but it would come at a price he didn't want to pay. But desperate times called for desperate measures. He finally requested his phone call.

"Who is this?" Mara's hard and angry voice asked when she answered the phone at the home they used to share.

"It's Winn," he said, feeling slightly lower than a worm.

"Why, Winn, I didn't expect to hear from you so soon," she said, slightly more cheerful now, a sound that made his stomach fill with acid. "I didn't think you'd be back yet. Your soon-to-be-ex-secretary thought you wouldn't be back until tonight."

"This call is not about Sara, and she has a job as long as she wants it. I'm calling about a little problem I'm having that I was hoping you could help me with."

"And what would that be? You know my services don't come cheap, my love," she said.

He cringed. Yes, he knew that only too well. He took a deep breath and plunged in. "I'm in jail, and I need someone to bail me out."

"Why, darling, of course I'll get you out of jail, providing you're not in for murder," she said in that sickeningly sweet voice he had come to abhor.

"Don't be ridiculous." He struggled to keep his anger in check. "I lost my driver's license and hadn't had a chance to get it back yet and—"

Mara cut him off before he had a chance to explain further. "Lost as in *lost,* or lost as in got it suspended?"

"Suspended," he said.

"That shouldn't be a very large bail," she said. "Surely you have enough in your wallet to cover that."

"I don't have my wallet with me."

"I see, ever the forgetful man I love," she said scornfully. "So you can't even hire a bondsman to help you out. Without your wallet, you probably don't even have a credit card."

"That's right," he admitted, feeling like he was going to choke on his words at any moment.

"Okay, Winn, how much is the bond?" she finally asked.

"I think it's around two thousand."

"You've got to be kidding," she yelled into the phone. "That can't be right. It can't be that much for driving on a suspended license."

"Well," he began, wondering how to phrase this in the least damaging way possible. "There are a couple other little things."

"Such as?"

"Well, I had a little accident, and they claim I was going too fast," he admitted.

"I see."

"Well and there was one other little problem. I was a bit confused," he said. "I had just rolled my car and—"

"Rolled your Cadillac?" she shrieked. "You said it was a *little* accident."

"In a manner of speaking, it was. I mean, you know, I don't have any major injuries."

"Just a bit of confusion," she chided. "So what did you do while you were confused?"

"I tried to get away," he said so softly he hoped she couldn't hear him.

But Mara was not hard of hearing. "You fled from the cops? On foot?"

"Well, yes," he agreed. "I didn't have a car anymore."

"And how did that work out for you?"

"Not too well. That's why I'm in jail. Can you come and get me, please?" Oh, how he hated to beg, especially to his ex-wife.

"Maybe I'll just leave you in jail and let you think about things for a while," she said snidely.

"Mara, for crying out loud, I've been here for over twenty-four hours. I've had plenty of time to think," he said, foolishly raising his voice.

"I'm guessing that you haven't been thinking about the right things. Call me in the morning, and I'll see what I can do."

"I can't wait till morning. Please, Mara, whatever you think I should think about, I can do that while you are driving to Tooele."

"Tooele! What are you doing in Tooele?" she demanded.

"I told you, I'm in jail."

"You know what I mean. Why are you in that part of the state? Where were you going?"

"We can talk about that while you're taking me home," he said.

"Yes, I suppose we can. Now, think about what you did that you didn't think I'd find out about. Think about what it would feel like to spend the rest of your life behind bars. And think about what you can do that will convince me to keep that from happening," she said.

"What are you talking about?" he demanded.

"That's what you need to think about. And when I get there in the morning, we'll talk."

"I can't sit in here that long," he said, approaching hysteria.

"What alternative do you have? Surely you aren't thinking about calling one of the attorneys in your office?"

"No, but I could call Sara. I'm sure *she* would help me."

That had the desired effect of convincing Mara to bail him out but also the expected effect similar to the detonation of a half dozen sticks of dynamite. When the smoke and debris had finally cleared, she said almost too calmly, "I'm on my way. And when we start for home, we're going to have a long talk about that smutty little Sara and her brother. I love you, Winn. I'll see you in a little while."

The phone went dead, and Winn was left with nothing to do but think about what she'd said—and what she'd implied. And it didn't make for pretty thoughts.

***

Sara was in the office by eight Monday morning. Nothing had changed from when she'd been here the night before. Her yellow legal pad was still on Winn's desk when she unlocked his door. Nothing further had been disturbed. As near as she could tell, the only thing that was disturbed was her. And she was very disturbed. She couldn't get the note from Winn's ex-wife out of her mind. The woman was wicked. Sara was also disturbed that she had no way to contact the man whose name and number she'd written down on the missing top sheet of the legal pad.

She carried the pad back into her office and ripped off the top page, the one that was right below the one someone else had taken. She held it up to the light to see if she'd pressed hard enough to leave an indentation. She hadn't pressed that hard. Then she had another thought. If Mara did have keys to Winn's office, might she have used one of their phones to make any calls, specifically to the person whose name was on the pad? Sara decided to check the phones' recent call history.

She didn't recognize most of the recent calls that had been made from Winn's phone. However, the time of the calls was helpful to her. Someone, probably Winn, had made some calls well before noon on

Saturday. Then, around eight that night there were three calls recorded. The first number she recognized—Winn's home number. The second was his cell phone. The third she didn't recognize but suspected that it might be the number she was missing.

The fact that calls had been made to Winn's numbers seemed to confirm that Mara was the one who had broken in. Sara dialed the third number and waited. It was a man that answered the phone. She spoke to him, saying, "This is Sara Noble at Winn Bertram's law office. I'm trying to reach—"

"Me, I hope," the man said. "I talked to you Friday and you said to come in around nine this morning, but I got a phone call last night from Mara, Winn's ex-wife. It was not a nice phone call. Would you care to explain how she got this number? It's unlisted."

He was angry and was clearly implying that Sara had given the number to Mara. Sara quickly replied, "I left your number and name on my desk because it was late and I'd already shut my computer off. Someone broke into the office—or rather, I should say someone with a key came in and found your number and called it from Winn's phone, the one in his personal office. That could only have been Mara."

She heard the man sigh deeply, and then he said, "I'm glad it wasn't you. Winn told me that you were very efficient. He seems to like you a lot."

"I try to do a good job, and I like him as well," Sara said, "although Mara is trying to get me fired."

"That sounds like Mara. My name, in case you've forgotten, is Ron Raynor. I used to be neighbors with Winn and Mara. I still live next door to Mara, but I avoid her like the plague. She's been hounding me about helping her get Winn to marry her again. I keep telling her it's none of my business. I made this appointment to meet with Winn this morning to see if he could get the woman to leave me and my wife alone."

"What did Mara say to you when she broke in here and called?" Sara asked.

"Well, at first, she was nice, if that word can ever be used to describe Mara. She thanked me for making an appointment to try to help convince Winn to take her back," Ron explained. "When I bluntly told her that the reason for my appointment was not that, she lit into me."

"Did she figure out that you were going to talk to him about just the opposite?"

"She might have, but she was mostly angry that I hadn't set up the appointment to do what she wanted me to do. Do you know her, Miss Noble?"

"Barely. What I do know is that she wants Winn to fire me," Sara replied.

"I'll bet. She told me that Winn was dating you, and I could tell that made her angry. It was Winn who filed for divorce, but no one who knew the two of them was surprised. In fact, I wondered what took him so long. She wanted the divorce too. She actually moved out on him before he filed. Apparently, she's changed her mind."

"I understand, Mr. Raynor," she said.

"Yes, well I guess you would," he agreed. "But I'll be there at nine like I told you, even though I'm not sure Mara won't try to do me bodily damage for it."

"Actually, that's why I'm calling," Sara began. "I came in last night to find the note and call you. That was when I discovered that it was gone. I didn't think until a few minutes ago to see if Mara had used one of our office phones to call you. That's how I got your number."

"I see, and why did you need to call me?" Ron asked.

"To tell you that Winn had to go out of town and won't be back in the office until tomorrow morning," she explained. "Winn asked me to reschedule all of his appointments for today. Would the same time tomorrow be okay?"

"Yes, that'll be fine," he agreed. "Where did Winn go?"

"He just said there was a family emergency," she said, discretely leaving out the fact that he had lied to her about that.

"I hope it's nothing too serious," he said. "I'll see you tomorrow then."

***

Donte was still at the hospital when Chey arrived a little before nine. Jessica was excited to see her. "I'm being released today," Jessica said.

"Really? That's great," Chey responded. But when her eyes met Donte's, he saw sadness there, and he had a feeling why.

"I'll let you two talk," Donte said. "I'm going down to the cafeteria to grab some breakfast."

"Go with him, Chey," Jessica said. "I'll bet you haven't eaten a bite yet this morning."

"Actually, I have," Chey told her. "Estela fixed a really nice breakfast."

"Go anyway. Donte's probably sick of my company and would like to spend a little time with you before we leave for home."

"I'd like that, Chey," Donte said with a smile, "even though I am not sick of Jessica's company at all."

"Okay," Chey relented, but there wasn't a lot of brightness in her voice.

"I'm really going to miss you," she confessed as she sipped on a hot chocolate and watched Donte eat some scrambled eggs.

He smiled at her. "You don't really know me. I'm a man with a lot of baggage and with skeletons in the closet."

"That doesn't change how I feel," Chey said. "Will you miss me?"

Donte swallowed hard, for he would miss her more than he cared to admit. But he didn't want to clutter her life with his problems. "Of course I will," he answered, thinking how he didn't miss the girl he had asked to marry him in even the slightest degree.

"But not much?" she pressed, a sadness on her face that made him feel like a knife was stuck in his heart.

"A lot," he confessed. "But believe me, Chey, if you knew all about me and my problems, you'd be grateful to see me gone from your life."

She just shook her head and looked down at the brown liquid in her cup. "I know I asked you this before, but if you ever get rid of those skeletons, will you look me up?"

"If you still want me to, I will," he promised. "But you need to understand that my life is a mess, and my problems will probably only get worse."

"I'll be praying for you," she said as she looked up and caught his eyes. "I've never met anyone quite like you before."

"You have no idea how true that is," he said. "I will promise you one thing. I'll e-mail you in a day or two to make sure you gals make it home okay."

"I'd like that," she said. "But there's something else I'm worried about."

"What's that?"

"Your bike and trailer are in Las Vegas. I won't be able to take you back there because of all of our stuff filling my little car," she said. "What will you do?"

Donte forced a chuckle. "That's the least of my worries. Dude and I can walk, hitchhike, whatever," he said. "I'm in no hurry to be anywhere."

"Donte, I wish you'd tell me what you're running from. That's what you're doing, isn't it?" she asked. "It's more than just Bo Gray, I think."

"You're right, but I really can't tell you."

They talked very little after that until Chey asked, "Where's Dude?"

"He's at Estela's brother's place, keeping another dog company," Donte replied lightly. "He's probably glad for someone of his own species to keep him company for a while."

"Do you have any idea what Marcos and his friends did to Bo Gray?" she asked.

He nodded his head. "Yes, a little. What I don't know is where the *other* guy is, the man who hired Bo. I walked around the parking area every hour or so last night, but I haven't seen the guy's car."

"How do you know he's coming?" she asked.

"I have my sources," was all Donte would say. "I'll be relieved, for your sake, when you two are on your way out of town."

"Do you need to borrow my laptop to check your e-mail again before I leave?" she asked.

"Is it at Estela's?"

"No, it's in my car."

"Yes, that would be great. Maybe when we finish here, we could go out and get it."

"Okay," she said. "We'll do that."

***

Sara was glad to be alone in her office. The door was open into the main reception area, but she'd only been disturbed a couple of times. Both times it had been another attorney inquiring about Winn. She gave them the standard answer and left it at that.

It was close to ten when she heard a beep inside her purse. She quickly retrieved her cell phone and opened her e-mail. As she hoped, there was a message from Donte. She opened it with shaking hands. *Scrunch. I'm doing fine. I am no longer where I was. Haven't seen W. Have you heard from him? How is the investigator doing? Is he making progress? I'm so sorry for all the trouble this has caused you. Miss and love you. Slurpee.*

She looked toward the door. She didn't see anyone. So she quickly typed a reply. She wrote: *Slurpee, I miss you too. I wish this would be over, not for me so much as for you. The investigator is making progress. He found a man who says he can confirm your alibi. They're at the police department this morning. I pray that what he has to say will change their focus. It should. Get back with me soon so that I can give you further updates. Love and miss you too. Scrunch.*

CHAPTER NINETEEN

So far, Clive had been very impressed with Lieutenant Jon Scales. As opposed to Detective Fields, Scales seemed like a motivated man, one who liked to get crimes solved. He was a sturdily built man of about fifty. His thick black hair was cut fairly short and combed to perfection.

"Detective Fields," he was saying, "is an experienced investigator. I'm sorry you're not satisfied with his work on this case. He is convinced that Donte Noble is the killer, and he has a lot of evidence to back it up. If you can show me something to the contrary, I'll see that the detective follows up on it."

"That's all we're asking," Clive said.

"That's why I'm here, Lieutenant," said the tall, lanky man in leather, Jacob Hickman. The old man's eyes narrowed. "I was with Donte in the mountains above Mirror Lake when that guy was murdered. I can personally vouch for him."

"Now that is significant," Lieutenant Scales said, his eyes widening. "I'll see that you get to talk to Detective Fields this morning. I wish we'd have heard this months ago."

"Nobody asked until this young fella came along," Hick said.

"Are you sure?" Lieutenant Scales asked.

"I ain't lying," the mountain man said darkly.

"I'm sure you're not," Scales agreed.

"There's more," Clive said and told Scales about Trevor Wells, about the overheard threat to kill Walker Aklen over back rent, and the repeated arguments that the neighbor had heard. Clive explained to Scales that Trevor had said that nobody liked Walker, that he couldn't keep friends. "He was always borrowing money, or drugs, or whatever, and he wouldn't pay it back. I checked again this morning before coming over here," he finished. "He wasn't home, and his neighbor doesn't think he's been home since he left with a man yesterday morning."

"It sounds like that's another lead Detective Fields will need to follow up on," the lieutenant said. "I appreciate what you've done. What line of work are you in, Mr. Granger?"

"This may sound crazy, but I'm a mystery writer. Novels. I have three—all bestsellers—and another one coming out in a few months. Before the death of my wife in a mass murder in a mall in Omaha, I was a writer for a major newspaper. I worked the crime beat," Clive explained.

"I'm sorry about your wife. That's tough," Lieutenant Scales said sympathetically.

"Thanks, I've finally moved on. But when I heard about Donte's troubles, I wanted to help if I could. He was a missionary in Omaha and was actually at the mall the day of the shooting. We're good friends. I know that Donte is simply not capable of murder."

"And I agree with Clive," Hick said with a shake of his fist.

"I understand your feelings, both of you," the lieutenant said, "but you both need to understand that we simply go where the evidence leads us."

"Which is why we're here today," Clive reminded him.

"Very well, and you have certainly given us a lot to work on. Is there anything else before I have you meet with Fields?" Lieutenant Scales asked.

"Yes, there is," Clive said. "Do you know a man by the name of Bo Gray?"

Scales slowly nodded his head. "Yes, I do. He's a private investigator but not, in my opinion, the most scrupulous. Why do you ask?"

"Donte's sister is a legal secretary and works for Winn Bertram," Clive told him. "He and Bo seem to have some kind of relationship, and she overheard something that makes her believe Bertram is paying Bo to find Donte. If that's true, it seems a bit strange to me."

"I've heard of Winn Bertram. He has a good reputation, although he doesn't do any criminal defense work. I do know that he had a messy divorce a few years back, and that his ex-wife is a colorful character, so to speak."

"Yes, she's threatened Sara, that's Donte's sister. She and Bertram have started dating, and from what I understand, the ex-wife strongly objects to it," Clive revealed.

"Does Miss Noble think that her boss might be involved in the murder?"

"Let's put it this way. Sara worries that Winn could be the killer although her heart tells her he's not. There's also one other thing," Clive said. "In talking to Detective Fields, there has been no motive established that would point to Donte wanting to kill Walker. That seems odd to me that the entire focus of your investigation is directed at Donte when others—such as Trevor Wells and other of Walker's associates—clearly have motive."

"Let me page Fields right now and you can meet with him. Mr. Hickman, I'll have him take a recorded statement from you," Lieutenant Scales said. "I'll see to it that your leads are followed up on."

"Thank you," Clive said.

The lieutenant got on the phone, but a moment later he put it down. "It seems Detective Fields is out on a case right now. I'll brief him on everything you've told me. Mr. Hickman, why don't I go ahead and take your statement. I'll see that Fields hears it as soon as he returns."

When they left the police department a few minutes later, Clive turned to Hick. "I feel a lot better now, don't you, Hick?"

"Oh, yes," Hick agreed. "I guess I'll mosey on back to the mountains now since we got things turned around."

"Thanks for your help. How can I keep you informed?"

"Give me your number, and I'll call you when I'm near a phone," Hick promised. "I sure want to see the right man arrested and Donte be able to get back to learning how to be a doctor."

***

Sara smiled when Clive walked in with a grin. "How did it go at the police station?" she asked after closing her door to ensure some privacy.

"I think it went well. We didn't get to see Fields because he was out working another case. But we did meet with Lieutenant Jon Scales. He seems like a sharp man and a good investigator," Clive reported. "He took a recorded statement from Hick and said he'd have Detective Fields follow up."

"That's great news," Sara said with relief. "Let me tell you about my morning now." She recited the things she had learned from Ron Raynor.

When she finished, Clive said, "Wow, that woman is a piece of work. You need to be really careful. Would you like some lunch?"

"That would be nice," she agreed. "There's a place just up the block where the food is good and the service is quick." When they left, she locked her office behind them. "Not that the lock will keep Mara out," she said with a huff.

***

Walking away from Kasiah had been easy; seeing Chey off and not knowing when or if he would ever see her again was very difficult. Donte wished he could have met her at another time, in another place, and under different circumstances. He would have loved to date her, to get to know her better, and to let her know who he really was.

He did allow her to hug him in front of Estela's apartment just before she got in her little Malibu. She said, "Now remember, you can always call the number I gave you for my parents and locate me. You remember it, don't you?"

"I remember it," he said. Then on an impulse, he asked, "I know your e-mail address, but if you don't mind, would you tell me your cell phone number?"

Her face lit up. "Yes, of course," and she recited it. He recited it back, twice, just to make sure he knew it. "You won't forget it, will you?"

"I won't forget," he promised. "And I'll use it to make sure you two get back to Vernal okay."

"I hope you use it after that too," she said wistfully.

"That'll depend on a lot of things," he cautioned her. "I hope someday . . ." He let his voice trail off and hugged her again. "Okay, you get Jessica safely home."

His heart in his throat, he watched Chey drive away. Estela, who had been standing there the whole time said, "You two are perfect for each other. Don't let her get away."

Donte smiled at her and said, "Right now, I'm anything but perfect for her."

"I think you are," Estela disagreed.

"Estela, thanks for taking care of her. You're a very special person. But you have no idea the troubles I have in my life. I can't burden Chey with them, no matter how much I care for her."

"Maybe someday," the young Hispanic girl said wistfully.

"Yes, maybe someday."

"What are you going to do now?" she asked. "You don't have a car, and my brother has your dog."

"I'll walk back to town and get some lunch. Then I'll go rest for a while at your brother's house. Later, Marcos and I have some plans." He grinned. "I like your brother. He's a smart guy."

"He is, isn't he?" Estela responded with a grin. "He's also stubborn. He won't tell me what he did to that Bo Gray guy. I know he didn't hurt him, but I wish he'd tell me."

Donte grinned. "Maybe someday he will. Now, I think I'll mosey back to town and get some lunch."

"I have a better idea," Estela said. "Why don't I fix you something to eat?"

"That would be nice," Donte agreed. "Chey told me what a wonderful cook you are."

***

As Clive and Sara were finishing their lunch, Sara got a call on her cell phone. She pulled it from her purse and answered. Clive was watching her closely as she began to speak. The look on her face was one of fright. He found himself holding his breath. With her free hand, she began teasing her long brown hair. "Yes, I wondered when you'd call," she said, her eyes catching Clive's.

"Why don't you just come to my office, Sawyer?" she said, letting Clive know who she was talking to.

She listened for a moment and then said, "You don't have to buy me dinner. Anyway, tonight won't work because I already have a date."

"I'm sorry, but I don't have to tell you who it's with," she retorted a moment later. Then, after listening for a moment longer, she said, "Okay, I understand. I appreciate that you're trying to help Donte. Yes, Tuesday evening would be fine." Again she listened, and then she said, "You don't have to pick me up, Sawyer. I'll meet you. Just tell me which restaurant, and I'll be there at seven tomorrow evening."

Again, she listened, her face frightened. She was wringing her hair so much that Clive reached across the table and took hold of her hand, freeing her hair. She let him hold it. "Okay, Sawyer, you can pick me up at my house at six thirty. Thank you. I'll see you then."

She closed the phone and looked at Clive, her eyes watery. "He scares me, Clive. I don't want to ride in his car, but he insists. He says what he has to tell me will convince the cops to drop the charges against Donte."

"I'll make sure you're safe," Clive promised.

"I can wear the wire, the one I'll wear tonight with Winn, right?" she asked.

"Yes, and I'll stay close by, Sara. I promise."

"I think he'll lie," she said a moment later. "I think he and Kasiah just want Donte to come home so they can have him arrested."

"You're probably right," Clive agreed. "We'll just see how it goes, knowing that we can't just accept whatever he says. I'll check everything out."

"Thanks for being here for Donte . . ." She hesitated. "And for me."

After walking Sara to her office, Clive went back to his pickup and looked at his notes. He had things to do that afternoon. First on his list was another visit to Brenda Finn. There was more he wanted to ask her, and now was as good a time as any.

***

"I have a date with Sara," Sawyer reported to Kasiah over the phone.

"Tonight?" Kasiah asked.

"No, she says she already has a date tonight. So it won't be until tomorrow night."

"You should have told her to break her date tonight. We need to get Donte back here and soon," she said fiercely. "He's been running around free for too long already. I want him to pay for what he did."

"So do I, but I don't want to make her suspicious," Sawyer said. "Tomorrow will be okay."

"If you say so," Kasiah relented. "Did she say who her date is with? I didn't know she was dating anyone."

"I don't know why she wouldn't be," Sawyer said. "I think she's a right good-looking gal. Not in your class, but very pretty."

"Then enjoy your date, and call me after you take her home."

"I'll do that—both enjoy my date and call you." Sawyer chuckled. Then he added, "Just don't tell my wife."

***

Clive concluded that Mrs. Finn was a lonely woman. She fixed him a cup of hot chocolate and cut a piece of pie for him. She obviously wanted him to stay and visit for a while. He guessed that was okay and hoped she would have a lot to tell him.

It wasn't until after she'd brought him refreshments, as she called it, that he got down to the business at hand. He started with some general questions about how long she'd been neighbors to Trevor and Walker. "Only a year . . . or maybe a little longer," she said.

"Did you ever meet any of their friends?"

"Just sort of in passing," she said. "They aren't my kind of people, you know. Except for that nice guy who wanted to get Trevor off drugs and alcohol. Of course, I didn't ever meet him; I just saw him."

Clive tried to get her to describe some of the people she'd seen coming and going over there. She gave some vague descriptions but nothing helpful. "There were also young ladies that occasionally came," Brenda suddenly revealed.

"Really? You didn't hear their names through those thin walls, did you? It would sure be helpful if you did," he said.

"Well, let me think. Some of them were kind of, you know, slutty girls. Not the kind I'd ever want my nephews to date, I can tell you that," she said. "She was thoughtful for a moment, and then she said, "I didn't get their names. But there were a couple of young women who came who looked like, I guess you'd say, classy girls?"

"Can you describe them?" Clive asked, knowing that the little recorder in the pocket of his shirt was picking up every word.

"Well, let's see. One of them might have been a movie star or a model or something like that. She was young, maybe twenty or so, with gorgeous, long blonde hair. I would have died to have hair so pretty when I was young," Mrs. Finn said wistfully. "Her skin was silky and smooth. I mean, she was simply stunning. I can't imagine why she would visit those guys."

Clive could. Mrs. Finn had just described Kasiah Aklen. "Did you ever hear her name?"

"Maybe, but I can't remember it if I did. The other nice-looking woman I remember well."

"We'll get to her in a minute, but first," Clive said, "I'd like to talk a little more about the first one. Could her name have been Kasiah?"

Mrs. Finn closed her eyes tight for a moment. "That could be it," she said when she opened them. "But I can't be sure."

"When did you last see her here?" Clive asked.

"Oh, it's been a while. She must have come to see Walker, because she'd come even when Trevor wasn't home. I can't imagine why she would come to see him. She was a classy lady, and he was a tramp, if you'll excuse me saying so," she said. "I think she might have come once or twice right after Walker was murdered, but I haven't seen her since."

"Now let's talk about the other woman," Clive said. "Can you describe her?"

"Oh, yes," she said. "She was older than the other girl, probably in her late twenties. She was attractive, but not like the other girl. And I remember seeing her face a few times, but it never had a smile on it. She looked mean or ornery. And she had a loud voice."

"What did she look like?" Clive pressed.

"Pretty, about the same size as the other girl. She also had blonde hair, but it was short. Her eyes, I remember them. They were set close together. Not in an ugly way, not at all, just close together," Mrs. Finn said.

"Did you hear her name?"

"Yes . . . I think it was Mara. I didn't ever hear a last name, but I'm sure that was her first name."

It was like a bolt of lightning hitting Clive. He had no idea how he would do it, but he had to find the connection between Mara, Walker, and Trevor. It worried him more than ever about Winn Bertram. And tonight Sara was having dinner with him.

Clive shrugged off the worries Mara's name had caused and concentrated on seeing if there was anything else Mrs. Finn could tell him. "After Walker died, the cops came to the apartment. Do you remember that?"

"Oh, yes, that's easy to remember."

"Did any of them talk to you?" Clive asked.

"No one talked to me," she said. "The cops that came were a couple of young fellows, and they spent some time with Trevor," she said. "I could, you know, hear them."

"Through the wall? I mean, you could hear the officers through the wall, right?"

"Yes, but not well."

"You say the officers who came here were young. About what age were they?"

She thought for a minute. "They couldn't have been over thirty, either one of them."

"So you didn't see an officer who might have been about forty-five?"

"Oh no, they weren't that old," she said. "They were more like your age."

Clive spent another half hour there, ate a second piece of excellent cherry pie, drank another cup of hot chocolate, and didn't learn anything more of value. But as he thanked her and left, he went with the knowledge that Mara Bertram had visited, both before and after Walker's death; that Kasiah had also been there; and that Detective Fields had not been to Walker's apartment, but a couple of other officers had.

Once again in his pickup, Clive thought about going back and checking with other neighbors, but he decided against it. He remembered that the only one who had been able to tell him anything when he and Sara had been there before was Brenda Finn. She might have missed seeing Detective Fields, but it was more likely that she was right and he had let others do the footwork—what little footwork had been done. It made Clive bristle. Fields was a lazy cop, and Clive wasn't convinced that even with the prodding of Lieutenant Scales the man would work any harder. That, Clive decided, put the burden on him, and he was okay with that. He would do whatever he could and go to Scales with his findings.

CHAPTER TWENTY

"HEY, MAN, I GOT THAT job done early," Marcos said when he arrived back at his house. "We can go anytime, if you still want to."

"Oh, yeah, I want to all right," Donte said. "I have a gun in my duffle bag. I don't plan to shoot the guy," he said. "But I'll feel better if I have it with me. It's self-defense, if I ever need it."

"Hey, I got no problem with that, man," Marcos said, grinning and showing him the butt of a pistol that was in the pocket of his pants. "A guy can't be too careful."

For well over an hour, they drove out into the desert. It seemed like it would be easy to get lost, but Marcos seemed totally at ease. They came to one fork in the road after another. The farther they went, the less used the roads were. They finally turned onto a road that looked more like a path. They had to go slow since it was so rough, but they kept going for another half hour. Finally, they turned off that road, or whatever it was, and drove over a couple of ridges, around some steep mounds, through a rugged ravine, and finally over one more ridge. There Donte saw a Ford Expedition with four flat tires.

A sunburned man in nothing but a pair of checkered boxer shorts and a very grimy t-shirt was standing beside it, looking quite relieved. "It's about time you came back," Bo snapped as Marcos and Donte climbed out of the truck. "And what are you doing here, Donte?" he asked, his eyes growing wide.

"I heard you'd gotten yourself into a jam," Donte said. "I just thought I'd have my friend bring me out here and let us get acquainted. I don't think we've ever actually met, and I wanted to see how you were doing."

"You can see how I'm doing," Bo hissed. "You better get my tires pumped up and fix whatever you did to my car so we can get out of here."

"Whoa, hold on there, Bo. I didn't say we were taking you any-where," Donte said. "I just said I'd come to check on you. Is your food and water holding out all right? Looks like you could use clean boxers and t-shirt. We did bring those for you, that is, if you have them in your suitcase. My friend here has it in the back of his truck with his tools. I'll grab the suitcase for you, although, of course, you can only keep those two items."

Bo's face was burned, and his lips were slightly blistered, as were his ears and the back of his neck. Donte was sure that contributed to Bo's irritable mood. The man was glaring at them, and when Donte spoke, it was like Bo was trying to keep from exploding. "You will get me out of here, Donte. This ain't no game here."

Donte leaned against the front fender of Marcos's truck and looked toward the young Hispanic man. Marcos had a big grin on his face. Donte said to him, "Kind of interesting, don't you think? Bo Gray doesn't think this is a game. I think it is, don't you, my friend?" He was being careful not to call Marcos by name. Bo didn't know his name, and Donte didn't want to be the one to reveal it.

"This is lots of fun." Marcos chuckled.

"That's what I was thinking," Donte agreed. He turned to face Bo again, studied the man's angry, sunburned face, and then asked, "You don't think this is fun, but you do think it's fun to harass and scare innocent young women? You have a warped sense of fun."

"I wasn't harassing anybody," Bo said.

"That sure wasn't the way it felt to them," Donte said. "Would you like to tell me what you were doing if you weren't harassing them?"

"I was just minding my own business, having a nice little vacation, when this thug here," he poked a finger toward Marcos, "and his friends decided to commit a bunch of crimes."

"Crimes?" Donte feigned surprise. "So have you called the cops and told them? My friend was kind enough to let you keep your cell phone." Bo said nothing, just squirmed uncomfortably. "There's a signal out here. My friend has called and checked on you a couple of times. Why didn't you call to report a crime?"

It appeared Bo didn't have an answer. "Speaking of games, what did you think you'd find in the bags on my bike, checkers or something?"

"I don't know what you're talking about," Bo said at last.

"Yes you do, Mr. Private Investigator Bo Gray. There is no need denying it. I saw you and so did one of the girls you were harassing. I knew you were after me. Why, you even called me by name when you inquired at the hotel desk about whether or not I had checked out. And you certainly recognized me when we got here. I suppose you're ready to tell me why, am I right?"

Bo kept his mouth closed except to run his tongue over his blistered lips.

"There is a way out of this mess," Donte continued. "I'll make it really easy for you. All you have to do is tell me why you're after me and who sent you, promise to leave me alone, and answer a few other questions. You do all that and I'll see that you get back to civilization."

The man's lips didn't part. Donte pushed himself up from the fender of the truck, turned to Marcos, and said, "I've seen enough. He's okay. Let's get back to town. It'll be dinnertime by the time we get there, and I'm already getting hungry."

"Whatever you say, boss," Marcos said with his big grin still in place.

Both men moved toward the doors of the truck. "Hey, you can't leave me here like this," Bo protested.

"Oh, that's right, I told you I'd let you get clean boxers and a t-shirt," Donte said. He moved around to the back of the truck, opened the tailgate, and reached in. He pulled Bo's suitcase out from where Marcos had put it earlier, right behind a portable air compressor. "Here you go, Mr. Gray. Come on over and find some clean stuff, and then we'll be on our way."

"You can't leave me here like this," Bo protested again. He made no effort to approach the truck.

"We found you like this," Donte said. "We're trying to make you more comfortable. Come on. Get over here. I'm not bringing it to you."

Bo still didn't move. Finally, Donte shoved the suitcase back into the truck, shut the tailgate, and headed back around to his door. Before he got in, Donte said, "I'll check back with you in a few days."

"You can't do this," Bo said again, his eyes angry slits on his sunburned face.

Donte nodded at Marcos, and the two of them got in. Marcos started the truck, and they drove off as Bo shouted at them to stop. They kept going. When they reached the nearly invisible road they had left earlier, Marcos stopped. "He's a stubborn man. Should we go back yet?"

"No, let's sit here for a few minutes and let him stew," Donte said.

"Do you think he'll talk if we give him a few more minutes?" Marcos asked.

"Honestly, I don't know. The man I think hired him could be a cold-blooded killer. Bo might be more afraid of him than of me," Donte said.

"Hey, that gives me an idea," Marcos said, grinning broadly. "We've both got guns, and he's still close enough to hear them. How about if we do a little target practice, then go back and talk to him?"

"You're a genius," Donte said. "And I know just what we can use as targets."

A minute later, Donte was sticking a pair of boxer shorts to one cactus while Marcos stuck a t-shirt to another. They took a few shots then returned the boxers and t-shirt to the suitcase and drove back toward Bo's location.

When they arrived, Bo was sitting on the ground in the shade of his SUV. He stood up, looking at the two men in alarm. "Was that you guys shooting over there?" he asked.

"Just a little target practice." Donte retrieved the suitcase, opened it, and picked up the shorts and t-shirt. He tossed them to Bo, who caught them with both hands. Then Donte said, "I know it's hot out here, so we made a few holes in those. Maybe that'll make them cooler while you wait to see if we come back in a few days."

"You won't leave me again," Bo said as he examined the clothes.

"I think you know better than that. We're both pretty good shots, and I've had three months to get very angry," Donte said. "Just be glad you didn't have those on when we ventilated them for you. Take care. We'll come back—sometime."

"Wait," Bo called. "Maybe I could tell you a few things."

"No, I don't think I'm interested," Donte said. "It's not like I don't already know who hired you. By the way, Winn Bertram's missing. Do you have any idea where he might have gone? Surely he wasn't going to come here and try to find you. That'd be impossible. Why, even though my friend here brought me out to check on you, I'm not at all sure *I* could find my way back again. In fact, I'm pretty sure I couldn't."

"He's not coming after me," Bo said. "I don't know where he is."

"But you admit Mr. Bertram hired you?" Donte asked. "Well, that's something, anyway." He turned to Marcos, who was enjoying the show immensely. "Let's go."

"Wait, wait! You said that if I told you what I was doing, you'd get me out of here," Bo whined, even as he held up the boxer shorts and looked nervously at the holes in them.

"Yes, I did, but you said you might be able to tell me a *few* things. That's not good enough."

"Okay, okay, I'll talk. I could die out here," Bo finally said.

"Then talk," Donte said. "I'm listening."

"Just you."

"It's okay for my friend to hear too. After all, he's been a big help." Donte glanced at Marcos. "So go ahead and tell me what happened. And start with how long you've known Winn Bertram."

Bo hesitated, and Donte said, pointing at the man, "Either talk or we leave."

"How do I know you won't shoot me anyway?" Bo asked.

"You don't. If I'm a killer, perhaps I'll do just that. If I'm not, then you're perfectly safe."

Marcos looked at Donte with a question in his eyes and the grin gone from his face.

"I'm not a killer," Donte reassured him. "But I'm not sure what Bo here thinks. I've been accused of a murder I had nothing to do with, a murder his boss—perhaps even with his help—might have committed."

"Hey, wait a minute, Donte. You got that all wrong. Winn didn't kill anybody and neither did I," Bo protested loudly.

"But you think I did?" Donte asked.

Bo looked down at his dirty bare feet. "No, that's not what this is about."

Donte felt a surge of hope flow through him. "Then tell me what it's about. And start by answering my question. How long have you known Winn?"

"This is awkward," Bo said. "How about if I put on some clothes and we sit in your friend's air-conditioned truck? Then we'll talk."

"I don't mind being in the sun. I've been out in the open for three months now, as you well know. And my friend here, I don't think he minds either."

"Don't mind at all," Marcos said.

"But I am tired of looking at your sunburned legs," Donte admitted. "So, come on over and get some clothes on. Then we'll finish this conversation. But get one thing straight, Bo. If I get the feeling for one second that you aren't being totally honest with me, we leave you here. Is that clear?"

"I'll tell you everything I know, and frankly, at this point, if Winn doesn't like it, that's too bad," Bo said.

"If Winn shows up, that is," Donte said darkly.

After Bo was dressed, Donte gave him some salve and even helped apply it to the blistered areas. "Why are you doing this?" Bo asked.

"I am used to helping people. I don't like to see people suffer," Donte said gently.

"That's right, you're training to be a doctor," Bo said, making Marcos's jaw drop. "Winn told me."

"Is that right?" Marcos asked.

"It *was* right, but when I was accused of murdering my fiancée's brother, it kind of foiled my plans," Donte said to an astonished Marcos.

"You have a fiancée?" he asked. "Does Chey know that?"

"I don't have a fiancée anymore, and no, Chey knows practically nothing about me."

"But she'd like to know more," Marcos pointed out.

"Maybe, maybe not," Donte said. "Okay, Bo, back to how long you've known Winn."

"Okay, I've known him and done a little work for him for several years. But he also hired me to help him when he was trying to divorce Mara, his ex-wife."

"What kind of work have you done for him?" Donte asked.

"He's had me look into the background of the companies his clients were thinking about investing in. That kind of thing."

"Has he ever had you do something like you were doing this time, something personal?"

Bo thought for a few seconds. "Sort of."

"Please explain," Donte prodded him.

"Okay," Bo said, "but you know you're asking me to divulge confidential matters."

"That doesn't bother me in the least, after all my sister and I've been through the past three months," Donte said coldly. "Tell me."

"Well, you see," Bo said, clearly uncomfortable. "Winn Bertram's mother and Kasiah's father are brother and sister. That makes Winn and Kasiah cousins."

"Kasiah and Winn are related?" Donte said, totally surprised. "That means Winn and Walker are also cousins."

"Yeah, but believe me, Winn has no use for Walker or his brother, Sawyer," Bo went on. "I've done some, shall we say, snooping into the lives of both of them. They're not nice guys."

"Did Winn kill Walker?" Donte asked.

Bo's head snapped back. "Good grief, no. He's not a murderer."

"Neither am I," Donte said.

"I know," Bo said.

"But does your employer?"

The answer that Bo gave set Donte back on his heels and had his head reeling.

CHAPTER TWENTY-ONE

SARA AND CLIVE WERE SITTING in her house, waiting to hear from Winn. "I wonder if something happened to him," Sara said, looking very worried.

"I suppose that's possible, but frankly, I doubt it," Clive said.

"He should have called by now. He was going to pick me up in a half hour," she explained.

"Maybe he'll just show up at the door," Clive speculated. "If he doesn't, then maybe it's time to worry."

"I'm already worried," Sara admitted.

"Why don't you try his cell phone," he suggested.

"I tried. It's not in service."

"I see. Well, then, I guess we wait. Let's check once more and make sure the wire's working," Clive suggested. He was worried too, but he was trying not to let her see that. He wasn't so much worried about Winn. He was more worried that he still hadn't heard back from Lieutenant Scales or from Detective Fields. That, in his mind, was a problem.

The wire was working fine. "Okay, we're ready if he comes. When he knocks, I'll go into the garage, and as soon as the two of you leave, I'll follow at a reasonable distance. I'll be listening to everything. So make sure one of you says which restaurant you're going to. That way I'll be sure not to lose you."

"Okay—if he shows up," she said.

For the next few minutes, they talked about the fact that Detective Fields had never gotten back with Clive. "It makes me angry. I'm going down there again in the morning," he said. "I won't rest until we get some action."

Ten minutes later, the doorbell rang. Sara hurried to it, peeked through the peephole, and then signaled to Clive. He hurried out to the garage, where he got in his truck, the garage opener in his hand. He listened as Winn and Sara talked. "Is everything better with your family?" she asked.

"Yes, they're fine now," Winn responded.

"You look like you've been hurt, Winn," Clive heard Sara say. "You're bruised all over your face, and you have a black eye."

"I have a confession to make," he said. "I didn't make it to Denver. I fell asleep and wrecked my car."

The little recording device and wire may have been inexpensive, but they were working just fine. Everything they said was being recorded, but it was also being fed directly into Clive's left ear via a small speaker. The gasp she gave when Winn mentioned a wreck came through loud and clear.

"Was it your Cadillac?" she asked.

"I'm afraid so, and it looks like it's a total loss."

"Oh, Winn, I'm so sorry."

"It can be replaced. So can my cell phone. I lost it in the wreck."

"That's why I couldn't reach you when I called," she said.

"That's why."

"What are you driving tonight?" she asked.

"My Jeep," he said.

"Oh, I forgot you have a Jeep," she responded. "I'm just glad you're okay and that we didn't have to miss our date."

"Me too," he said. "I've been looking forward to it."

"Where are we going?" she asked.

He told her, and she said, "That will be nice."

Clive didn't have any trouble following them. He pulled up outside the restaurant and parked in the parking area across from it. He'd heard every word spoken by both Sara and Winn, but there was nothing that alarmed him. In fact, it rather bored him. Mostly it was about office matters, Winn's schedule for the next day, and on and on.

Clive slid the seat of his truck back as far as it would go, reclined a little, and settled in for a long wait, and hopefully, a boring one.

It was just that for the first thirty minutes, but he sat up straight when he heard Winn say, "I'm afraid I've got a little bad news for you, Sara."

"What's that?" she asked. Clive could feel apprehension in her voice.

"I've got to let you go," he said.

"Let me go!" she cried in alarm. "Do you mean you are firing me?"

"Yes, that's what I mean," he said. "I'm truly sorry."

It was silent for a minute, and then she said, "I guess if I'm not good enough, then I'll have to accept it. But I'm deeply hurt, Winn." Suddenly, she cried out, "Winn, what are you doing?"

It was silent again. Clive was already out of the truck and running toward the restaurant. He paused at the door when Winn said, "I'm doing what I should have done earlier."

There was a crackling sound, and then Sara said, "You were wearing a wire!"

"I'm afraid so," he admitted.

"Why?" she demanded.

"For the same reason I fired you."

"But the note you slid over to me says I'm not really fired. Winn, I'm really confused."

So was Clive. He stood just outside the entrance and continued to listen. "So was I, Sara, but not anymore," he said. "There are some things I need to confess, Sara. I've never been around anyone who does to me what you do. You're a wonderful woman. Just being with you makes me feel like I'm on a cloud. But my ex-wife is jealous. She hates you. I had to wear this wire so she could hear me fire you. But I could never really fire you, no matter what happens to me because of it."

"Winn, if you think you're making sense, you're wrong. You divorced her. What possible hold does she have on you now?" Sara asked.

"I've been a coward. It's something that happened, something that could land me in jail, but . . . but . . ." Winn's voice trailed off.

"Winn, did you by any chance go to the office tonight before you picked me up?" she asked.

"No, why?"

"I have a confession to make too."

Clive held his breath and slipped farther from the door. He was embarrassed listening to Sara, especially if she was about to say something that he didn't want to hear. When she went on, he let the breath out. She said, "Mara broke into your office and left you a note."

"She did, and you found it?"

"Yes, I was snooping," she confessed.

"That's okay, Sara. I don't have any secrets in my office that you can't look at. After all, you are my secretary and my . . . ah . . . my best . . . friend," he stammered.

"Thanks, Winn," she said, "that means a lot."

To Clive, it hurt a lot. He knew he should never have let Sara make a place in his heart, a heart that had already been wounded so badly many years ago in a mall in Omaha. But despite himself, it had happened. She had slipped right into that damaged heart of his, and now it was being hurt again.

Winn's voice came again through the earpiece. "Do you remember what the note said?"

Clive knew she did, and so did he. But she didn't tell Winn. Instead, and to Clive's surprise, she said, "I have a copy of it right here in my purse. You can read it for yourself."

It was silent on the earpiece for a minute or so, and then Winn said softly, horror in his voice, "This note is crazy, Sara! She thinks I murdered Walker. That's what she meant when she kept telling me that she would turn me in and I would go to jail. Oh, that woman. It's time I stood up to her. I've been such a coward."

"Did you?" Sara asked.

"Did I what?" Winn asked.

"Did you kill Walker Aklen?"

"Sara, surely you don't think I'd do something like that, do you?" he asked with no less horror in his voice.

"Did you?" she pressed. Clive waited in suspense for the answer.

"No, Sara, I did not. I admit he was a creep, a selfish and bad man. He borrowed money from me and would never pay me back, but I wrote that off," Winn said. "I should have known better than to loan it to him. But when he came begging, all filled with sad luck, I gave in. After all, he was my cousin."

Clive guessed that Sara must have been as stunned as he was at that revelation because he heard her now-familiar gasp, and then there was silence once again.

"Winn," Sara finally said. "Why didn't I know this? If you and Walker are cousins, so are you and Kasiah. She was my friend, was planning to be my sister-in-law, and she never bothered to tell me that she was my boss's cousin? And you didn't tell me either. That's unbelievable."

"It really isn't," he said. "Not if you know her and her family. They're capable of anything."

"I guess so!" Sara exclaimed. It was quiet again for a moment, and then Clive heard first Winn and then Sara say, "Thank you."

Clive could only assume that their food had arrived. That was confirmed a moment later when Sara said, "This looks good, but I'm not sure I feel like eating now."

"Yeah, I know what you mean," Winn said. "But I suppose we should try."

"Yeah, I suppose so," she agreed.

Another period of silence and then, "Sara, maybe if I get some more things off my chest, I would get my appetite back."

"Okay, what else can you tell me? I don't suppose I can go any deeper into shock than I already am." Nor could Clive, he decided as he adjusted his earpiece.

"Well, first let me say this. Please, don't think I'm a horrible person, Sara. I care for you, deeply," he said. So did Clive, but there was nothing to be done about it now. He just wished it was him sitting in the restaurant across from the girl he had come to admire and, yes, have tender feelings for.

"Winn, let's don't move too fast. After all, we do have a boss-employee relationship. Maybe we should keep it at that for now," said Sara, sensible, beautiful Sara. Clive wished he could whisper into a little speaker in her ear and tell her she should never let it go deeper than that with Winn. But now he was just an eavesdropper, and he felt guilty. This was her life. What business did he have in it?

Winn spoke next. "I realize now what Mara was accusing me of. It's clear she thinks I killed Walker. She knows he owed me several thousand dollars. She kept pressing me to collect it. She must have thought I'd killed him when he wouldn't pay up. But I was thinking it was something else entirely."

"Something bad enough that she could blackmail you?" Sara asked.

"Yes, it's something I'm ashamed of," he admitted. "What I thought she was referring to was something that really wasn't my fault, but four years ago, Mara told me she'd see me in prison if I ever told anyone what had happened. She said she'd make what *she* had done look like *I* had done it. That's what I was thinking, that's why I let her bully me, and that's why I'm so ashamed and wouldn't blame you if you not only refused a personal relationship with me but quit working for me as well."

Clive's interest piqued again. Apparently, Sara's had too. "Tell me about it."

And that is what he proceeded to do. "Mara and I, before we divorced, were in a partnership with a friend of mine, a little business venture. Neither he nor I could figure out why it went under. But it did. Six months after the business was dissolved and the partnership ended, I discovered that Mara had a large bank account. She was the bookkeeper for our business, and I realized that she had embezzled our money. When I confronted her, she threatened to ruin me."

"She would do that," Sara agreed.

"Oh, would she ever. Anyway, she made me promise never to tell my former partner and said that if I did, she would make it look like I took the money. And she could do that," he said. "To my shame, I never did tell him. But that's going to end now. I'll call him tomorrow, confess to what happened, and set up a repayment schedule. Then let Mara do what she thinks she has to. She can't touch me on that then, and she certainly can't touch me when it comes to the murder of my deadbeat cousin."

Even as Clive thought it, Sara spoke the words that were in his mind. "Don't kid yourself, Winn. Donte didn't kill anyone, yet on the word of his fiancée, there's a warrant out for his arrest."

"I know he didn't do it," Winn said, much to Clive's surprise.

He guessed it was also a surprise to Sara, for she again asked the question that he would have. "Then why did you hire Bo Gray to find Donte?"

"Now that, Sara, is not at all what you think," he said. "But how did you know about that?"

"I have my ways, Winn," she said. "Now, would you like to tell me why you hired him?"

"Of course," he said.

"I'd like a friend of Donte's to hear this too, in person. Actually, he's a friend of mine too," she said, and Clive could have hugged her.

"Now I'm the one who's confused," came the reply.

"As well you should be," she retorted. "Clive, why don't you come join us in here? We have food enough and some to spare." He headed for the door as she went on, "Winn, that look on your face is priceless. You're not the only one that can wear a wire."

"Don't tell me someone has listened to everything we've said."

"More than that, he's recorded every word. Oh, here he comes now." She leaped to her feet and ran toward Clive. She hugged him briefly and then took him by the hand and led him back to the table. "Waiter," she said, signaling with her free hand.

The waiter came over, and Sara said, "Bring another place setting, please." Looking slightly bewildered, the young man agreed and moved quickly away.

"Winn, this is Clive Granger. He's a very dear friend of Donte's and of mine. He has a talent for investigating crime, and he's been helping me try to clear Donte's name. And frankly, he's been doing a great job."

"So you both thought I had something to do with Walker's death?" Winn asked.

"We wondered about you, among others," she confessed. "Clive, this is Winn, my boss, and he's also a good friend of mine. Now, let's sit down and listen to him explain why Bo Gray caused so much trouble."

Winn laughed uncomfortably. "I suppose you know about what happened to Bo?" he asked.

"Not really," Clive said. "But I know that something did. I expect to learn what that was soon."

"Okay, Winn, we don't have to fill Clive in on what we've already talked about, but would you please tell us what Bo was doing and why?"

"Yes, but first, I have one more confession to make," he said. "I lied to you. I wasn't ever planning to go to Denver. My family there is fine. I was going to try to find out what had happened to Bo. The last I knew he was in Tonopah, Nevada. That was where I was going."

Sara and Clive exchanged glances, and Winn noticed. "Did you figure that out?" he asked.

Sara explained, "We were pretty sure because we knew Bo had been in Tonopah. And it only took one phone call to your father to discover that everything was fine in Denver and that you were not going there."

"You'll never trust me again," Winn said, his head bowed in shame.

"I didn't say that."

"I wasn't quite through with my confession," he said without looking at either Clive or Sara. "I *was* in a wreck, and my Cadillac was destroyed. I got arrested and thrown in jail."

"For wrecking your car?" Sara asked. "Couldn't they have just given you a ticket?"

"That's the problem. I've had a bunch of those, and as a result, my license was suspended."

"And you went to jail for that. Why didn't you just pay the bail?"

"I would have, but there were two problems. First, I'd left my wallet at home, and second, I did another stupid thing," he said. "I tried to get away from the officer at the hospital. I'm facing that charge as well."

"So how did you get out of jail?" Clive asked.

"Blackmail," he said.

"You called Mara," Sara guessed.

"It was the only thing I could do," he admitted. "And she put conditions on it."

"That you fire me," Sara said sadly. "She's so pathetic."

"And so am I," Winn said.

Sara didn't disagree. Instead, she said, "Okay, so tell us about you and Bo."

For the next ten minutes, he did just that. He had barely finished his story—one told to a captive audience of two—when Sara's cell phone buzzed in her purse. She pulled the phone out and opened the incoming e-mail as her heart raced.

CHAPTER TWENTY-TWO

"IT'S FROM DONTE," SHE ANNOUNCED to both her boss and her partner. "Let me see what he has to say."

"You've known where he was all the time." Winn shook his head. "I suspected as much."

"No, I've been in touch with him, but I haven't known where he was," she explained. "I didn't want to know so that no one could make me tell them."

"Like me," a very humble and subdued Winn Bertram said.

"That's right."

"So what does Donte have to say?" Clive asked.

Sara opened the e-mail and began to read. *Scrunch. I found Bo. He was working for W. and neither is a threat. He and Bo are on our side. Bo was trying to keep track of me and was prepared to help me get away if any cops tried to arrest me. Here's the kicker. W. is in love with you, and he was doing this to impress you. I'll admit it impresses me. These are pretty extreme measures to take in the name of romance. Still don't know who killed Walker. Will continue to try to stay out of sight until I am cleared. Can't say where I am now. Bo says he'll help if needed. Oh, say hi to C. for me if you see him. And keep your investigator working. I want to come home. Delete this message. Love and miss you. Slurpee.*

"Winn, I don't think we need to impress upon you the importance of keeping this communication secret," Clive said sternly. He was impressed with Winn's efforts to protect Donte, but Clive didn't like the man and hoped that Sara could see that Winn wasn't right for her, no matter how much he expressed his love.

"I understand," he assured them. Then he looked wistfully at Sara. "I'm sorry, Sara. You won't quit will you?"

"No, I won't quit."

That seemed to relieve him, but he still said, "Will you give me some time to straighten out my life and to take care of my trouble with Mara?"

"Yes." She nodded. "But that doesn't mean that we'll have a personal relationship. I like you, Winn, but I'm not in love with you."

"Could you ever be?" he asked, making Clive wish he was anywhere else at the moment.

"That remains to be seen," she said. That was not what Clive wanted to hear. "Now, we have a bunch of really good food to eat. Let's get it done. You guys start while I answer Donte."

***

Donte was back in Tonopah. He and Bo Gray were eating dinner when Donte received a reply on Bo's phone from his sister. With much anticipation, he read: *Slurpee. We're making progress. Detective Fields is stubborn. Our investigator has gone over Fields's head, but so far it hasn't helped. We hope to learn more in the morning. We have some ideas who the killer could be, but those ideas are nothing much more than guesses so far. C and I are having dinner right now with W. I think we know everything with regard to W. It's good to have another ally. However, his ex is a major problem. Keep in touch as much as you can. Things could change in a day, and I'd hate to have you out there any longer than you have to be. Miss and love you. Scrunch.*

Donte was discouraged. He couldn't understand why Detective Fields was so stuck on only him as a suspect. Someone else did it, and surely there would be a way to prove that. Even someone coming forward to back up his alibi apparently hadn't helped. He wondered who that person was. Maybe he should ask. Or . . .

He looked up at his new ally. "Bo, you say you want to help me. I wouldn't blame you if you didn't after what I put you through."

"Hey, I understand. This whole thing is crazy. My car's okay, I'm still getting paid, and I'm eating well. What more can I ask?" he said with a grin on his obviously sore lips. "What do you need me to do?"

"Would you find and speak to the witness who's established my alibi?" Donte asked. "Apparently Detective Fields isn't buying it. Or at least my sister doubts he is because she hasn't heard from him since they told the cops about it."

"I can do that," Bo said. "I'll get right on it first thing in the morning."

"That would be great," Donte said.

"And I'll take you to Vegas in the morning so you can go wherever you want to go next," Bo added.

"Would it be too much trouble if you hauled me to another state and let me go from there?" Donte asked. "I've been here too long. You found me, and who knows who else might be closing in on me here."

"That could be. Let's do this. I'll check you into a hotel, probably the one you were in a few days ago. I'll do the check-in and then give you the key. They won't even need to know you're there."

"That'd be great, Bo. I owe you," Donte said gratefully.

"No, I owe you. I'd still be out there in that desert if it hadn't been for you."

Donte closed his eyes. "I'm sorry. You aren't what I thought you were."

"Don't worry about it," Bo said graciously. "It's not your fault. I would have done the same thing." He chuckled. "Someday, when I have grandkids, I'll tell them what happened, and they won't believe it."

"Well, I really am sorry," Donte said. "There's something else I'd like to do. Could I use your phone again and make a call to Chey and Jessica?"

***

"I don't recognize this number," Chey said when her phone began to ring. "I don't know if I should answer it."

"What if it's Donte?" Jessica asked.

"Oh, I don't think he'd call already," Chey said. "If at all."

"But what if it is him and you don't answer? You know he won't have many chances to call."

"Okay." Chey gave in and took the call. "Hello," she said tentatively into her phone.

"Chey, it's Donte."

Chey grinned and then spoke rapidly. "Donte, I'm so glad you called. I didn't recognize the number, but Jessica talked me into answering. I would have felt terrible if I'd missed your call."

"If you knew whose phone I'm using you'd feel worse," he said with a chuckle.

"Why?" she asked. "Whose phone is it?"

"This phone belongs to Bo Gray."

"Oh no, Donte! Are you okay?"

"Yeah." He chuckled. "Bo's a friend now. He wasn't out to hurt me, and he would never have hurt you gals. Bo is okay. He's even forgiven us for what Marcos did to him."

"What did Marcos do?" Chey asked.

"I guess it's okay if you know now," Donte said. He gave her a condensed version of Bo's ordeal.

After listening to it, she said, "That's awful. The poor man."

"Yes, it is awful, but Marcos did it for us, and for that I thanked him. Bo is okay now, just sunburned and embarrassed. However, I'm still in danger, and I'll be going someplace else soon. But Bo will be helping to keep my real enemies from finding me," he said. "But enough about me. I called to see how you guys are doing."

"We made it as far as Salt Lake, but we decided not to try to go on to Vernal. Another three hours today would have been too much for Jessica," Chey said. "And for me too, for that matter. I'm exhausted."

"Are you at a hotel?" he asked.

"Yep, and sometime tomorrow we'll drive the rest of the way home. I miss you, Donte."

"I miss you too, but we'll both just have to get used to it," he said. "My life is such a mess. Tell Jessica hi for me. And you guys get some good rest tonight."

"You too," she said.

***

Mara was furious, as angry as she had ever been. She couldn't believe Winn had disconnected the wire. Well, she knew a quick way to get partial payback. The best way to hurt Winn was to hurt his girlfriend, and Mara knew just how to do that. She called the police department and asked for Detective Jaren Fields. When told that he wasn't in, she told them it was an emergency, that she had some crucial information on a murder case he was working on.

She was told to give them a name and a number and that they would see if the detective was available to call her back. In about ten minutes, she got a call. Detective Fields was very grouchy. "This had better be good. I'm a busy man."

"Oh, it's good all right," she said. "My name is Mara Bertram. My ex-husband, Winn, is the boss and current boyfriend of Sara Noble. And I have some information about her brother that I think you'd like."

"Hold on, Mrs. Bertram. Let me get a pen." She waited for a moment, and then Detective Fields came back on the line. "I assume this is about Donte Noble," he said, sounding a whole lot less grouchy.

"Yes it is, and I know where he's hiding," she said.

"I'm listening," he told her. "First, how do you know where he is? I've been looking for him for months."

"Well, it's like this. My ex-husband hired an investigator, and that investigator found Donte. He did something to the investigator, and so Winn headed out to catch Donte himself," she said.

"Winn Bertram knew where Donte was and didn't tell me?" The officer sounded angry.

"That's right," Mara said as she realized there was another way she could hurt Winn. And she had every intention of doing it.

"He's broken the law," Fields said. "I could arrest him for that."

"And you should," Mara agreed. "And you should also arrest Miss Noble. She's the one who told me where he is. She had no idea I'd tell you, but I'm not willing to break the law or to protect a wanted murderer—even for a friend."

"I knew it," Fields said. "I just knew that girl was lying to me. Okay, I'll have them both charged, but of greater importance right now is the killer himself. Where is Donte Noble?"

Mara smiled. She had no idea if Sara knew where Donte was, and Mara certainly hadn't learned anything from Sara, but a little lie or two mixed in with some truth didn't matter as long as she got her revenge. "He is in Tonopah, Nevada."

"Thank you. Do you know exactly where in Tonopah?"

"No, but it's a small town. I'm sure he's in a hotel there. But you need to hurry if you're going to catch him," she said.

"I'll get right on it, Mrs. Bertram."

"Thank you, and when you catch my ex-husband, I think I should tell you something else that he did," she said. "Something quite bad."

"I'll get that from you tomorrow," Detective Fields said. "If you learn any more about Donte, you call me. I don't care what time it is." He then gave her his number and promised to fill her in the next day.

After the officer was off the line, Mara took time to smirk. Winn, the fool, didn't know that she had figured out where Donte was by the bits and pieces that she had wheedled out of him. And he must not believe that she would carry out her threat to expose him. She'd already alluded to it when she spoke to Detective Fields. She hadn't been bluffing when she'd told Winn that if he ever tried to expose the embezzlement, she'd turn the tables.

He hadn't tried that, but she would turn him in for it anyway. And he would go to jail for a very long time. If she couldn't have him, no one would, especially that prissy Miss Noble.

***

There was a knock on Donte's door just as he was finally drifting to sleep. He looked through the peephole and was surprised to see Bo standing there. He opened the door, and Bo rushed in. "Grab your stuff and the dog and get out. I'm not sure what they want, but some cops have been in and out of two other hotels tonight. I think they'll hit them all before they're through. They are clearly looking for someone, probably you. Since you're on the ground floor, maybe you should just go out the window. I'm parked just up the street. I'll walk out the normal way. Give me five minutes, and I'll drive down the road. Come into sight and jump in my car when you see me. We'll head out of town."

Donte didn't know if the cops were after him or not, but he wasn't taking any chances. He did as Bo instructed, and within a couple of minutes, he was hiding a block or so from the hotel. Three minutes later, he was in the Expedition, hiding with Dude on the floor in the back. Bo drove slowly since they didn't want to attract attention as they left the city limits.

"Which way should we go?" Bo asked. "The cops aren't at the hotel yet, but they soon will be, not that it matters since you aren't registered there."

"Go west," Donte said. "It's not that far to some bigger towns. I can get my bike later, or I'll just get another one."

"Or I can get it for you and meet you somewhere," Bo suggested.

"Maybe. We'll worry about that another day. For now, I want to be someplace where there are more people and I can get lost in a crowd," he said.

Twenty minutes later, Bo said, "Why don't you come up here now? There isn't a lot of traffic, and you'll be a lot more comfortable."

Leaving Dude in the back, Donte climbed into the front seat. "I wonder how they found me, if it was even me they were after," he said. "Winn wouldn't have told them, would he?"

"No, I can guarantee you that," Bo said. "But he did tell me on the phone earlier that he'd called Mara, his ex-wife, to get him out of jail.

She might have put two and two together. She's a mean woman. She wants Winn back, but he doesn't want her. Like I told you, Winn wants nothing more in this world than to win your sister's heart. I do think the cops are after you, though. They were just going into another hotel when we passed, so it might be a while before they get to yours."

"Since you checked in for me, the fellow at the front desk won't have a description of me," Donte said. "Or any record of me being there. I'm glad you suggested that."

Bo chuckled. "I didn't use my real name or ID. I have spares for when I need them. A little trick of the trade. They won't know you've been in town at all. We should be just fine."

"They will learn, if they try hard enough, that I was registered there a few days ago. And a lot of people have seen me eating in a couple of different cafes. So at some point they'll have my description. But for now, I should be okay. Thanks, Bo. If I ever can, I'll make it up to you," Donte said.

***

Mara called Detective Fields at seven o'clock the next morning. She had hardly slept at all, and she wanted to know if Donte had been arrested yet.

"No, I'm afraid not. They've been searching all night. They did confirm that he'd been registered in one of the hotels a few days ago and that he and another man had eaten dinner in a local café that night. I think the other man may have been Bo Gray," Fields told her. "Your ex-husband is in a lot of trouble."

Mara smiled. That was what she wanted to hear.

CHAPTER TWENTY-THREE

THE FIRST PERSON TO WALK into Winn's office that Tuesday morning was Winn's former neighbor, Ron Raynor. He was there a few minutes before eight. He was only in the office for a couple of minutes, and then he came out smiling. He stopped beside Sara's desk for a moment. He told her he was glad that the problem was about to be solved, what a nice guy Winn was, and how he and his wife could have some peace now.

Sara told Ron that she was glad for him. What she didn't say was she wasn't at all sure that would happen, not with a woman like Mara living next door.

Winn came out of his private office a moment later. "Sara, I am so ashamed," he said. "How can you ever forgive me for being such a fool?"

"That's not a problem," she said with a grin. "How many girls have a man go to so much trouble and expense to impress her? Frankly, I'm flattered." And truly she was, but that didn't mean she was in love with him. She wasn't sure she ever would be, although she still thought he was a good guy. She liked working for him.

"Sara, would you mind coming into my office for a minute? There's a call I need to make, and I'd like you to be a witness. Just let your phone go to voice mail. It'll only take a minute."

He shut the door then picked up his phone and dialed a number that he clearly knew by heart. "I'm calling my former business partner," he said. "I'm going to beat Mara to the punch on this just in case she tries to cause me trouble over it."

He reached his former partner at home and explained that he had something he needed to talk to the man about and that if he could spare a few minutes, Winn would work him in whenever. As it turned out, that was sooner rather than later, and the fellow walked in twenty minutes later, a full forty minutes before Winn's first client was due to arrive.

They shut the door behind him, and Sara prayed that the man would see things Winn's way and that Mara wouldn't be able to bring the embezzlement back to hurt Winn. The men were in there for twenty minutes before Winn came back out and dropped a handwritten paper on her desk. "Sara, would you type this up and print two copies? I'll have you notarize both of them when we sign in a few minutes."

It was a legal document that did a couple of things. It was a contract for the repayment by Winn to his former partner of his portion of the money that Mara had stolen, with interest. The document was also a written promise that the partner would not attempt to either bring or support any legal action against Winn for the theft, either criminally or civilly. She typed it, they signed it, and she notarized it. Winn's former partner left with a big smile.

***

At nine o'clock, Clive walked into the office of Lieutenant Jon Scales. After greeting each other, Scales asked, "So did Detective Fields get in touch with you?"

"No," Clive said. "I haven't heard a word from him."

"He said he'd try," Scales said. "But I know he was very busy yesterday. He's here this morning, so let's have him come in right now, and we'll see if we can get some things going."

"Thank you, Lieutenant," Clive said. "I'd like that."

The lieutenant made a call on the intercom. He put the phone down a moment later. "He went to see the prosecutor, but he'll be back any minute. He'll join us as soon as he gets back. If you don't mind waiting out in the foyer, I'll call you in as soon as he gets here."

While he was waiting, Clive called Sara at her office and asked her how things were going. She told him what had happened over the money that Mara had embezzled. She finished up, saying, "I think that should just about end her troublemaking."

Ten minutes later, Clive was still waiting when Sara called him back. From the tone of her voice, he knew she was upset. "What's wrong?" he asked her.

"I just got a message from you know who, and he said that he nearly got caught last night. Someone tipped the cops off about where he was. He and Bo think it was probably Mara, although I have no idea how she knew."

"I'll see if I can find out when Detective Fields comes in—if he does," Clive said. "Right now he's over at the prosecutor's office on some case or another. I just wish he'd get something done on this one."

Clive had barely finished that latest call from Sara when he was summoned back into Scale's office. He was actually surprised to see Jaren Fields sitting there with an angry scowl on his face. Clive's stomach rolled, but he sat down when Lieutenant Scales asked him to and tried to mentally prepare himself for the worst.

"The detective and I have been talking for a moment," Scales said. "He spent most of the day yesterday following up on your leads."

"And what did you learn, Detective?" Clive asked the man directly while trying to keep the dislike out of his voice.

"Several things, actually," Detective Fields said. "First, about Mr. Jacob Hickman, I'm afraid the man lied to you. I did interview him right after the murder. And he denied having seen Donte Noble at all during the week in question. I couldn't find him yesterday, but I'm afraid that his attempt to manufacture an alibi does nothing more than point to the guilt of your friend. I'm sorry, but that's a fact."

Clive was stunned. "He certainly seemed sure of himself to me."

"I'm sure he did, but he was lying. Now," Fields said, "let's talk about Trevor Wells. I also interviewed him right after the murder. It's true that Walker owed him some money, but he said they'd worked out a repayment plan. He also has an alibi, a solid one, for the time of death. And contrary to what his neighbor Mrs. Finn supposedly told you, I also interviewed her. She's not exactly young, and I suppose that over three months she could have forgotten. But she didn't tell me that she had overheard a threat by Trevor to kill Walker. She didn't even tell me that she could hear anything through the walls. Nor did the neighbor on the other side. Not that it matters, with Trevor's alibi."

"Did you talk to either one of them yesterday?" Clive asked.

"No, but I tried. I went by their apartments three times. Neither of them was home. I know Noble is a friend of yours, but the evidence is what it is."

Clive was even more stunned. He leaned forward and asked, "According to what Trevor told me, there are others Walker owes money to. Have you tried to locate any of them?"

"He did mention a couple of men that I did interview earlier, and I did again yesterday, but once again, Mr. Granger, you've gotten bad information. I don't know of anyone else that Walker owes. If you can give me a name, I'll follow up on it today," Fields promised.

Clive was sure he saw a smirk cross the officer's face, so he decided to provide a name. "I have a name," he said.

Lieutenant Scales took immediate interest. "Let's hear it and how you know it," he said.

Rather than talking directly to Scales, Clive decided to address Fields. He wanted to watch his eyes closely. "Winn Bertram is a cousin of Walker's, and he personally told me that Walker owed him ten thousand dollars."

Clive was sure he saw a glint in the detective's eye, but it was fleeting. Fields shifted in his seat and looked over at the lieutenant. "I can check into that, Jon, but I know what I'll find. Anyway, it wasn't Bertram," he said. "However, Bertram is going to be in a lot of trouble as soon as I can check some things out and get back with the prosecutor. Actually, it was Bertram, as well as his secretary, Donte Noble's sister, that I was discussing with the prosecutor this morning."

"Why were you doing that?" Lieutenant Scales asked with a furrowed brow.

"I got a call last night from Bertram's ex-wife. It seems that Sara Noble told Mrs. Bertram where Donte has been hiding and—"

Clive couldn't take any more, and he cut in. "Surely you don't believe anything that woman says. She's pure poison."

"Actually, she was very helpful," Detective Fields said with that trace of a smirk once again. "As I was saying, your friend, Miss Noble, told Mrs. Bertram that Donte has been staying in Tonopah, Nevada. Mr. Bertram also knew that. When I find him, a private investigator by the name of Bo Gray can verify it. The prosecutor is reviewing the matter, and I expect to have warrants issued for both of them today."

"That's crazy, Fields," Clive said angrily.

"Wait a minute here, Mr. Granger," the lieutenant said sternly. "I hope you're not accusing one of my officers of making this up."

"Not at all," Clive said. "It's Mara Bertram who made it up."

"Well, well," Detective Fields said. "For your information, she was right. I had some local officers there working all night. They were able to confirm several things. First, Donte Noble had stayed in a local hotel a few days ago. He was also seen as recently as yesterday there at the hospital, where a girl he knew was being treated. He was also seen several times at local restaurants where he had eaten several meals. He had a dog for a companion and has changed his appearance quite dramatically," Fields continued. "That's pretty solid evidence that Mara Bertram was telling me the truth."

Clive didn't know what to say. There was nothing he could say without making things worse for Bo, Sara, or Winn. "It looks like I've wasted you gentlemen's time." He stood. "I'm sorry. But before I go, I still would like to know what motive Donte had for killing Walker."

A triumphant smiled crossed the face of the detective. "You said it yourself, Mr. Granger. An unpaid debt. Money borrowed and not paid back."

"Can you prove that?" Clive asked.

"Not yet, but I'm working on it. You were right about one thing you learned in your little investigation. Walker borrowed, and he didn't pay back. There are people who kill over such things. Your friend, Donte Noble, is one of them. He would, and he did."

Clive walked out the door, deflated, angry, and determined. Someone was lying, and it was neither Donte nor Sara. He had to find out who it was, and that was exactly what he intended to do.

Back in his truck, he mentally reviewed everything he'd been told, every witness he'd talked to and recorded. Detective Fields had provided an answer for every one of them. Clive shook his head. If he could only find Trevor again. But at this point, Clive didn't expect that would happen. Someone didn't want Trevor talking. But if that was the case, it would mean that Trevor wasn't the killer. Of course, Trevor could just be on the run.

Right now, Clive decided, it was time to go see Winn and Sara. He had to warn them about Fields's threat to get warrants for their arrests. The whole thing made his blood boil. Fields was so blinded against Donte that it seemed nothing would change his mind.

***

Sara was busy typing a contract when she looked up to see Clive walking in, his face a mask of anger. "Uh-oh, what happened?" Sara asked.

"Lots of things and none of it good," he said.

Her heart began to pound. "Was Fields a jerk again? Did you even get to see him?" she asked.

"Oh, I saw him all right, and yes, he was a jerk. Is Winn in his office?"

She nodded. "He has a client."

"How serious would it be if he were to be interrupted?"

"It depends on what it's for, how important it is."

"It's critical," Clive said. "I've got to talk to both of you right now. It can't wait." His tone of voice was all it took to get her to reach for her phone and dial into Winn's office.

"What is it, Sara? You know I'm with a client," he said.

"Clive just came in. He says he needs to talk to both of us, and he says it can't wait. He just came from the police department."

"Okay, I'll be right out," he said.

He came out a moment later and closed the door behind him. "Hello, Clive," he said. "I take it there's a problem."

"You could say that," Clive said, his words clipped, his eyes hard and angry.

"We'll have to talk in here because I have a client in my office," Winn said.

"That's fine. I won't take long," Clive said. As soon as the door was shut, Clive said, "I just came from a very disturbing meeting with Lieutenant Scales and Detective Fields."

"Don't tell me Fields still believes Donte is guilty after all the evidence you've produced," Winn said.

"That's exactly what he thinks, but I'll work on all that later," Clive said, as he stood bunching his fists. "Right now you guys have got to prepare for what Mara has done." Sara felt the blood drain from her face, but Clive didn't wait for her to comment. He went on, "She called Fields last night and told him that Sara told her where Donte was hiding."

"I never—" she began.

Clive silenced her with a wave of his hand. "I know, but Mara convinced Fields that the two of you both knew that Donte was in Tonopah."

"I knew he *had* been there, but that's all," Winn said. "And I certainly didn't tell Mara."

"I'm sure you didn't. But she figured it out somehow," Clive said. "At any rate, Fields has already been to the prosecutor and thinks he'll be getting warrants for both of you sometime today."

That was too much for Sara, and had Clive not been standing near, she would have gone to the floor. He helped her back to her desk and got her seated. "You don't need to worry too much. It isn't true and—"

Sara cut him off. "That doesn't seem to matter much to the police. Donte didn't hurt anyone, and look at what he's going through."

Winn hadn't moved, but suddenly he slapped his head with his hand. "I know what happened," he said. "And it's my fault. The officer that arrested me in Wendover asked me where I was going, and I told him Tonopah. He didn't ask why, and I didn't tell him. But he was at the jail when I was released, and I think he and Mara talked for a minute."

"Yes, that would explain it," Clive agreed.

"Sara, as soon as I can get through with this client, I'll get an attorney, a good criminal attorney, and get him right on this," Winn said. Then he turned to Clive. "I don't suppose she tried anything else, did she?"

"Apparently she also accused you of embezzlement," Clive told him. "He'll be going after you for that as well."

"A fat lot of good that will do him," Winn said angrily. "Sara, I've got to get back in there. Why don't you show Clive the contract that my former partner and I signed today."

"I can do that," she agreed.

"Also, why don't you fill Sara in on the Donte thing and what Fields is up to on that," Winn said. "I'll hurry so we can get an attorney to work on this other problem." The door to his private office shut behind him.

"That should take care of the embezzlement matter," Clive agreed a few minutes later. "Did Winn draft this contract?"

"Yes, he's good at that kind of stuff," Sara said. "The other guy was excited about the whole thing. I didn't see any sign of animosity. Mara is the problem, and they both agree on that."

"Do you have a minute so I can tell you what Fields is claiming now?" Clive asked.

"It'll be lunchtime soon. Could we talk over lunch?" she asked.

"That would be great," he agreed.

"You can wait here if you want."

Clive sat in the chair she had indicated. He watched her as she worked, and he realized more than ever how fond he'd become of her.

CHAPTER TWENTY-FOUR

WHEN WINN AND HIS CLIENT came out of the private office a few minutes later, Sara told him she'd be going to lunch with Clive so they could discuss the case. Winn said, "Bring me a sandwich when you come back, would you, Sara? I don't have time to go out. By the time you get back, I should have someone ready to take on Mara and Detective Fields and their nonsense."

By the time Clive had finished telling her what had transpired in Lieutenant Scales's office, Sara was feeling keen disappointment. "Does Scales believe him?"

"I'm sure he does," Clive said wearily. "What I've got to do is talk to Mrs. Finn again, try to find out where Trevor went, and then try to locate Hick."

"How are you going to find Trevor?" she asked.

"It'll take some work, but I'm sure he has family somewhere. I'll begin there. I'll also check the jail both here and in surrounding counties. Who knows, it could have been a cop that took him away that day."

"I wish I didn't have to work. I'd love to go with you," Sara said regretfully.

"No more than I'd love to have you with me," Clive said. "Whatever I do, I'll be back at your house well before Sawyer Aklen comes to pick you up."

"I'm trying not to think about that. I dread it." Sara sighed.

***

Donte ate lunch in an outdoor restaurant in Carson City, the capital of Nevada. He shared a couple of hamburgers with Dude and then went in search of a library. He had to tie the dog outside while he went in and located a computer. He hurriedly typed an e-mail to Sara, asking for an update, and then went back outside and passed the time playing with his dog. He waited twenty minutes then went back inside. A reply to his e-mail was waiting for him. Sara had written: *Slurpee. Sorry, no good news. Fields claims he's already interviewed our witnesses and that they told him a completely different story. He said that the man who confirmed your alibi hadn't seen you at all that week. The roommate of Walker's, Trevor Wells, told the investigator that Walker owed him money, but he's nowhere to be found. A neighbor said she overheard Trevor threatening to kill Walker. Fields says she told him a different story. Fields also says that Walker owed you a bunch of money. That's what he's claiming your motive is. I'm sorry I don't have better news, but our man will keep looking. You are innocent, and we'll prove it. Oh, and you were right. Mara figured out where you'd been and told Fields. Love and miss you. Scrunch.*

Donte deleted the e-mail and then found a public phone. He called Bo's number. "Bo," he asked, "I know it's awful soon, but have you been able to learn who the alibi witness is?"

"I have. A contact of mine in the Provo PD got it for me. His name is Jacob Hickman. Do you know him?"

"Yes, I know him very well. He and I both love the mountains; although, for me it's an occasional vacation, for him, it's his life," Donte said.

"He claims he was with you the day of the murder," Bo said.

"He and I did cross paths. We were both on snowshoes since the snow hadn't melted yet," Donte responded.

"Detective Fields says Hickman denies seeing you up there at all on that trip."

"Then Fields is lying," Donte said. "But, there is one problem. I saw Hick the day before the murder. I suppose Fields could argue that I had time to hike out and be home before Walker was killed."

"Listen," Bo said. "If you don't mind me being gone from the neighborhood for a couple of days, I'll go find Hickman. Maybe he saw you later but didn't talk to you."

"That could be. I sure hope so. Anyway, you go ahead; I'll be fine."

What Donte didn't tell Bo was that he was planning to change his hair and beard color and get all new clothes—or at least different ones. The bike and trailer would just have to stay in Vegas for the foreseeable future. He hoped to be able to get an old truck or car of some kind, if he could figure out a way to put it in a false name. If he couldn't buy a car, he'd take a bus out of the state.

Either way, he wasn't going to tell Bo where he was. Bo was tough—he'd proven that—but it was too dangerous for Bo to know where he was. Whoever had killed Walker was probably very much in favor of Donte's being convicted, and if Bo were caught and tortured, he just might give Donte up to save himself. After all that had happened, Donte wouldn't put anything past his enemies, including torture. He would call Bo from public phones on occasion, but that would be the extent of the risk he'd take.

***

Clive found Mrs. Finn at home, just like he'd expected to. "My memory is as good now as it was when I was a teenager," she protested when Clive told her that Detective Fields claimed he had interviewed her right after the murder.

"I believe you, Mrs. Finn. Now for the next question. Where were you yesterday?" he asked.

"Right here like I always am," she said. "Why?"

"Detective Fields told me that he came by several times to talk to you and that you weren't home."

"That's not . . ." she began, then she paused, rubbed her chin, and said, "I just remembered, I did go to the grocery store yesterday, but I was gone less than an hour. Other than that I was home all day."

"What time did you go to the store?" he asked.

"Early afternoon. I'd just had lunch and used the last of my milk. So I went right after that. He could have missed me then," she said. "But to have missed me several times—there's no way."

"Did you take a nap yesterday?" Clive asked. He was trying to be thorough.

"No, I don't take naps often. I have a quilt on, and most of the day I was quilting. I'm making a quilt for my grandniece," she explained.

"Okay, so let me make sure I have this right. You have not been interviewed by Detective Fields at any time since Walker was killed?"

"I don't think so. If I saw a picture of him, I'd know for sure. I never forget a face," she said.

"I'll find a picture and come back," Clive promised. "It might not be until tomorrow, but I will be back. And just for the sake of the little recorder I'm using, when was the last time that Trevor Wells was at home?"

"The last time I saw him was when that nice man took him to get him help," she said.

After leaving the apartment, Clive went back to Sara's house and made some calls. The first one was to Detective Stu Colwell, the police officer in Grand Junction who had given Clive the report on Walker, Sawyer, and Kasiah Aklen. "I'm sorry to bug you again, Detective," Clive began, "but I need some more information on the Aklen family."

"Tell me what you need, and I'll see what I can do," Stu said.

"I appreciate the criminal records you found for me on Walker and his brother, Sawyer. In my investigation, I've learned that Walker owed money to a lot of people. He was a sponge and deadbeat and refused to repay people—or couldn't. At any rate, I'd like to know if there were any calls to any residences where any of the Aklens lived. You know," Clive said, "domestic disturbances or fights, things that might have been reported but no arrests made."

"I don't recall any, but I'll check our records," Detective Colwell said. "They only own one home that I know of. From what I remember, Sawyer lives there with his wife."

"Sawyer has a wife?" Clive asked in surprise.

"Sure does. I'll go over there and see if either one of them will tell me anything."

"That would be great, but I know Sawyer won't be there." Then Clive explained.

"Well, I'll just talk to his wife and some of the neighbors then."

"Perfect," Clive said.

"I'll get back with you as soon as I have something to report," Stu promised.

The upcoming meeting between Sara and Sawyer was worrying Clive. If Sawyer and Kasiah were as determined to get Donte as he suspected they were, Clive couldn't help but think they had a motive beyond mere anger. Who knows, he thought, maybe Walker had been in debt to Sawyer or Kasiah and wouldn't pay them. If either of them was the killer, that would be reason enough to lie to Detective Fields. But in fairness, maybe Clive would find that he was totally wrong and that they sincerely wanted to clear Donte's name and had the evidence to back it up. He hoped that was the case, but it was a feeble hope at best.

Clive then made several calls to various county jails. He was trying to determine if, by any chance, the man who had picked Trevor up had been a police officer and had booked him into jail somewhere. Every call had the same negative result. It was time-consuming work, but Clive felt like it was important.

Still hoping to learn more about Trevor, he scoured the Internet looking for any information. He suspected that Trevor might have a criminal record, but he couldn't find anything. Fields or other officers would have access to those kinds of things, but citizens didn't. What Clive really wanted was to find some relatives. He looked on his laptop at phone listings and found so many Wells listed that he knew it would take too long to locate someone who might be related to him. He decided he'd do that later if he had to.

Next he decided to check with the hospitals, but he hit a dead-end on his very first phone call. Patient confidentiality made it so that hospitals wouldn't release any information except to next of kin. Fields could do it with a court order, but at this point, Clive knew it would be hopeless to even ask. Only if he could find some compelling evidence would he be able to do that. And at this point, if he found that evidence, Clive was determined to take it to Lieutenant Scales. And when he did, he'd ask Scales to personally see if he could get whatever court orders were needed.

Clive spent a little while reviewing his notes. Without a list of Walker's former associates—possible enemies—the list of suspects wasn't very long. One of them was Sawyer, and thinking about him prompted Clive to call the officer in Grand Junction again. He wanted to ask the man to do one more thing.

"I don't have anything for you yet, Clive," Stu said as soon as Clive had identified himself.

"I didn't expect you would. That's not why I'm calling. I was hoping that you could do something else for me. Would you see if there is anyone either related to Sawyer or a close friend who would have had access to controlled drugs and would know how to give a person an injection? Walker died from an overdose of an injection of Fentanyl. Not just anyone can get the stuff or knows how to reduce it to a liquid and inject it," Clive explained.

"I was just about to head out to Sawyer's neighborhood," Stu told him. "I'll see what I can find. So far, I've found nothing here about any disturbance calls to the Aklen residence, but I have another officer digging a little deeper."

"I sure appreciate all the effort you're making."

"You're more than welcome. Anything I can do to help bring a killer to justice," Stu said.

Clive wished Detective Fields had that same kind of motivation. Maybe he'd had it earlier in his career, Clive thought, but he certainly didn't now. Thinking of the officer reminded Clive that he needed to get a picture of Fields to show Mrs. Finn.

He went back to work on his laptop. It took a few minutes, but he finally found what he needed. He printed two copies each of two different pictures of Fields on his small portable printer. If he could prove that Fields had lied about interviewing Mrs. Finn, maybe that would be enough to get Scales to take some independent action.

Clive was surprised when the door to the garage opened and Sara walked in. "Is it that late already?" he asked.

"It's after five," she said.

"I guess I lost track of time," he admitted.

"That means that either you've been busy or you took a little nap," she said with a half-hearted grin.

"I've been busy," he said. "I'm glad to see that you're not in jail."

This time her grin was more real. "Winn and I are both still free, but I'll tell you one thing, Mara is hopping mad. And so is Detective Fields."

"Really? What happened?" Clive asked as he got up from the table where he'd been working at his computer and stretched the stiffness from his legs and shoulders.

"Winn found a really good criminal defense attorney," she said. "He met with us, called whoever he called, and then he met with the prosecutor that Detective Fields had met with this morning. Our attorney says he poked so many holes in the cases that the prosecutor said not to worry, there wouldn't be any charges filed against us."

"Good. At least that's one thing we don't have to worry about." Clive was grateful for one positive outcome after a frustrating day.

"There's more." Sara put her purse down. "The prosecutor thinks that Mara should be investigated and possibly have charges brought against *her* for providing the police with false information," Sara told him. "Apparently, Fields blew his stack and stormed out of the meeting with the prosecutor—at least that's what our attorney said. And the prosecutor called our attorney later and said Mara had called, reading him the riot act. The prosecutor didn't much like that. He was quite offended."

"Sounds like fun times may be ahead with those two. Fields will probably be even less cooperative than he has been, and who knows what Mara will try next. We need to keep a lookout. Speaking of Mara, I've just been going over my notes, and I'm not sure that Mara wasn't involved somehow in Walker's death. I can't back it up with anything yet other than the fact that she knew Walker owed Winn money," Clive said. "Maybe she tried to get it herself."

"But she thought Winn killed Walker." Sara was shaking her head. "If she did it, she'd have known it wasn't Winn."

"She might have just wanted him to think she thought he did it," Clive said. "After all, he didn't embezzle any money, yet she was ready to accuse him of that."

Just then the doorbell rang. "You could be right," Sara agreed. "She's an awful woman. That will be Joanie from our firm. Her car broke down today, and she needs a car tonight. I told her that if she could get someone to bring her here she could take mine. I didn't expect her so soon. I told her I could get a ride to the office in the morning with you and that I'd pick the car up when I was ready to go home. I hope that's okay." It was certainly okay, and he told her so.

As Sara was answering the door, Clive's cell phone rang. It was Detective Stu Colwell. "I have learned a few things, Clive," he said. "I'm surprised the officer working the case hasn't already found what I did. He must not be working very hard."

"That's the understatement of the year." Clive rolled his eyes. "I wish someone like you was working the case. We sure wouldn't be where we are now. So what have you learned?"

"All right, here it is," Stu began, and for the next few minutes, he explained what he'd learned.

Sara had seen her friend off in the late model silver Ford Focus and had just reentered the room as Clive finished the call. "Who were you talking to?" she asked.

"Detective Stu Colwell from Grand Junction," Clive answered.

"Did he find anything that'll help?"

"I'd say, and it makes me even more nervous about your meeting tonight with Sawyer."

CHAPTER TWENTY-FIVE

"I GUESS IT'S ALL ABOUT point of view whether it's good or bad," Clive said. "It certainly should help us. What time is Sawyer supposed to be here?"

"He said six-thirty."

"Okay, we've got some time, so let me tell you what Detective Colwell discovered," Clive said. "First, there was a domestic abuse call at Sawyer's house about eight months ago. It was called in by a neighbor. When the cops got there, Sawyer, Walker, and Sawyer's wife were all at home."

"Wait, Sawyer's married?" Sara exclaimed. "Kasiah never told me that. For that matter, neither did Winn."

"I'm thinking there are a lot of things Kasiah didn't tell you—or Donte, for that matter," Clive said. "As for Winn . . . I don't know what to say."

"I have a date with a married man?" Sara said with a look of disbelief on her face. "I don't do that, Clive."

"Tonight's not a date. Tonight's part of an investigation. And you and I will be working together, *partner*," Clive stressed with a grin. "And just like last night, I'll be close enough to come on the run if I need to."

She took a deep breath then let it out. "Okay, I guess for Donte's sake I can do this. So, what else did Detective Colwell tell you?"

"Again, when the responding officers arrived, the three I mentioned were there," Clive began. "The report was brief, and all it said was that the home's occupants said there was no problem, that they couldn't imagine why anyone would have called the cops. No arrests were made, and that was the end of it."

"That's not much help," Sara said.

"Ah, but there's more. When Detective Colwell went there today, Sawyer's wife wasn't home, and of course, neither were Kasiah or Sawyer. It gave Colwell a chance to talk to the neighbors. The woman whose husband had called in the domestic disturbance was at home. She remembered the incident well. She said there was often a lot of shouting and threatening when Walker was around, which wasn't often. She called her husband at work, and he talked to Colwell.

"The evening of the domestic disturbance call, according to the neighbor, it was a particularly bad argument. The fellow said that he'd been working on his car in the garage. It was chilly outside, but he had the garage door up a little to let the fumes out whenever he started his engine. His garage apparently is right next to what would be the living room in Sawyer's house. The neighbor remembered hearing a car drive up, and he'd looked out his garage window and saw that it was Walker. He said Walker hadn't been in the house more than ten minutes when the ruckus began. It was loud, a lot of shouting and cursing.

"At one point, Walker and Sawyer came out to Walker's car. The neighbor was watching it all at this point. Walker leaned into the passenger side of his car like he was getting something. Walker said something about not being able to find whatever it was he was looking for. Sawyer then kicked him in the rear, and Walker fell forward into the car. A moment later, Walker came out with his fists up and took a swing at Sawyer. Sawyer kicked him in the stomach. Walker stood bent over for a minute or so. When he straightened up, Sawyer told him to get back in the house. As they walked up the sidewalk, Sawyer yelled that if it ever happened again, he'd kill Walker. The neighbor remembers Sawyer saying that it wasn't a threat, it was a promise," Clive concluded.

"It must have happened again." Sara's eyes went wide. "I bet the man I'm having dinner with tonight killed his brother. If Fields was doing his job, he'd know that."

"I agree," Clive said. "But there's more. Get this; Sawyer's wife is a nurse, works at a nursing home in Grand Junction. She would likely have access to Fentanyl, and she knows how to give shots."

"We've got to get this information to Lieutenant Scales," Sara said with sudden urgency. "Surely this will get them moving."

"Maybe, but at this point I'm honestly not sure. We've got to be especially careful tonight. At the smallest sign anything is going bad, I'll get you away from Sawyer," Clive said.

"I'm scared, Clive. I don't know if I can do this. I don't think Donte would want me to."

And Clive was sure he didn't want her to either. He decided right then and there that he wouldn't let it happen. "Let's go for a ride," he said. "I don't want you to take the risk. Anyway, there's no way he is going to give you anything but a bunch of baloney designed to convince you it's safe for Donte to come home."

"Where are we going?" Sara asked after the alarm on the house was set, all the lights turned off, and the pair sat in the truck.

"We need to eat. How about if we go up to Salt Lake and eat somewhere up there?" he asked.

"That's fine with me," she agreed, and so they left.

***

Donte had succeeded in buying a used truck. He'd done it without going through a dealer, from an ad in a newspaper. The truck was old, and the fellow didn't even bother taking the plates off or removing the registration. He simply took Donte's cash, signed the title, and watched Donte drive away. The seller hadn't even asked for his name.

It was an old Dodge but seemed to run okay. It used a lot of gas, but that was the least of Donte's worries. He filled up at a station in Klamath Falls, Oregon, a town just north of the California border. He got a handful of quarters from inside and then stepped out to a pay phone. He dialed Chey's number from memory. She answered after a couple rings.

"Hello," she said.

"Hi, Chey, it's me."

"Donte, I was afraid you wouldn't call," she said. "Jessica and I made it back fine. She's not feeling well, but I'm sure it's the travel. At least she's home now, where her family can take care of her and she can rest for as long as she needs to."

"That's what I wanted to hear."

"Are you doing okay, Donte?"

"I'm fine," he said. "As fine as I can be under the circumstances."

"Where are you?" she asked.

"I can't tell you that. I'm not telling anyone," he said. "I just wanted to make sure you were okay."

"I'm fine, but I miss you, Donte."

"Yeah, I know how it feels. Well, I can't talk long. But it's good to hear your voice," he said.

"It's good to hear yours too," Chey responded.

"There is something I need to mention to you," he said. "If anyone asks you if you know me, I need for you to lie. Tell them no. And, Chey, please ask Jessica to do the same. I don't think anyone ever will, but just in case, it's best if you pretend you've never even heard of me."

"Okay," she said. "But that seems extreme."

"I'm a dangerous man to know."

"You're a good man," she said quickly.

"I didn't say I was bad; it's just dangerous to know me. Please remember that. I need to go now."

"Will you call me again?" she asked.

"Honestly, I don't know. You might want to just forget me."

"I can never do that," she said. "No matter how hard I try, I don't think I'll ever forget you. I don't want to."

"Thanks for all you've done for me. Good-bye, Chey," he said.

"Good-bye," she echoed, and he was sure he heard a catch in her voice.

He put the receiver down, leaned against the wall, and fought back the tears that threatened. Why, oh, why couldn't he have met her instead of Kasiah? he asked himself. How different his life would be.

Donte finally got his fractured emotions under control and bounced the remaining quarters in his hand, wondering if he should try to call Bo. He decided against it. It was unlikely Bo would be in Kamas yet, and even more unlikely that he could have located Jacob Hickman. After all, even Donte didn't know where the old man lived. Right now, Hick was probably high in the mountains, living his dream. Hick was a man who'd been born a hundred years late.

Donte shoved the quarters back in his pocket and walked back inside the convenience store. He stepped into the men's room, and as he washed his hands, he studied himself in the mirror. The man with the jet-black hair and beard scarcely resembled the blond man he used to be. He put his dark glasses back on and walked out. A few minutes later, he and Dude were on the road once more, headed to . . . wherever.

***

The unofficial investigators were enjoying a lovely dinner when Sara's cell phone began to ring. She answered it, dismayed to see that it was the company that handled her burglar alarm system. She was told that her house had been broken into and that the police had been notified. She thanked the man who had called and said to Clive, "Someone broke into my house. You did bring your laptop, didn't you?" she asked, wondering silently why that was the most important thing or, at least, the first thing she thought of that could have been stolen.

"Yes, and my notes and the recorder," he said. "Why?"

"Since someone broke into my house, I just wanted to make sure your recorder hadn't been stolen. I wouldn't want our work to be lost."

"Nor would I. I'm sorry about your house," he said. "I'll bet Sawyer knows who did it."

She nodded her head. "I'm sure he does. The cops are on their way."

"We better head back to Provo," he suggested.

"No, let's finish eating first. It would be a shame to waste all this good food," she said so calmly that it scared Clive.

"Sara, are you okay? You should be hysterical about now," he said.

"I've been hysterical before," she told him, "and it didn't help at all. Anyway, the only thing I care about right now is my brother. Nothing else really matters."

"A lot of things matter, Sara," Clive said, knowing he sounded awkward, but he had to say something.

"Maybe, but if we were to leave here now, it wouldn't make any difference as far as my home is concerned." She shrugged. "So let's just try to enjoy our dinner."

"If you say so," Clive said.

"Clive," she said, looking across the table at him. For a long moment, their eyes were locked. Finally, she spoke again. "I was wrong, Clive. There is something else that matters."

"And what would that be?" he asked, wondering what she could be referring to—the Church, her faith?

So he was totally unprepared for what she said. "Clive, you matter to me. You matter a lot." She ducked her head then and picked up her fork.

"Sara," he said, "please look at me."

She slowly raised her eyes, her misty, pretty blue eyes. "You matter to me too. You matter more to me than I ever imagined anyone could after . . ."

Slowly, a smile crossed her face. But she said nothing, just resumed her meal. A few minutes later, one of the cops who had responded to the alarm called and reported that they had been to her house and that other than a broken window, everything was secure. She thanked him and told him she would be home soon. He told her that none of the neighbors had seen anything. That didn't surprise her. She didn't tell him that she was pretty sure she knew who had done it.

They were finally on their way back to Provo an hour later. Clive had held her hand when they left the restaurant, and it had felt right to her. She was thinking as he drove south on the freeway what a big mistake it would be to ever get serious with Winn. It was true, she admitted to herself, that she didn't know Clive very well, but she knew her own heart, and her heart was telling her that here was a man she could care for, a man she could . . . love. Maybe someday after Donte was home, she'd let her heart go.

They were on Interstate 15 driving past the Point of the Mountain when her cell phone rang again. It was another police officer. He asked if she owned a silver Ford Focus. She said she did, and he asked if she knew where it was. She told him that a friend had borrowed it. She felt hysteria building. He asked if the friend's name was Joanie. She said that it was. He informed Sara that Joanie had been in an accident and was in the hospital. She had serious injuries but was expected to live. The Focus was a total loss. Sara wasn't even aware that Clive had taken an exit and was surprised when she realized he was pulling up to the side of a convenience store. He stopped the truck and got out as she continued to listen to the officer on the phone.

When the call was completed a moment later, Clive opened her door, reached for her hand, helped her from the truck, and took her in his arms, holding her tight. She began to cry hysterically.

Clive continued to hold her, stroking her long brown hair, and saying nothing.

She calmed down and finally said, her head against his chest, listening to the strong beat of his heart, "Mara is dead."

***

Donte had spent the night in his truck. He'd cleaned up in a rest area and then driven for a while in the early morning hours, crossing the Columbia River, leaving Oregon and going into Washington. When he pulled into a convenience store in Goldendale and began to put gasoline in his truck, he noticed a pay phone near the door. It was around nine o'clock now, so after paying for the gas, he made a call to Bo. Donte didn't expect to learn anything, but he didn't know when he would be near a phone again.

"This is Bo," the investigator answered.

"Bo, it's Donte."

"It's about time you called. A lot has happened." Donte just listened as Bo went on. "Mara Bertram is dead."

"What?" Donte asked. He had not expected something like this. And from the serious tone of Bo's voice, he was sure there was a lot more that the man was about to say.

"Last night, your sister loaned her car to another secretary from the law firm. The police think that Mara believed Sara was driving, so she intentionally rammed the car. The other girl is going to live, but she's hurt badly. In trying to hit Sara's car, Mara drove into the path of a large truck. She didn't survive the crash."

Donte was trembling so badly that his knees felt like they could buckle. He braced himself. "She tried to kill Sara?"

"That's what it looks like."

"Why would she do that?" he asked.

"I met just a few minute ago with Sara and your investigator. I think he said his name is Clive Granger," Bo said.

"Clive Granger! He's not an investigator, he's a writer," Donte protested even as he realized that his friend was probably doing exactly what he'd told Donte he wanted to do.

"He might not be an official investigator, but he can come work with me anytime," Bo said with admiration in his voice. "He discovered a whole lot of stuff that the cops haven't been able to or, maybe I should say, that they haven't tried very hard to find. There's a chance that Mara was somehow involved in the murder of Walker Aklen, but Clive admits that's only speculation. He's also looking closely at Walker's brother, Sawyer, and his wife."

"Is Detective Fields still stuck on me being the one?"

"He's a fool," Bo said. "And lazy."

That was all the answer Donte needed. He still couldn't go home, but maybe it was time to get Sara to join him. Mara Bertram might not be the only one who wanted his sister dead. "I'll call you later, Bo."

"No, wait," Bo said. "You haven't told me where you are yet. And there's more I need to tell you."

"Thanks for what you're doing, but later, Bo," Donte said and hung up the phone.

Throwing caution to the wind, he fed more quarters into the slot and dialed Sara's cell phone.

CHAPTER TWENTY-SIX

SARA, CLIVE, AND WINN WERE all sitting in Winn's office. Winn and Sara were feeling pretty glum. Clive was angry. "Detective Fields says that what Mara did was caused entirely by the two of you lying to your attorney, Mr. Evenoff, and your attorney in turn lying to the prosecutor," Clive said. "That man is unbelievable."

"He is that," Winn agreed.

"Even after I showed him the note that was attached to the hammer Sawyer tossed through your window, he says we can't prove who threw it. He says I'm barking up the wrong tree." Clive was ranting. "Maybe I haven't found the exact tree yet, but I think I'm close. A little more sniffing, and I'll find it. Detective Fields isn't even looking in the right forest." He shook his head. "I have some things to get done. Sara, are you sure you're okay working the rest of the day?"

"Yes, I'll be fine," she said as Clive got to his feet.

"Hey, you two mentioned a note, but you never did tell me what it said. And why are you sure it's from Sawyer? Surely he wasn't fool enough to sign it," Winn said.

"That's right. It wasn't signed," Clive told him. "But there's no doubt it was him that threw it. Sara left him a note, taped to the door, explaining that she'd learned he was married and that she didn't go out with married men."

"Sawyer's married?" Winn looked surprised. "I guess I should have known that. Shows how close I am to them, even if we are related. How long has he been married?"

"I have no idea how long it's been," Clive told him. "Anyway, the note was written on the back of the one Sara had left him. It's handwritten. A very simple handwriting comparison should confirm that Sawyer wrote it."

"I see," Winn said. "Where's the note now?"

"The police took it—not Fields, but a pair of uniformed officers. Anyway, it said something about Sara learning that it's a dangerous thing to stand some people up."

"That sounds like a threat," Winn said.

"Yes, it does," Clive agreed. "That's why Sara and I got hotel rooms last night. Her house didn't feel safe after that."

Clive started toward the door when Sara's phone began to ring. She looked at Winn, who said, "You probably better answer it."

"Hello," she said.

"It's me. Are you okay, sis?"

She began to sob and only got one word out. "Donte."

Clive gently pried the phone from her fingers, lifted it to his ear, and said, "Donte, this is Clive Granger. Give your sister just a moment. It's good to hear your voice, my friend."

"It's good to hear yours too, Clive, even if you didn't honor my wishes," Donte chided.

"Sorry, Donte, but I couldn't help myself. Please don't be angry," Clive said.

"Actually, I appreciate what you've done. But now I have another favor to ask," Donte said.

"What's that?"

"Bring Sara to me so that I'll know she's safe. We can both live the nomadic life until you get this case solved."

"I'm not sure she'll agree to that," Clive said. "But I see your point, and I'll do my best to persuade her. We will need to know where to meet you."

"That won't be a problem. And thank you," Donte said. "Now, if she's ready to talk, I want to know exactly what's going on there."

"She's reaching for the phone. So I'll let you talk to her while I get back to work. Take care of yourself, Donte. By the way, how did you know something had happened?" Clive asked.

"I called Bo Gray a few minutes ago. He told me."

After handing the phone to Sara, Clive gave a little wave to her and Winn. "I'll pick Sara up at five," he told Winn. And then he was out the door.

***

"What do you mean, she stood you up?" This morning was the first Kasiah had talked to Sawyer since he left for his *date* with Sara. Kasiah had slept well, thinking that Donte would soon be on his way home, stepping into their cleverly laid trap. She'd called her brother this morning expecting the good news. She was angry now and shouted into the phone, "Sawyer, how could you let that happen?"

"I didn't let it happen," he said. "That girl is a lot like her brother."

"You should have pounded on the door until she let you in," Kasiah said. "This isn't like you. You are a persistent man."

"I did pound. I knocked several times and kept ringing the doorbell, but there was no one home. She'd left a note on the door saying she didn't go out with married men."

"How did she know you were married? I never told her—or Donte either, for that matter. And I don't think Winn knew."

"I don't know how she knew, but I think that man she's running around with had something to do with it," he said.

"I want to see the note," Kasiah said. "I know her handwriting. I'll bet she didn't write it. I'll bet her nosy friend did."

"I don't have the note."

"What did you do, leave it on the door?"

"No, I tied it to a hammer that I had in my car and threw it through the window," he said.

Kasiah seethed as she thought about what he'd done. Finally, she said, "Please tell me you didn't write anything on it before you returned it."

"That's exactly what I did. Nobody stands me up and gets away with it."

"Get the note back, Sawyer. The last thing we need right now is your handwriting on a note that has been used in the commission of a crime."

"What crime?" he asked.

"Sawyer! You can't go around breaking people's windows. That's against the law," she said.

"So how do I get it back?" he asked. "Go up to Sara and say, 'Please, give me my note and my hammer back?'"

"That's exactly what you do. You call and offer to pay for the window. You tell her you did it in a fit of anger, that you are sorry. And then make arrangements to meet with her again," Kasiah ordered.

"She won't go out with me," Sawyer reminded her.

"Of course she won't, but you can arrange to meet her at her house," Kasiah said. "Just do whatever it takes. We have a good story. When she hears that story, she'll get Donte back here. He deserves to be in jail. I'm going to hang up now. Call me back as soon as you know when you'll be meeting with her."

***

Sara was still sitting in Winn's office. She had just filled Winn in on the details of her and Clive's investigation.

When she finished, he said, "I know I've blown it with you on a personal level, Sara, and I'm deeply sorry about that. You're the exact opposite of Mara. I care deeply for you. But even though I'm pretty sure that all we'll ever be is friends, I at least want that."

"And you'll have it," she said sincerely.

"Thank you." He hung his head, and she started to get up. "No, wait. I have a suggestion. Let me arrange a meeting with Barry Evenoff, the attorney I hired for us yesterday. He wields a powerful influence with the right people. If you two tell him everything you know, I think he can get Detective Fields pointed in the right direction."

"Yes," she said firmly. "That's a great idea. I'll call Clive right now."

As she pulled her phone from her purse, it began to ring. "I don't recognize this number," she said nervously. She answered, immediately recognizing the voice on the other end. "Sawyer! I can't believe you have the nerve to call me after what you did. You threw a hammer through my window," she said angrily. "And you threatened me."

"Sara, I'm sorry. Please, listen to me," Sawyer begged. Surprised by the pleading, almost humble tone of his voice, she listened. "I did that in a fit of anger. I have a bad temper. Please, I need to talk to you. Kasiah is begging me to talk to you. We have information that can clear Donte."

"I'm listening."

"It's got to be in person," he said. "There are some things I need to show you. I'm sorry if I gave you the wrong impression. I'm not asking you to go on a date. Meet me at your house," he said. "You name the time, and I'll be there."

"Are you going to break another window?" Her anger still boiled just beneath the surface.

"No. Of course not," he confessed. "I'm sorry. I'll pay for the damage. And I'll take my hammer back and get rid of that stupid note. I didn't mean what I wrote. I'm sorry. When can I meet you there?"

Sara quickly decided that it would not be a good idea to mention the note was in the possession of the police. She didn't want to set Sawyer off again. After all, she still believed he could have killed his own brother. She was as certain as she'd ever been that this was still a desperate game with him. She spoke again. "I'll meet with you, Sawyer. I want to hear what you have to say and see what you have to show me." She ignored Winn, who was shaking his head violently. "But I won't meet you alone. It must be with you and Kasiah." Winn was still shaking his head. "And I want my friend Clive there too," she finished.

"Okay," Sawyer said. "I'll talk to Kasiah and see if she'll agree."

"Her being there isn't negotiable," Sara said firmly. "Neither is having Clive there."

"I understand," he said. "I'll see what I can do. Give me a time, and we'll come by your house. I'll call and make arrangements to get your window fixed." She was sure she heard him chuckle before he added, "That was my best hammer. I'll pick it up when I meet with you."

Winn was still shaking his head but not quite so vigorously. "Sawyer, I won't meet with you at my house," she said, even as she was scribbling a note and pushing it across the desk to Winn. He nodded and she went on. "It must be here in my office. Well, actually, in Winn's office. He won't sit in on our meeting, but it must be here."

There was a long pause. Finally, Sawyer said, "Okay, I'll get Kasiah to come. Let's say an hour. And you be sure to have my hammer and note."

"Sawyer, I have a lot of work to do. This is a law office, and we have a full schedule today. Be here at five. I'll be free by then," she said firmly.

There was a long pause. "Okay," he said finally. "I'll see you at five."

"With Kasiah," she reminded him.

"Yes, with Kasiah. And bring the note and hammer."

After she had ended the call, Winn asked, "Do you think they actually have something to tell you?"

"Yes, but whatever it is, it will be a lie. That I'm certain of. The only way I'll believe him is if he says something like he killed Walker so he knows it couldn't be Donte."

"What else did he say?" Winn asked. She told him, and he said, "But you don't have the hammer or the note."

She smiled. "That's right, but he won't know that until I've heard what he has to say. Now, I better get that contract typed. Oh, and Winn, I'm sorry about Mara."

"I guess in a way I am too. But I'm grateful you didn't get hurt."

"But our friend did. Would you like me to have some flowers sent to her hospital room?"

"Please do," he said. "While you do that, I'll call Barry Evenoff and see if I can arrange to have him meet us here at three. Have Clive come then too. That way Barry can begin working on the case while you meet with Sawyer."

***

Clive had just pulled up in front of the apartment complex where Brenda Finn lived when he got a call from Sara. He listened intently as his truck idled. "Are you sure this is a good idea? Sawyer is a dangerous man," he said when she'd finished explaining her plan.

"But you'll be there," she said. "And Winn will be in my office. And there will be others close by."

"Okay, I guess," he said, shutting off the engine and pulling his key from the ignition. "So you need me there a little before five, I take it."

"Actually, I'll need you here by three," she said. "Winn is arranging to have Barry Evenoff meet with us."

"Isn't he the attorney that you two hired yesterday?"

"Yes, and he'll be here to listen to what we've learned. And I intend to hire him to represent Donte too," she said. "If anyone can get Detective Fields on the right track, it's him, or at least Winn thinks so."

"It's certainly worth a try. I'll see you at three," he said. "And now I'm going to go have a talk with Mrs. Brenda Finn. I have a picture to show her." He hung up, and a minute later he stood on Mrs. Finn's doorstep.

"Come in, Mr. Granger," Mrs. Finn said with a smile. "I wondered when you'd be back. I can have some hot chocolate ready in just a minute, and you must taste my berry pie. I made it fresh yesterday after you left. I made it just for you."

With that introduction, there was no way Clive could turn down the pie, even though he didn't really have the time. "Thank you, Mrs. Finn." He smiled politely.

"Trevor still isn't home," she said. "Did you find a picture for me?"

"I did," he said, but before he could get the two photos of Detective Fields out of his jacket pocket, she was bustling off to the kitchen. "I'll just be a moment. Please have a seat," she said.

Clive sat and waited. He was getting fidgety by the time she reappeared carrying a silver tray with a cup of hot chocolate and a large piece of pie. She placed it down in front of him and said, "Now, I'll look at that picture while you enjoy the pie."

"There are two pictures," he said, handing them to her.

He sipped the chocolate and watched as she looked at the pictures, first one, then the other, and then repeated them again. Finally, with a puzzled expression on her face, she said, "I do recognize him." Clive felt a great disappointment. He had so wanted to prove that Detective Fields was a liar. "Yes," she said. "I certainly do remember this man. He was so nice."

"Nice?" Clive asked, confused.

"Yes, he was so nice when he came and got Trevor that day and promised to help him get off drugs and alcohol."

Clive nearly choked on the hot chocolate. He set the cup down before he could spill it. "Are you sure?"

"Oh, yes, Mr. Granger. I never forget a face. So this is Detective Fields. He's such a nice man." Then her face clouded over. "But why would he lie about talking to me? I never talked to him. I would never forget such an important thing."

Yes, why indeed? Clive was asking himself. And where had Fields taken Trevor? Not to jail, so the only answer could be to a rehab center or a hospital. Clive had to find out so he could talk to Trevor. Detective Fields was going to have to do some tall talking to get out of this one. Clive barely tasted his pie as he shoveled it down, and he nearly burned his throat drinking the chocolate so fast. When Mrs. Finn offered him more, he said, "Oh, no thanks. That was very good, but I really have to go now. Thank you so much for your help."

He didn't bother to shut the recorder off until he'd reached his truck. And he didn't start the ignition until he had called Lieutenant Scales. "This is Clive Granger. I can prove that your detective isn't doing his job. And I can prove that he lied to you as well as to me."

"This is a very serious accusation," Scales said. "Why would he do that?"

"That's my question," Clive snapped. "But I think I know the answer. He's a lazy slob. He's so sure he has the right man in Donte that he isn't willing to lift a finger to see if he might be wrong. I'd like to meet with you."

"Certainly, but I think you should tone it down until we see what's going on."

"I don't want Fields there when I talk to you. I'll show you what I have, and you can deal with him in whatever way you deem appropriate."

Even as Clive was speaking, a thought entered his mind. He tried to shove it out, but it hung on tenaciously. "Lieutenant," he said, anxious now to get off the phone. There was something else he needed to do. And it was urgent. It needed to be done before he met with Barry Evenoff at three. "Can you come to Winn Bertram's office at three o'clock?" he asked. "I'd like to meet with you there."

"Sure, I'll be there, but again, I caution you to be sure of your facts before you make any allegations. I am assuming this is all about Detective Fields? Or is it about Mara Bertram's attempt on the life of Sara Noble."

"Both and more," Clive said. "And please bring the hammer and note that were taken from Miss Noble's house. The officers who responded to the alarm have it. The man who threw it through her window will be in Winn's office at five."

"Who's that?" Scales asked.

"The brother of your murder victim, Sawyer Aklen, and his sister Kasiah. They say they can clear this matter up, and maybe they really can. Be there at three, please. And I'll need you again at five. With you there, I'm sure that Mr. Aklen and his sister will be most helpful."

"I'll see you then," the lieutenant said.

Clive started his truck and pulled into the street. He'd left his laptop at the hotel. He needed it, and he also needed to make contact with Detective Colwell in Grand Junction. There was one more thing he needed the detective to do.

CHAPTER TWENTY-SEVEN

CLIVE DID A SEARCH ON his laptop, but he couldn't find what he was looking for. So he called Detective Colwell. "I'm sorry I'm such a bother," he said when the detective was on the phone. "The information you gave me has been extremely helpful. But there's one more thing I'd like to know. I may be way out in left field, but then again I might not be."

"I'll do what I can," the officer promised. "Tell me what you need."

Clive told him, and Colwell said, "Wow! That is some request. I assume you have a reason for asking."

"I do," Clive said. "If things go the way I think they will, I'll let you know."

"That's fair," Detective Colwell said. "I'll call you back."

The next call was to Sara. "I need you to get me a little piece of information. I'd do it myself, but it'll take me longer than it will take you. Anyway, I'm very, very busy and don't want to miss the meeting at three."

"I want to help. What information are you looking for?" she asked.

When Clive told her, she asked, "Why do you need to know that?"

He told her that he just wanted to know. She pressed him for a more definitive answer, but all he would say is, "I don't want to say what I'm thinking until I'm sure of myself. And Sara, please, whatever you do, don't let Winn know."

"I won't say a word to him, that's for sure. I'll take a break and take care of it outside the office. But, Clive, are you sure you're not stirring things that would be better left alone?" she asked.

"Yes, I am."

"What if you're wrong?"

"Then I'm wrong. I'll live with the consequences, and we'll press on. Would you get on it as soon as you can and then get back with me?" he asked.

"Yes, I will, Clive."

"And one more thing," he said. "If Donte calls, stall him on his idea of you joining him. Tell him that before Kasiah and Sawyer leave your office tonight, we may have enough information to wrap this thing up. If that happens, then he'll be able to come home real soon. If not, then tell him I will personally bring you to meet him."

"I don't know that I should go," she said. "I have—"

Clive cut her off. "Sara, if Mara had succeeded in her plans last night, you'd be dead. The very thought makes me so sick I can hardly stand it. Your life is what matters most right now. I won't let anyone hurt you, and neither will Donte."

"Okay, Clive," she said meekly, "I'll go if you and Donte say I should."

***

After speaking on the phone with both Bo and Sara, Donte had turned around and headed south, back into Oregon. From there he had driven east on Interstate 44. He wanted to be closer to Utah so Sara could join him. Once she was safely with him, they would go much farther away.

He was stopped now, eating some lunch in La Grande, Oregon. When he had finished, he once again found a pay phone and called Bo. "Any luck yet?" Donte asked.

"As a matter of fact, I found your friend Jacob Hickman, or Hick, as he told me I should call him," Bo reported. "He is as colorful a character as I have met in a long time. We had a great visit."

"I'm sure you did," Donte smiled, remembering his friend. "He can be a very entertaining soul. But what I want to know is if he's going to be of any help or if I was right about him visiting with me the day before the murder."

Bo chuckled. "You were right, but that doesn't change anything. He did see you the next day. Hick described a trail that he was on, and he said he saw you far above on a pass. He admitted that he had the first day wrong, but he saw you the next day as well."

"But will anyone believe him?" Donte asked, having a hard time not feeling discouraged. "He's a man who was born after his time, and to some, he might seem like a crazy old man."

"He's not crazy. I can attest to that," Bo said with a chuckle. "I told him what your friends did to me in Tonopah, and he laughed until I was afraid he would have a stroke. He told me what he would have done if he'd been in my place. He said, 'That wouldn't have kept this old man from going to find help.'"

"Really?" Donte said.

"Yeah, when I told him that I had a small pocket knife in my car, he lit up like a campfire," Bo said. "He told me that he would have cut up the leather seats of my Expedition and made breeches, a shirt, a backpack, and some moccasins. Even without a knife, he said he'd have sharpened a rock on some of that sandstone out there and done it anyway. Then he told me that by using the sun or stars as a guide, it would be a simple matter of traveling in a straight line until I came across a road."

"That sounds like Hick."

"That story would convince anyone that the man is not only sane but as smart as a whip," Bo said. "So, yes, his testimony destroys Detective Fields's theory of you as the killer."

"Will you see that Sara knows that?" Donte asked.

"If you'd like me to, or you can call her yourself," Bo suggested.

"Why don't you try to reach her?" Donte asked. "And if she doesn't answer, then call Clive Granger." He made sure Bo had both numbers.

"I will be moving on. But I'll call later," Donte said. "Oh, and remind them that I still think it's terribly important for Sara to meet me and stay out of sight until this whole mess is wrapped up. I nearly lost her last night. I can't take that chance again."

After the call ended, Donte realized that Bo had not asked him for his location. He guessed the PI was learning that Donte would do what he thought best and that no one would change his mind. And right now, it was best that no one know his location.

***

By one o'clock, Detective Colwell had reported back to Clive. "I don't know how you ever guessed it, but you were right," he said. "Three other officers and I worked on your request."

"Okay, I was right. But exactly how was I right? I need facts," Clive said.

So Detective Colwell gave him facts, revealing facts. Clive got a call at one thirty from Bo Gray. When Bo reported on his meeting with Jacob Hickman, Clive asked, "How soon can you be in Provo?"

"If I left right now, I could be there around three," Bo said.

"Then get on your way. Go straight to Winn's office. There will be a meeting there at three, and I think you can contribute," Clive said. He then explained what the meeting was about.

"I am on my way, Clive."

It was almost two o'clock before Clive received a call back from Sara, giving him the information he sought. "Winn had to leave for a little while, so I was able to make the calls from right here in my office," she told him. "I'll see you at three."

"I'll be there," he said. "But until then, I'll be working."

"You're getting close, aren't you?" she said, sounding very hopeful.

"I hope so. I'll let you know how close when we meet with the lieutenant and Mr. Evenoff."

Clive was running out of time. He had a hospital to visit. The question he had was a straightforward one. Since it didn't involve any patients, Clive was able to persuade the hospital administrator to tell him what he wanted to know. That was the last piece of information he needed. On the way to the meeting in Winn's office, Clive called Lieutenant Scales. "I'm on my way to Winn Bertram's office," he said. "I've changed my mind. I know it will be hard to believe after how hard I've been on Detective Fields, but I need him there as well."

"I'll bring him," Scales promised. "I'm glad you changed your mind, because it'll be better if he hears your evidence straight from you. I'm guessing, considering his good record, that he'll be willing to look into any discrepancies in the case and make any necessary adjustments in his investigation."

"I sure hope so," Clive said, "because I can prove that Donte is not the killer. I fully expect his help."

"I look forward to hearing what you have to say," Scales said. "And I can guarantee you that both Detective Fields and I will cooperate fully."

"That's all I ask," Clive said.

***

Sara looked around. By five minutes to three, all but one of the parties invited to the conference were there. That meant four were in attendance. Sara was there, of course, as were the two attorneys, Winn Bertram and Barry Evenoff. Clive had come in just a minute earlier. He'd winked at her, slipped close, and whispered, "I got a call from Bo Gray. He's confirmed Donte's alibi and is trying to get here but might be a minute or two late."

"Oh, that's great," she whispered back. "So I don't have to go on the run with Donte?"

"I didn't say that. Let's see how the afternoon goes. Then we'll decide," he said.

So there were actually two who were not at the meeting yet, Bo and Lieutenant Scales. Once again, Clive whispered to her, "Oh, I invited Detective Fields too. I decided we needed him here. Scales seemed relieved."

That made three missing. She was wound tight, and the acid in her stomach was stirring around. She slipped out to her desk and got an antacid from her purse. That helped, but she was anxious to get this meeting underway.

Bo walked in just one minute after three and took a chair where Sara pointed. Finally, three minutes late, the two officers arrived. "Sorry we're late," Lieutenant Scales said. "Detective Fields is busy, and it's difficult for him to get away."

"Thank you all for coming," Clive said. "We need to get started right away. So first, let's make some introductions."

When that was done, he continued, "Now, if you'll all indulge me, I have been doing some digging, and I'd like to tell you what I know."

"Sounds like a waste of time," Detective Fields said with a huff. "I have work to do. Your digging about, as you call it, has already caused unnecessary delays and diversions that impacted my time negatively."

"Detective," Lieutenant Scales said, "I will repeat what I said in our office a few minutes ago. Mr. Granger might have uncovered something that will be helpful. We're going to hear him out, and then we'll go from there."

"If you say so, but I think this is a waste of time," Fields insisted. "I've investigated the case thoroughly. And I have one more objection. I think Mr. Evenoff should be excused. He represents Mr. Granger and Miss Noble in a matter that I find most objectionable. If he's here, then I will have nothing to say."

"That's fine, Detective," Clive said. "You don't have to say anything if you don't feel like it. All I ask is that you listen."

Clive laid his small digital recorder on the table. "I do have a few matters that I think bear closer scrutiny. On this recorder—and backed up on my computer and two thumb drives—is every interview I conducted. The recordings will be made available for any of you to inspect. Now, let me first begin with the basic matter of Donte Noble, the accused killer, and his alibi. I have already given a copy of his statement to Lieutenant Scales."

"And it's bogus," Fields said angrily. "I already addressed that matter. Mr. Hickman told me that he didn't even know anyone by the name of Donte Noble."

"I thought you didn't have anything to say." Clive feigned surprise, making Sara chuckle. "Apparently you've changed your mind. But please humor me, Detective. I happen to think you are wrong about that. So please, hear me out."

Fields started to speak again, but Scales shut him down by putting a hand firmly on the detective's arm. Clive went on. "I have invited Bo Gray here to confirm Hickman's statement."

"He calls himself an investigator," Detective Fields grumbled just loud enough for everyone to hear. For a man who claimed he had nothing to say, he certainly couldn't keep his mouth shut, Sara thought.

Bo said, "I met with Mr. Hickman earlier today. I recorded my interview with him. It's rather lengthy, but I will make it available to whoever wants a copy. I'll see that you officers get one for sure."

"Thanks," Scales said. "We'll consider it."

"To save time," Bo continued, "I will summarize. First, Mr. Hickman denies ever speaking with Detective Fields—not recently, not early in the investigation, not ever."

"That's because the man is nuts," Fields blurted out.

"He's far from that," Bo said. "In the tape you'll hear some things he said to me that would convince any jury in the country that he is not nuts, as you say, but is a highly intelligent man. But I digress. The second thing he told me is that he did in fact speak with Donte on a trail high in the mountains the day before the murder and that he then saw Donte again on the day of the murder. His interview will speak for itself."

"The lying old coot," Fields mumbled, getting himself another frustrated glance from Lieutenant Scales.

"Thank you, Mr. Gray," Clive said. "The second matter I want to discuss is a matter of motive. I have been unable to find anyone who can point to any kind of motive, any reason at all that Donte would want to take the life of the brother of the woman he was engaged to."

"I told you the motive," Fields thundered. "Walker owed him money."

"Yes, you did mention that. Perhaps you would like to present some proof," Clive said. "You told me before that you didn't have any but that you'd get it. Do you have it?"

"Not yet," Fields mumbled. "I was working on that when Lieutenant Scales told me that he would like me to come to this little meeting."

"So you don't have it yet?" Clive asked, catching Sara's eye and giving her a very tiny smile. She thought he was doing great. He went on. "That brings me to my next point. That very motive has application to others. To name just two, a roommate of Walker's was owed money for back rent. Trevor Wells is his name. He was overheard threatening to kill Walker if he didn't square the debt."

"I have already proven that not to be true." Fields sounded exasperated. "I interviewed both Mr. Wells and his neighbor Mrs. Brenda Finn. Only when you came along, Mr. Granger," Fields added angrily, "did any mention of such a thing come up. You're so anxious to prove the innocence of your friend that you've been manipulating people."

Clive didn't even respond to Fields this time, and it made Sara smile. "Unfortunately, Trevor Wells seems to have disappeared," Clive said.

"I can't say I blame him, with you throwing around unsubstantiated accusations against him," Fields said, once again causing the lieutenant to attempt to quiet him.

"However, I have spoken with Mrs. Finn on several occasions. The latest was today." Clive addressed the entire group. "She denies that Detective Fields ever spoke to her."

"She's a forgetful old biddy," Fields put in. Sara could tell that Lieutenant Scales was getting annoyed. She wondered how many more interruptions he would let the detective make before he blew his stack. She also kept an eye on Mr. Evenoff. He was taking notes at a furious pace, and every time Detective Fields spoke he would smile. He probably enjoyed cross-examining stubborn officers like Fields.

Clive didn't even look at Detective Fields. "Since the allegation of her senility had earlier been made to me by the detective, I decided to put her memory to the test. So today I took her two pictures of Detective Fields. She told me, and it is recorded, that she did recognize him." Clive paused, and Fields smirked. "She recognized him, but not as a man who interviewed her, rather as the man who escorted Trevor Wells from his apartment, promising Trevor that he would help him beat his drug and alcohol addictions. I have made dozens of phone calls, but I can't locate Mr. Wells. Perhaps, Detective, you would like to tell us where you took him?"

The smirk was gone, and Detective Fields's face was filled with rage. "You don't listen well, do you, Mr. Granger? I said I'd stay and listen, that's all. I have nothing to say to your slanderous insinuations."

"That's fine," Clive said with a smile. "I'll go on to my next point. I've learned that Walker's own brother threatened to kill him for an outstanding debt. That is the second person with the very same motive that Detective Fields—while he was only observing—just mentioned."

Fields opened his mouth again, but the lieutenant had reached the limit of his patience. "Jaren, be quiet. Mr. Granger has raised some valid points. We're going to hear him out. Remember, if this case ever goes to a jury, what we're hearing today will be raised by the defense attorney. So far, Clive has succeeded in poking several holes in your case. We're going to *listen* to what he has to say. And if there is something we need to act on, we will!"

Sara noted that Mr. Evenoff was smiling and relaxed while continuing to take copious notes. But he didn't say a word. Clive said, "Thank you, Lieutenant. Let me mention one more person to whom money was owed by the deceased. He also owed you money, did he not, Mr. Bertram?"

Winn's face went red. "We were cousins, not close at all, but yes, I lent him money. But I did not—"

Clive cut him off. "I'm not accusing you of anything," he said. "I'm just stating a fact. But let me ask you this. Did Mara, your ex-wife, know Walker owed you money?"

"Yes," Winn admitted. "And she kept hounding me to collect it."

For the first time, Barry Evenoff quit making notes and spoke. "Winn, I would advise you not to say anything further at this time."

Winn looked thoroughly rattled. He nodded his head, his face flushed.

"That's fine," Clive said evenly. "Now to my next point. The manner of death has been established as a lethal injection of a pain killer known as Fentanyl. It's typically used in the form of a patch. However, if it were to be reduced to a liquid and then injected, it would be fatal. Such is the case here. That's how Walker was killed. Fentanyl is a controlled substance, so very few people have access to it, and even fewer would know how to make a liquid of it. As we know, Donte is one who'd know how to do it. Detective Fields has, I think unwisely, chosen to hang his hat on that bit of evidence. However, I have learned that Sawyer Aklen, a man who threatened to kill his brother, is married. His wife is a nurse in a Grand Junction nursing home. She, like Donte, had both the knowledge and the access, but she also had something else. She had motive." Clive paused and looked around the room as Sara did the same. He had everyone's attention. "She and her husband were out thousands of dollars, thanks to the victim's unscrupulous borrowing practices."

Lieutenant Scales asked, "Did you know this, Jaren?" The detective didn't answer. Scales shook his head. "You should have. This is critical information. We'll discuss this later."

Clive then dropped the biggest bombshell of the night. "I have discovered one other person who made a loan to Walker. He's an impatient man who's also married to a nurse. She has been invited to join us. Sara, she's seated in the next office over. And she has something to say."

Sara found the lady where Clive had said she would be. Sara had never seen her before. The woman's eyes were red and puffy. Once the two women were in Winn's office, the woman shouted, "Jaren, how could you? You used me. Walker was your cousin. You . . . you. . ."

Jaren Fields turned white.

Clive spoke up. "Lieutenant Scales, let me introduce you to another cousin of Walker, a man who also lent a large sum of money to Walker, and a man who asked his wife—no, coerced his wife—to get him some Fentanyl for some pain he was having in his shoulder. The man who accused Donte Noble of the crime he himself had committed. Let me introduce you to Detective Jaren Fields, a cold-blooded killer."

Almost everyone in the room was stunned. The only one who wasn't tried to make a break for it, but his own lieutenant wrestled him to the floor, snapping on handcuffs and arresting him for murder. After Scales had Fields secured, Clive said, "I suspect that Fields also knows where we can find the body of his second victim, Trevor Wells."

The day's drama was not yet over. At five o'clock, Kasiah and Sawyer arrived. After a short, tense meeting, Kasiah turned angrily on her brother. "You made it all up," she screamed. "You blamed Donte and convinced me of it because you knew that they could have arrested you. I didn't know he owed you money. I didn't know you had threatened him. You . . . you beast! You made me accuse the man I love."

Sawyer didn't deny it. He simply walked out of the office. No one attempted to stop him.

Later, as Sara and Clive enjoyed a quiet dinner, she said, "I can't believe it. You did it. You really did it. Thank you."

"You helped," he reminded her.

"But I didn't have any idea it might have been Fields. When you put Winn on the spot and Mr. Evenoff told him not to say anything, I honestly thought it had been him after all. I almost fainted."

"I'm sorry. I wanted to keep Fields off balance," he said. "But you were a great help, Sara, and you put your life on the line for your brother."

"I hope Donte contacts me soon. I can't wait to tell him he can come home now," she said wistfully.

Clive grinned. "He called Bo already. He's on his way."

Sara cried out with joy. "God answered my prayers," she said reverently.

"And mine," Clive said.

"And Donte's."

"That's true. But Donte owes you." Clive grinned. "You prayed, and then you backed those prayers up with hard work and perseverance."

"No, I owe Donte," she said.

"Why do you say that?" Clive asked.

"Because of him, I met you."

"Then we both owe him," Clive said.

They ate, they gazed into each other's eyes, and they talked and laughed. At one point, Clive asked, "I saw you talking to Kasiah before she left Winn's office. How did that go?"

Sara shook her head sadly. "She says she loves Donte, that everything she did was because of Sawyer. She says she'll win him back."

"What did you say?" he asked.

"I told her that time would tell."

"Will he take her back?"

"What do you think?" Sara asked.

"I don't think so. Bo told me there was a girl Donte met in Tonopah. Apparently, there was a spark there."

"Oh, so I guess time really will tell, won't it?" Sara said as she reached across the table and took hold of Clive's hand.

***

Chey was watching TV in the family room when the doorbell rang. She was the only one home, so she paused the program, got to her feet, and headed through the house. She opened the door—and gaped. Standing there was a clean-cut man with short, dark blond hair; a clean-shaven face; and the most beautiful blue eyes she had ever seen. It was the eyes that brought recognition, and with a squeal of delight, she threw herself into his arms. "You came," she said. "You found me."

Donte hugged her tightly and then held her back where he could look deep into her eyes. "I thought it was time we got to know each other," he said. "If it's okay with you, that is. Oh how I've missed you."

ABOUT THE AUTHOR

CLAIR M. POULSON WAS BORN and raised in Duchesne, Utah. His father was a rancher and farmer, his mother a librarian. Clair has always been an avid reader, having found his love for books as a very young boy.

He has served for over forty years in the criminal justice system. Twenty years were spent in law enforcement, ending his police career with eight years as the Duchesne County Sheriff. For the past twenty-plus years, Clair has worked as a justice court judge for Duchesne County. Clair is also a veteran of the US Army, where he was a military policeman. During his time in the Military Police, Clair became very well acquainted with two accused killers. In law enforcement, he has been personally involved in the investigation of murders and other violent crimes. Clair has also served on various boards and councils during his professional career, including the Justice Court Board of Judges, the Utah Commission on Criminal and Juvenile Justice, the Utah Judicial Council, the Utah Peace Officer Standards and Training Council, an FBI advisory board, and others.

In addition to his criminal justice work, Clair has farmed and ranched all of his life. He has raised many kinds of animals, but his greatest interest is horses and cattle. He's also involved in the grocery store business with his oldest son and other family members.

Clair has served in many capacities in the LDS Church, including full-time missionary (California Mission), bishop, counselor to two bishops, young men president, high councilor, stake mission president, scoutmaster, and high priest group leader. He currently serves as a Gospel Doctrine teacher.

Clair is married to Ruth, and they have five children, all of whom are married: Alan (Vicena) Poulson, Kelly Ann (Wade) Hatch, Amanda (Ben) Semadeni, Wade (Brooke) Poulson, and Mary (Tyler) Hicken. They also have twenty-three wonderful grandchildren. Clair and Ruth met while both were students at Snow College and were married in the Manti temple.

Clair has always loved telling his children, and later his grandchildren, made-up stories. His vast experience in life and his love of literature have contributed to both his telling stories to children and his writing of adventure and suspense novels.

With this book, Clair will have published over two dozen novels. He would love to hear from his fans, who can contact him by going to his website, *clairmpoulson.com*.